CHRISTOPHER BUSH
THE CASE OF THE
TUDOR QUEEN

CHRISTOPHER BUSH was born Charlie Christmas Bush in Norfolk in 1885. His father was a farm labourer and his mother a milliner. In the early years of his childhood he lived with his aunt and uncle in London before returning to Norfolk aged seven, later winning a scholarship to Thetford Grammar School.

As an adult, Bush worked as a schoolmaster for 27 years, pausing only to fight in World War One, until retiring aged 46 in 1931 to be a full-time novelist. His first novel featuring the eccentric Ludovic Travers was published in 1926, and was followed by 62 additional Travers mysteries. These are all to be republished by Dean Street Press.

Christopher Bush fought again in World War Two, and was elected a member of the prestigious Detection Club. He died in 1973.

By Christopher Bush

The Plumley Inheritance
The Perfect Murder Case
Dead Man Twice
Murder at Fenwold
Dancing Death
Dead Man's Music
Cut Throat
The Case of the Unfortunate Village
The Case of the April Fools
The Case of the Three Strange Faces
The Case of the 100% Alibis
The Case of the Dead Shepherd
The Case of the Chinese Gong
The Case of the Monday Murders
The Case of the Bonfire Body
The Case of the Missing Minutes
The Case of the Hanging Rope
The Case of the Tudor Queen
The Case of the Leaning Man
The Case of the Green Felt Hat

CHRISTOPHER BUSH

THE CASE OF THE TUDOR QUEEN

With an introduction
by Curtis Evans

DEAN STREET PRESS

To

MOLLY PETRIDES

with love and good wishes

INTRODUCTION

THAT ONCE vast and mighty legion of bright young (and youngish) British crime writers who began publishing their ingenious tales of mystery and imagination during what is known as the Golden Age of detective fiction (traditionally dated from 1920 to 1939) had greatly diminished by the iconoclastic decade of the Sixties, many of these writers having become casualties of time. Of the 38 authors who during the Golden Age had belonged to the Detection Club, a London-based group which included within its ranks many of the finest writers of detective fiction then plying the craft in the United Kingdom, just over a third remained among the living by the second half of the 1960s, while merely seven—Agatha Christie, Anthony Gilbert, Gladys Mitchell, Margery Allingham, John Dickson Carr, Nicholas Blake and Christopher Bush—were still penning crime fiction.

In 1966--a year that saw the sad demise, at the too young age of 62, of Margery Allingham--an executive with the English book publishing firm Macdonald reflected on the continued popularity of the author who today is the least well known among this tiny but accomplished crime writing cohort: Christopher Bush (1885-1973), whose first of his three score and three series detective novels, *The Plumley Inheritance*, had appeared fully four decades earlier, in 1926. "He has a considerable public, a 'steady Bush public,' a public that has endured through many years," the executive boasted of Bush. "He never presents any problem to his publisher, who knows exactly how many copies of a title may be safely printed for the loyal Bush fans; the number is a healthy one too." Yet in 1968, just a couple of years after the Macdonald editor's affirmation of Bush's notable popular duration as a crime writer, the author, now in his 83rd year, bade farewell to mystery fiction with a final detective novel, *The Case of the Prodigal Daughter*, in which, like in Agatha Christie's *Third Girl* (1966), copious references are made, none too favorably, to youthful sex, drugs and rock and roll. Afterwards, outside of the reprinting in the UK in the early 1970s of a scattering of classic Bush titles from the Golden Age, Bush's books, in contrast with those of Christie, Carr, Allingham and Blake, disappeared from mass circulation in both the UK and the US, becoming fervently sought (and ever more unobtainable) treasures by collectors and connoisseurs of classic crime fiction. Now, in one of the signal developments in vintage mystery publishing, Dean Street Press is reprinting all 63 of the Christopher Bush detective novels. These will be published over a period of months, beginning with the release of books 1 to 10 in the series.

Few Golden Age British mystery writers had backgrounds as humble yet simultaneously mysterious, dotted with omissions and evasions, as Christopher Bush, who was born Charlie Christmas Bush on the day of the Nativity in 1885 in the Norfolk village of Great Hockham, to Charles Walter Bush and his second wife, Eva Margaret Long. While the father of Christopher Bush's Detection Club colleague and near exact contemporary Henry Wade (the pseudonym of Henry Lancelot Aubrey-Fletcher) was a baronet who lived in an elegant Georgian mansion and claimed extensive ownership of fertile English fields, Christopher's father resided in a cramped cottage and toiled in fields as a farm laborer, a term that in the late Victorian and Edwardian era, his son lamented many years afterward, "had in it something of contempt. . . . There was something almost of serfdom about it."

Charles Walter Bush was a canny though mercurial individual, his only learning, his son recalled, having been "acquired at the Sunday school." A man of parts, Charles was a tenant farmer of three acres, a thatcher, bricklayer and carpenter (fittingly for the father of a detective novelist, coffins were his specialty), a village radical and a most adept poacher. After a flight from Great Hockham, possibly on account of his poaching activities, Charles, a widower with a baby son whom he had left in the care of his mother, resided in London, where he worked for a firm of spice importers. At a dance in the city, Charles met Christopher's mother, Eva Long, a lovely and sweet-natured young milliner and bonnet maker, sweeping her off her feet with a combination of "good looks and a certain plausibility." After their marriage the couple left London to live in a tiny rented cottage in Great Hockham, where Eva over the next eighteen years gave birth to three sons and five daughters and perforce learned the challenging ways of rural domestic economy.

Decades later an octogenarian Christopher Bush, in his memoir *Winter Harvest: A Norfolk Boyhood* (1967), characterized Great Hockham as a rustic rural redoubt where many of the words that fell from the tongues of the native inhabitants "were those of Shakespeare, Milton and the Authorised Version.... Still in general use were words that were standard in Chaucer's time, but had since lost a certain respectability." Christopher amusingly recalled as a young boy telling his mother that a respectable neighbor woman had used profanity, explaining that in his hearing she had told her husband, "George, wipe you that shit off that pig's arse, do you'll datty your trousers," to which his mother had responded that although that particular usage of a four-letter word had not really been *swearing*, he was not to give vent to such language himself.

Great Hockham, which in Christopher Bush's youth had a population of about four hundred souls, was composed of a score or so of cottages, three public houses, a post-office, five shops, a couple of forges and a pair of churches, All Saint's and the Primitive Methodist Chapel, where the Bush family rather vocally worshipped. "The village lived by farming, and most of its men were labourers," Christopher recollected. "Most of the children left school as soon as the law permitted: boys to be absorbed somehow into the land and the girls to go into domestic service." There were three large farms and four smaller ones, and, in something of an anomaly, not one but two squires--the original squire, dubbed "Finch" by Christopher, having let the shooting rights at Little Hockham Hall to one "Green," a wealthy international banker, making the latter man a squire by courtesy. Finch owned most of the local houses and farms, in traditional form receiving rents for them personally on Michaelmas; and when Christopher's father fell out with Green, "a red-faced, pompous, blustering man," over a political election, he lost all of the banker's business, much to his mother's distress. Yet against all odds and adversities, Christopher's life greatly diverged from settled norms in Great Hockham, incidentally producing one of the most distinguished detective novelists from the Golden Age of detective fiction.

Although Christopher Bush was born in Great Hockham, he spent his earliest years in London living with his mother's much older sister, Elizabeth, and her husband, a fur dealer by the name of James Streeter, the couple having no children of their own. Almost certainly of illegitimate birth, Eva had been raised by the Long family from her infancy. She once told her youngest daughter how she recalled the Longs being visited, when she was a child, by a "fine lady in a carriage," whom she believed was her birth mother. Or is it possible that the "fine lady in a carriage" was simply an imaginary figment, like the aristocratic fantasies of Philippa Palfrey in P.D. James's *Innocent Blood* (1980), and that Eva's "sister" Elizabeth was in fact her mother?

The Streeters were a comfortably circumstanced couple at the time they took custody of Christopher. Their household included two maids and a governess for the young boy, whose doting but dutiful "Aunt Lizzie" devoted much of her time to the performance of "good works among the East End poor." When Christopher was seven years old, however, drastically straightened financial circumstances compelled the Streeters to leave London for Norfolk, by the way returning the boy to his birth parents in Great Hockham.

Fortunately the cause of the education of Christopher, who was not only a capable village cricketer but a precocious reader and scholar, was taken up both by his determined and devoted mother and an idealistic local elementary school headmaster. In his teens Christopher secured a scholarship to Norfolk's Thetford Grammar School, one of England's oldest educational institutions, where Thomas Paine had studied a century-and-a-half earlier. He left Thetford in 1904 to take a position as a junior schoolmaster, missing a chance to go to Cambridge University on yet another scholarship. (Later he proclaimed himself thankful for this turn of events, sardonically speculating that had he received a Cambridge degree he "might have become an exceedingly minor don or something as staid and static and respectable as a publisher.") Christopher would teach in English schools for the next twenty-seven years, retiring at the age of 46 in 1931, after he had established a successful career as a detective novelist.

Christopher's romantic relationships proved far rockier than his career path, not to mention every bit as murky as his mother's familial antecedents. In 1911, when Christopher was teaching in Wood Green School, a co-educational institution in Oxfordshire, he wed county council schoolteacher Ella Maria Pinner, a daughter of a baker neighbor of the Bushes in Great Hockham. The two appear never actually to have lived together, however, and in 1914, when Christopher at the age of 29 headed to war in the 16th (Public Schools) Battalion of the Middlesex Regiment, he falsely claimed in his attestation papers, under penalty of two years' imprisonment with hard labor, to be unmarried.

After four years of service in the Great War, including a year-long stint in Egypt, Christopher returned in 1919 to his position at Wood Green School, where he became involved in another romantic relationship, from which he soon desired to extricate himself. (A photo of the future author, taken at this time in Egypt, shows a rather dashing, thin-mustached man in uniform and is signed "Chris," suggesting that he had dispensed with "Charlie" and taken in its place a diminutive drawn from his middle name.) The next year Winifred Chart, a mathematics teacher at Wood Green, gave birth to a son, whom she named Geoffrey Bush. Christopher was the father of Geoffrey, who later in life became a noted English composer, though for reasons best known to himself Christopher never acknowledged his son. (A letter Geoffrey once sent him was returned unopened.) Winifred claimed that she and Christopher had married but separated, but she refused to speak of her purported spouse forever after and she destroyed all of his letters and other mementos, with the exception of a book of poetry that he had written for her during what she termed their engagement.

Christopher's true mate in life, though with her he had no children, was Florence Marjorie Barclay, the daughter of a draper from Ballymena, Northern Ireland, and, like Ella Pinner and Winifred Chart, a schoolteacher. Christopher and Marjorie likely had become romantically involved by 1929, when Christopher dedicated to her his second detective novel, *The Perfect Murder Case*; and they lived together as man and wife from the 1930s until her death in 1968 (after which, probably not coincidentally, Christopher stopped publishing novels). Christopher returned with Marjorie to the vicinity of Great Hockham when his writing career took flight, purchasing two adjoining cottages and commissioning his father and a stepbrother to build an extension consisting of a kitchen, two bedrooms and a new staircase. (The now sprawling structure, which Christopher called "Home Cottage," is now a bed and breakfast grandiloquently dubbed "Home Hall.") After a falling-out with his father, presumably over the conduct of Christopher's personal life, he and Marjorie in 1932 moved to Beckley, Sussex, where they purchased Horsepen, a lovely Tudor plaster and timber-framed house. In 1953 the couple settled at their final home, The Great House, a centuries-old structure (now a boutique hotel) in Lavenham, Suffolk.

From these three houses Christopher maintained a lucrative and critically esteemed career as a novelist, publishing both detective novels as Christopher Bush and, commencing in 1933 with the acclaimed book *Return* (in the UK, *God and the Rabbit*, 1934), regional novels purposefully drawing on his own life experience, under the pen name Michael Home. (During the 1940s he also published espionage novels under the Michael Home pseudonym.) Although his first detective novel, *The Plumley Inheritance*, made a limited impact, with his second, *The Perfect Murder Case*, Christopher struck gold. The latter novel, a big seller in both the UK and the US, was published in the former country by the prestigious Heinemann, soon to become the publisher of the detective novels of Margery Allingham and Carter Dickson (John Dickson Carr), and in the latter country by the Crime Club imprint of Doubleday, Doran, one of the most important publishers of mystery fiction in the United States.

Over the decade of the 1930s Christopher Bush published, in both the UK and the US as well as other countries around the world, some of the finest detective fiction of the Golden Age, prompting the brilliant Thirties crime fiction reviewer, author and Oxford University Press editor Charles Williams to avow: "Mr. Bush writes of as thoroughly enjoyable murders as any I know." (More recently, mystery genre authority B.A. Pike dubbed these novels by Bush, whom he praised as "one of the most reliable and resourceful of true detective writers"; "Golden Age baroque, rendered remarkable by some extraordinary flights of fancy.") In 1937 Christopher Bush became, along with Nicholas Blake, E.C.R. Lorac and Newton Gayle (the writing team of Muna Lee and Maurice West Guinness), one of the final authors initiated into the Detection Club before the outbreak of the Second World War and with it the demise of the Golden Age. Afterward he continued publishing a detective novel or more a year, with his final book in 1968 reaching a total of 63, all of them detailing the investigative adventures of lanky and bespectacled gentleman amateur detective Ludovic Travers. Concurring as I do with the encomia of Charles Williams and B.A. Pike, I will end this introduction by thanking Avril MacArthur for providing invaluable biographical information on her great uncle, and simply wishing fans of classic crime fiction good times as they discover (or rediscover), with this latest splendid series of Dean Street Press classic crime fiction reissues, Christopher Bush's Ludovic Travers detective novels. May a new "Bush public" yet arise!

Curtis Evans

The Case of the Tudor Queen (1938)

Menzies looked up at the ceiling. "Almost makes you expect to find a spotlight up there. She wasn't an actress, was she?"

"Mary Legreye," Wharton said. "If that conveys nothing to you, then I'll add that she was an actress."

Menzies pursed his lips. "Well, she certainly finished up like one."

The Case of the Tudor Queen

CRIME FICTION emphasizing the realistic workings of police investigation, known today as the police procedural subgenre, really took its full strut upon the stage, as it were, only after the Second World War, in the hands of such postwar authors as, in the United States, Hillary Waugh and, in the United Kingdom, Maurice Procter, yet significant strides in the development of the police procedural were made in both countries in the 1930s. In the UK authors like Basil Thomson, a former Assistant Commissioner of Scotland Yard and Director of Intelligence at the Home Office, and Henry Wade (pseudonym of Henry Lancelot Aubrey-Fletcher), a landed baronet and former High Sheriff of Buckinghamshire, produced notable proto-police procedurals (Thomson's recently have been reissued by Dean Street Press), while more traditional British detective writers, such as Freeman Wills Crofts and Christopher Bush, published excellent examples of crime novels with unusually credible police procedure for the period, the former in *The Loss of the "Jane Vosper"* (1936) and the latter in the book you hold before you, *The Case of the Tudor Queen* (1938), the eighteenth Ludovic "Ludo" Travers mystery and one of Christopher Bush's most impressive essays in fictional murder detection.

One of only a pair of Christopher Bush detective novels reprinted in the UK as a green-and-white Penguin paperback after the Second World War, *The Case of the Tudor Queen* in my view was especially well-chosen by Penguin editors as an introduction to Christopher Bush's detective fiction, in that in it time has been taken carefully to introduce readers to key series regulars in the Bush canon: canny gentleman detective Ludovic Travers, dignified manservant Palmer ("the very spit of an archdeacon in mufti"), amiably gruff Superintendent George "the General" Wharton, stolid Chief-Inspector Norris, dour Police-Surgeon Menzies and cheeky Detective-Sergeant Lewis. Yet in its emphasis on detailed police investigation and material clues the novel is somewhat atypical of pre-war Bush mysteries. On the other hand, the emphasis on alibi-busting is pure Bush, and fortunate first-time readers of the novel will encounter one of the finest alibis found in Bush's detective fiction—which means one of the finest alibis found in detective fiction, period. Additionally, although the non-series characters in the novel are seen only through the eyes of the investigators and thus are sparely (though quite capably) portrayed, Bush in *The Case of the Tudor Queen* in my estimation does a brilliant job of portraying a mystery with a theatrical milieu--all about the murder of a stage actress, Mary Legreye--in which this specific milieu is absolutely essential to the plot.

To be sure, the presence in Ludo Travers of a gentleman amateur investigator who is allowed not merely to sit in on but to participate equally with high police officials is implausible, to say the least. But this, as all readers of Golden Age detective fiction will know, was a confirmed convention, however unlikely, of the period that gave us such ingenious dilettante sleuths as Lord Peter Wimsey, Albert Campion, Philo Vance, Ellery Queen and Lancelot Priestly, to name but a few members of this distinguished company. It is also improbable that Travers, Palmer and Wharton, while taking time during a drive through Hampshire to visit the village of Wharton's birth, would just happen to encounter a woman, exiting in something of a flurry from a cottage gate, who will drop a bizarre murder case into their laps: Edith Bunce, dresser to Mary Legreye, the stage actress who has just come off a great success in the play *Stony Heart*, wherein she wowed audiences as Mary Tudor (the Tudor queen of the title).

It seems that Mary Legreye has vanished from her Hampshire cottage, The Briars, leaving behind her hat, coat, fur and gloves and a copy of the *Daily Record*. It is at Arden, Legreye's house in Westmead, near London, that Travers and Wharton discover the actress's corpse, displayed in a spectacularly ghastly fashion:

> What [Wharton] saw was the strangest sight of his long career. . . .
>
> [. . .]
>
> "My God!" he said. "Did you ever see anything like it?"
>
> Travers shook his head, finding no words. Mary Legreye sat regally in that chair, arms along its arms and fingers hooked over its ends, like a queen poised to give an audience. . . .

In regal death Legreye eerily presides over a mortal tableau reminiscent of something out of a P.D. James novel. More gruesomely yet, Legreye's servant Fred Ward--"an old-time trouper who had fallen on hard times . . . a kind of permanent charity on the part of Miss Legreye . . . employed as an indoor servant, with odd gardening jobs to fill in his spare time"--is found sprawled on the floor of another room in the house, likewise dead. Both victims—whether by their own hands or another's--have been poisoned. By whose fatal hand was death twice dealt becomes the question for Bush's dedicated team of criminal investigators.

In *The Case of the Tudor Queen* Christopher Bush seemingly effortlessly conveys a complex and fascinating criminal investigation in multiple locations, with a panoply of fingerprints, photographs, analyses of stomach contents and good old material clues, such as a missing pair of valuable eighteenth-century miniatures, a lost cameo brooch, a couple of minute flecks of green paint and the crushed cap of a pen. Nor is psychological insight lacking, or a frank (for its time) portrayal of contemporary sexual mores in London's theatrical word, which Bush portrays economically but with the sure hand vintage mystery fans expect from another, rather more famous, Golden Age detective novelist: revered Crime Queen Ngaio Marsh.

Eventually in the novel it is the amateur, Ludo Travers, who brings murder home to its remarkably clever but revoltingly callous perpetrator, yet Ludo's triumphant solution is triggered by a singular piece of good fortune, inadvertently brought about by certain entertainment proclivities of his man Palmer. This happy happenstance in no way diminishes the genius of Travers' demolition of an alibi that is one for the ages. "The visionary Travers," at the time commented the exceptionally perceptive London *Observer* crime fiction reviewer Torquemada of the sheer wonder of it all, "seems to be crooning to himself with considerable justice: 'We are the alibi breakers; we are the dreamers of dreams.'"

PART ONE

*

Presentation

1

DOUBLE DISAPPEARANCE

Superintendent George Wharton of Scotland Yard returned from Jersey by the late afternoon boat, and Ludovic Travers, who had had business of his own in Hampshire, met him by arrangement at Southampton. Wharton, who had been born at Limpyard, asked if Travers would mind going through that village on his way to the main Portsmouth Road. The time of year was early April, the day a Wednesday, and the weather fine but somewhat misty, especially near the coast.

As for the three men in the Rolls, Ludovic Travers himself was driver; George Wharton sat alongside, and Palmer, Travers's man, sat behind. The three were diverse in type and yet each might have been taken for a somebody. Ludovic Travers had six foot three of lean, lamp-post length, and his monstrous horn-rims gave him the air of a benevolent secretary bird. He looked the author and the expert on social economics that he was, and though five minutes in his company would have made one aware of a first-class brain and a delightful manner, it would have taken much longer to know that the diffident Travers was a man of fine courtesies and rare generosities, a good listener but fertile in invention. An even longer acquaintance would have shown him as unconventional and even communistic in the things that really matter but holding tight as a limpet to those canons of living whose outward and cheaper expressions are an Oxford accent and the old-school tie.

George Wharton – the General, as the Yard not unaffectionately knew him – wore a huge weeping-willow of a moustache that gave him the air of a harassed paterfamilias, so that Travers once observed that his natural and only footwear should be carpet-slippers. But George Wharton could be more men than one. Acting and showmanship were in his blood, and he loved the dramatic moment and the sudden pounce. When in his eyes the means justified the ends, he could be various things to various men: wheedling, flattering, deferential, dignified, judicial, scowlingly suspicious, indignant to the point of apoplexy and the next moment chuckling away with a dig in the ribs for the man he had scared.

As for Wharton and Travers in conjunction, they were the perfections of the opposite that make the unique fit. To the suave theories of Travers, Wharton would oppose hard common-sense. Travers was always looking for the short cut; Wharton had learned from the experience of a life-time the value of what he called the tried and true, which meant patient inquiry, slow accumulation and the gradual elimination of the unwanted. Travers in fact was the amateur, to whom deduction and the chase were the most thrilling of hobbies; Wharton lived by the law and its accepted standards were his own, so that in his dignified moments one could perceive in him something of its slow tenacity, its cold impartiality, and a vague frightening something which can make the most innocent of us quake at its very mention.

As for Palmer, he had a face more patrician than his master's, and with his white hair and philosophic cast of countenance, looked the very spit of an archdeacon in mufti. Travers had been born with a gold spoon in his mouth, but Palmer, like Wharton, had risen from the ranks. Some would not have called the position of personal servant much of a rising, but Palmer, who had been promoted in the dim past from houseboy to the valeting of Travers's father, would have changed his status and place for nothing under the known heavens. In his case the ironic adage was disproved, for not only was the master a hero to the man, but each had for the other a respect and an affection that were remarkable.

So much for the occupants of the Rolls that nosed its way through the quieter roads of Hampshire that early evening of a Wednesday of April. It was about six o'clock when Travers all at once slowed down the car and looked tentatively about him.

'Something tells me we're off the road, George. What do you think?'

Wharton grunted – his usual preliminary to expostulation or defence.

'You were right at the last fork, weren't you?'

'I know,' Travers said, 'but we seem to have lost the telegraph poles.' He swivelled round to Palmer. 'We haven't overshot a road, have we?'

Palmer gave his little incipient bow. 'We passed one about a mile back, sir.'

'Push on, push on,' Wharton said impatiently. 'All these roads lead into one another. I'll keep an eye out for a direction post.'

But the road became a narrowish lane, and dusk was already in the sky when they came in sight of a house that lay on the outskirts of what looked like a tiny village. The land sloped steadily upwards to the left, and below, to the right, ran a stream which was wider than a mere brook and yet hardly wide enough to be called a river. On the left another lane could be faintly made out in the dusk, and as Travers slowed down at the direction post, Wharton was suddenly peering ahead.

'There's a woman. Better draw alongside and ask her to tell us where we are.'

The woman had emerged from the gate of that cottage which lay at the entrance to the village, with its garden running back to the river. She had first looked each way about her, and then had started off at a curious kind of trot. Her brown dress had something of the nature of a uniform about it, and she was wearing neither hat nor coat though the evening was chilly. If Wharton had uttered his thoughts aloud he would have said that she was running to the village shop to fetch, before it closed, something urgently needed in the house.

The car drew almost abreast and Palmer was ready at the door. Then Travers switched the sidelights on and the woman halted in her tracks and turned towards the car with frightened eyes. Then she came forward as if to look inside, and Travers and Wharton watched her amazedly.

'Would you mind telling us where we are?'

She stared frightenedly at Palmer, and now Wharton could see that she was a youngish woman; tall, not bad-looking, but with a face that had in it something calculating and hard. All at once he got out of the car.

'You were in a hurry to get somewhere,' he said. 'Can we give you a lift?'

She shook her head and her eyes went from Wharton to the car, then to Palmer and to the car again. She moistened her lips.

'I really wanted to go to the station.'

'And which way is that?' Wharton said.

'Straight on,' she told him. 'About half a mile.'

Wharton waved a hand at the car door.

'Get in then, and we'll take you. What's the name of this village, by the way?'

He had motioned to Palmer to go to the front and now as the car moved on again he shot a look at her and the scared flush of her face and the shaking hands.

'We were making for Limpyard,' he said cheerfully, 'only I'm afraid we've got lost. Where we are I don't know, except that this isn't Limpyard – I know that.'

'You're right off the road,' she said. 'I don't know this part very well but Limpyard's miles away. I think you ought to have taken a road to the right, over a bridge.'

Travers called back. 'What about the Portsmouth Road? How far is that?'

'I believe it's about seven miles,' she said, 'and you keep straight on.'

The car was moving dead slow through the narrow street of the village, and the post-office sign told Wharton they were passing through Arneford, whereat he faintly remembered the place from his boyhood, if only by name.

'You're meeting someone at the station, are you?' he said, still wondering why she had set out on a half-mile walk without a hat.

'Yes, my mistress,' she said, and with a touch of pride: 'She's Mary Legreye, the actress.'

'Really?' said Wharton, with a raising of eyebrows. 'A very charming actress too. I saw her in that last thing of hers at the Odilon. What was it now? Oh, yes, *Stony Heart*.'

She smiled. 'Lovely in it, wasn't she? I'm her dresser as well, you know, only the play came off week before last and we're coming down here for a holiday. Miss Legreye has a cottage.'

Travers was drawing the car in at the tiny yard, and at once the woman was all nerves again, fingers on the handle of the door as if ready to spring out, and eyes peering at the station and at the dim line of track beyond. Then when the car stopped before the ticket-office door, out she sprang with never a thank-you and was scurrying inside. Travers swivelled round to Wharton with a grimace.

'A rather jerky young person, wasn't she?'

'Yes,' said Wharton and his eyes narrowed. 'Don't move on yet though. One or two things I'd like to know more about.'

He got out of the car and lighted his pipe. As he afterwards confessed, there was nothing more in his mind than common curiosity, or, as he put it himself, a wish to know why a maid should trot a hatless half-mile to meet a mistress who could her-self have ordered some kind of conveyance at the station. Then, almost at once, the woman was coming out again and a man's voice gave a good night behind her as she shut the door. She moistened her lips nervously again at the sight of Wharton.

'There isn't another train – not to-night.'

Wharton smiled like a father. 'Look here, young lady, let's get all this clear. Do you mean that Miss Legreye told you she was coming down to-night, and now you've found out she can't come after all?'

'I didn't know how she was coming,' she said. 'I thought per-haps when I saw your car, she was in it.'

'So that's why you looked in the car,' Wharton said, and nod-ded. 'Anything else we can do for you before we go?'

She stood for an indecisive moment, then gave a quick shake of the head.

'I don't like going back . . . I'm afraid.'

'Afraid?' said Wharton. 'What have you got to be afraid of?'

But it took the best part of five minutes before they had her story clear. Her name was Edith Bunce and she had been maid and dresser to Miss Legreye for the last two months, having taken the post on the death of an old family servant who had been in Miss Legreye's employ for many years.

The story began on Sunday, at Miss Legreye's house at Westmead – a suburb which is accessible enough to town, being at the junction of the Portsmouth and Great West Roads. During the week before that Sunday, at Arden, the Westmead house, Miss Legreye had said that Edith might have three days off as a kind of holiday, but by tea-time on the Wednesday she was to be at The Briars – the Arneford cottage. The necessary luggage would be sent by Fred Ward, who would also be coming down on the Wednesday and would be taking some kind of a holiday till tea-time that day.

Fred Ward, an old-time trouper who had fallen on hard times, was a kind of permanent charity on the part of Miss Legreye, of whom he was a very distant relation. He was employed as indoor servant, with odd gardening jobs to fill in his spare time. He and Edith Bunce apparently ran the Westmead house.

'You'll pardon me,' Travers said, 'but didn't he once do a juggling act on the halls?'

'That's right,' she said. 'At least, so he's told me himself. I never saw him myself because he's much older than me.'

'I remember him,' Travers said. 'A short, thin man with quite a humorous face.'

Edith left Westmead immediately after lunch on Sunday, and, as far as she knew, Fred Ward was taking the luggage to the station the same afternoon, and the two would meet again at tea-time on Wednesday at the Arneford cottage. There had been such holidays and arrangements before, and Edith had supposed that her mistress would arrive about four o'clock. She herself had arrived at The Briars at just after three, and had let herself in with her own key. Since the door was locked she had naturally expected to find the place as it had been left a month before, but to her amazement she saw on the oak settle in the living-room her mistress's hat, coat, fur, and gloves, together with a copy of the *Daily Record* bearing Monday's date!

'Well, why shouldn't she have come down on Monday?' asked Wharton, who had gathered from the tone of the maid's voice that she had expected him to be tremendously surprised.

'But she told me and Fred she wasn't coming till to-day,' she said. 'Besides, if she came Monday the cottage wasn't aired or anything. There wasn't a thing in the house either. I was to order everything, like I always did, as I came through the village. And not only that. Soon as I got there I knew someone had been in, because drawers and things were open like as if there'd been a burglary.'

Wharton raised his eyebrows. 'A burglary, was there? Anything missing?'

She shook her head. 'Not that I could see.'

'You told the local police?'

'Well, no.' She shook her head again. 'You see, I expected Miss Legreye to come at any moment and then I'd have told her – or Fred.'

'Ah, Fred,' said Wharton. 'I was forgetting Fred. What happened to him? Hasn't he turned up either?'

'No,' she said. 'That's what's worried me and made me afraid.'

'A telephone in the cottage, is there?'

'Yes, but something's gone wrong with it. I couldn't get any reply.'

Wharton grunted and frowned, then thought of something else.

'Were any of the beds slept in?'

'No,' she said. 'The beds weren't even made up. They were just as we left them.'

Wharton turned to Travers. 'You're in no particular hurry and neither am I. What about going back to that cottage and calling in at the local police-station on the way? Besides, we might find Miss Legreye arrived when we get there.'

It was almost dark as they turned back to the village and Edith Bunce was hazy about the whereabouts of the local police. The station turned out to be an ordinary house where the constable lived, and Wharton found himself received with considerable deference. The telephone, the constable explained, was in the parlour, and Wharton did his phoning there with the maid at his elbow. But all that was reported about Westmead 223 was that there was no reply.

'Well,' said Wharton, 'that certainly shows your mistress isn't there. The house is shut up just as you expected it to be, so now we'll go on to the cottage and see if anyone's turned up.'

The constable put on his tunic and made a fifth in the car. As they drew near The Briars, eyes were searching the darkness for a light, but the cottage was still empty. Travers parked the car and the five made their way along the path to the front door, Wharton leading. The maid opened the door with her key and plucked up courage to reach round and switch on the light. Wharton stepped inside and the others followed.

'Peaceful enough here,' Wharton said, and let his eyes rove round. 'And this is the living-room, I see. That's the settle where you found her hat and things. And that's the newspaper. I think I'll take that; and you, Miss Bunce, go with the officer here through the upstairs rooms and see if everything's all right.'

He waited till they had mounted the stairs, then turned to Travers with a suggestive nod.

'Fishy business, don't you think? And what about that telephone?'

He hunted round till he found the cut piping and flex along the skirting board.

'Hacked through with a knife,' he said. 'Looks as if there has been a burglary after all. If so, how did the burglar get in? That front lock is a Yale. What about the back door?'

The dining-room faced south alongside the living-room and a door led through it to the kitchen, the door of which was locked and bolted. Then Palmer noticed a draught in the dining-room, and there above the catch of the window was a neat hole in the glass where the burglar had cut a way for his hand.

'Very pretty,' Wharton said, and pointed to the remains of stickiness where the paper had been stuck that pulled the circle of glass away. Then he cocked an ear. 'They're coming down again. Draw those blinds, Palmer. We don't want that maid to be scared stiff.'

'Everything all right?' he asked the maid.

'Nobody's been up there,' she said, 'I mean, not again.'

'They had been up before, had they?'

'Oh, yes,' she said. 'They'd thrown things out of the drawers just like they had down here. 1 had a rare job tidying up.'

Wharton was thinking what a self-possessed young woman she now was. That hard, calculating look had gone from her face, or maybe it hadn't been anything of the sort but merely watchfulness and fright.

'Let me have a look at those things of Miss Legreye's,' he said.

But there was nothing to gather from the black hat with its white trimming, the silver fox fur, or the black and white gloves, except that, according to the maid, Miss Legreye must have come down in her black costume with the white revers.

'And no bag?' asked Wharton.

'Nothing but what you've seen,' she said, 'and the news-paper.'

'What about the luggage?'

'It's at the station,' she said. 'I brought two of the bags with me and I thought Fred would bring the rest.'

'Any dirty plates or cups to show she'd had a meal here?'

'Nothing at all,' she said.

'No attempt at lighting a fire?'

'No,' she said, 'it was just as if she'd come in and sat down, then snatched up her bag and gone out again.' She hesitated a moment. 'You know, like as if she'd seen someone go past on the road.'

'Exactly,' said Wharton, and nodded portentously. 'She might have gone somewhere in someone's car, for instance. This fire here, of course, you lit yourself.'

He frowned for a moment or two, then gave another nod.

'I'll go back to your place, officer, and ring local headquarters, and you'd better stay here as company for Miss Bunce till you're relieved, or till Miss Legreye or someone comes. And as it won't be too far out of our way, Miss Bunce, I think I'll look in at the Westmead house and make sure Miss Legreye isn't ill or anything. That telephone cable's been cut, by the way. Anyone in the village who could do a quick repair?'

The constable suggested the garage proprietor.

'Right,' said Wharton. 'You get the exact locality of the West-mead house, Mr Travers, and borrow Miss Bunce's key, if she has one. I'd like a word or two with the officer.'

Travers waited with the Rolls outside the garage while Palmer interviewed the local electrician and Wharton did his telephoning. Wharton was late in getting back but was satisfied with results.

'They're buzzing a detective-sergeant and a man along at once,' he said, 'and taking up the burglary business.' The tone became rather too offhand. 'It's all no business of ours, of course, as I told them.'

Travers smiled. 'You're a delightful old humbug, George. You know you're simply bursting to find out what's happened, just as I am.'

Wharton waved an airy hand. 'Natural curiosity, perhaps.' Then, as the car turned left up the inland slope, 'That looks like the last of the river. Many a tiddler I've caught in it as a boy.'

'The Arne, isn't it?'

'That's right,' Wharton said. 'It widens out considerably lower down. Joins the Solent at Arnemouth.'

There was silence for quite a time while Travers pushed the car on through the quiet lanes. Then at last the junction came and the wide main road, and the Rolls moved on in earnest.

'Remarkable business, all this,' Wharton suddenly said. 'But I've thought of one possible solution. She didn't know that telephone line had been cut and she's been trying to phone and tell the maid where she is. As soon as it's mended, then everything'll be explained.'

'I'm glad you said it so regretfully,' Travers said. 'Personally I'd hate an anti-climax like that. In any case you're probably wrong. Your solution doesn't account for quite a lot of things.'

'Such as what?'

'That she left the cottage some time on Monday and therefore had all yesterday and most of to-day to send a message or telegram. Also it doesn't explain the disappearance – or non-appearance – of the man Ward.'

Wharton grunted. 'Do you think I don't know that? But by the way, I suppose there isn't any chance that she might have gone off with the man?'

'You mean eloped?'

'Something of the sort.' Then he shook his head. 'But he isn't the type for that sort of thing. An oldish man too, I gathered. What's she like herself?'

'The small and dainty type,' Travers said. 'A bit of a shrew according to popular rumour, but quite a good actress. Some say that Mary Tudor of hers in Stony Heart was just a mechanical reproduction of Harold Quintock –'

'Who's he?'

'The producer. They say he drilled her so well that she never varied a tone or gesture. Pure scandal perhaps – I can't say, for I only saw the play once.'

'Too highbrow for me,' Wharton said grumpily. 'I go to the theatre to be entertained, not to be harrowed. But this business we've got ourselves mixed up in is a devilish queer one, if you ask me. Why did she come down on Monday instead of to-day? Why did she leave everything except her bag and bolt out of the house?'

Travers smiled dryly. 'Explanations are easy, George. I'd say she had reason to go there on Monday when she knew the two servants wouldn't be there. Then, soon as she set foot inside the door she saw someone else had got there first – had beaten her to it, if you like – and that scared her so that she bolted.'

'Without hat, fur and gloves?'

Travers shrugged his shoulders. 'I know the loopholes well enough, George. That's what makes it all so intriguing; why, in fact, I'm pushing on this car to Westmead and you're not making your usual protests about speed.'

Wharton gave a little chuckle. From the rear seat came a deprecatory cough.

'You'll pardon me, sir, if I suggest something?'

'Go ahead,' Wharton told him quickly. Palmer was a great reader of the Sunday press and in his time had put in many a promising word at a ticklish moment in a case.

'Then why shouldn't Miss Legreye have been kidnapped, sir?'

Wharton grunted. 'Promising – yes. A car might have called up and a man she knew might have taken her for a trip and said she wouldn't need her hat and things. But how does that explain the non-appearance of the man Ward?'

'And the burglary,' said Travers, and then, hastily: 'Not that Palmer's wasn't a perfectly good theory.'

'The more I think about everything, the less I like it,' Wharton said. 'Between ourselves, the sooner we get to Westmead, the better I shall be pleased.'

Travers pushed the car on still faster. Wharton, usually so timorous of speed and scornful of Travers's hell-wagon, as he called it, leaned back in his seat with eyes closed, and only an occasional grunt betrayed the fact that he was awake and thinking. As the Rolls passed the clock tower on Westmead town hall, it was ten minutes to nine. A few yards on came the left turn and the bridge which the maid had mentioned. Two minutes later, Palmer was left with the car and Wharton and Travers were moving along Morfield Road, making for the third house, which, according to the maid, was the one known as Arden.

2

DOUBLE ENDING

MORFIELD ROAD, Westmead, is an old-fashioned backwater, with houses that were built in mid-Victorian times, and built leisurely and with ample space. One side only was built on, with the fronts facing south across a small strip of public gardens, beyond which lay the sunken line of the Underground. The houses therefore could not be overlooked from the south, and since each had a fair-sized front, most of which were bordered by well-grown trees and shrubberies, there was perfect privacy for each front door. And since moreover the road itself was a cul-de-sac, there was no through traffic and its pavements were deserted after dark except for such occupants of its houses as chanced to be out.

There were only twelve houses in all, and their modern convenience lay not only in their privacy and freedom from noise, but in the further fact that they were now only some four hundred yards from the Underground Station, with its direct connexion with the West End. Some of the houses were quite large, and Arden was sandwiched between two of them. It was a two-storey house, looking rather like a demure and squat country vicarage: an effect which was added to by the twin gates and the miniature crescent of gravelled drive. Tradesmen's entrances were at the rear, where a road as yet unnamed connected with Westmead High Street.

That precise situation of the house was important, as Wharton was to come to know, but in the half-light of that night he was aware of nothing but the darknesses which were the houses and shrubberies of Morfield Road. It was he who first made out the name-plate *Arden* on the brick pillar of the first of its twin gates.

'Here we are,' he said quietly to Travers. 'Not a soul inside by the look of it.'

They stood for a minute surveying the grey outline of the house with its central door and twin flanking bay-windows. The late moon was not yet up but the air was lightening, and there was a singular quiet in the trim secluded road enhanced somehow by the faint sound of traffic in the busier streets beyond. Then all at once Wharton's fingers closed on Travers's arm.

'Sh!... what's that over there?'

The moving darkness against the grey of the stucco-fronted house resolved itself into human shape. A man was coming from the back and he seemed to be stooping by the left bay-window as if listening. A moment or two and he was moving to the front door, and with their eyes accustomed to the light, and the door much nearer, they could see him stoop again as if listening at the crack of the door or the keyhole. Then he straightened himself and stood for an indecisive minute. He turned again, as if to make for the way he had come, and then, as Wharton moved to open the gate and call, he shifted his course abruptly and came straight towards them. Wharton drew back to the cover of wall and hedge and Travers stepped behind him.

The gate opened and the man came out, making queer muttering noises to himself. As he backed to the pavement, closing the gate behind him, Wharton stepped forward.

'You can't make anyone hear then?'

The man started round. There was a moment or two's silence while he peered at Wharton in the dim light.

'Suppose I can't. Anything to do with you, is it?'

'As a matter of fact, it is,' Wharton said mildly. 'I happen to be connected with the police –'

What happened then was grotesque, because it scarcely seemed to happen at all. As Wharton mentioned the police, the man was there, but as he hunted for his next words and shaped his lips to utter them, the man was not there. Before Wharton had realized he had gone, he was a blackness yards away, and then even the blackness went as he slipped down a side passage that, unknown to Wharton, ran between Arden and its neighbour. Then Wharton began to run, and it was the side passage that told him he was far too late.

'Well, I'm damned!' he said as he came pantingly back to Travers. 'What're you going to make out of that?'

But Travers was polishing his glasses – a trick of his when perplexed in thought or on the edge of discovery – and blinking away at the dark like an owl at the sunlight.

'Soon as I mentioned the police, he bolted,' Wharton went on fretfully. 'That proves he hadn't lawful business there.'

'A pity you scared him,' Travers said.

'I spoke quietly enough, didn't I?' Wharton rounded back.

Then he gave a shake or two of the head. 'A damn fishy business all this. I've half a mind to have a look through the house.'

'Isn't that what we came for?' asked Travers bluntly.

'What's that?' Wharton glared. 'You can't do things like that without informing the local police.' Then he shook his head again. 'Yet I don't know. We were given the key and we're just making a friendly call on behalf of that maid. Isn't that right?'

'You needn't trouble about easing my conscience,' Travers told him dryly. 'I'm proposing to go inside, right or wrong.'

'Come on, then,' Wharton said, and made for the door. Then he halted. 'What was that fellow doing round at the back? Better have a look there first.'

They moved off round the side passage, with trees and shrubberies belonging to the house making a dense blackness on their left. That embowering of the houses of Morfield Road, and their concealment, seemed indeed to have been a main object of the gardening of the neighbourhood. So dark was it that Wharton and Travers overshot the side door. It was locked and the side and back windows were fastened, and from nowhere inside the house came a glint of light.

'We'll have a peep inside,' Wharton said, and led the way back.

He opened the front door and struck a match to find the switch. He and Travers found themselves in the usual hall, with its cloak-room with washbasin and downstairs lavatory. A poorish-quality towel, still slightly damp, hung over the rail.

Wharton fingered it.

'Can't tell when that was used,' he said. 'Might have been on Sunday.'

From the hall, stairs led upwards to a landing. To left and right of where they stood were doors, and Wharton tried the one to the right.

'The living-room,' he said, and then, quickly: 'No, it isn't. What do you make of it? A spare room?'

'Looks to me like the sitting-room of Ward and the maid,' Travers said. 'If so, there's probably a drawing-room upstairs. Where's this door lead?'

Wharton opened it and found himself in a scullery. Neither room revealed anything of immediate interest and he led the way to the hall again and the left-hand door. That opened to what was most certainly the dining-room, its pictures heavy and its furniture massive and mahogany.

'This door'll lead to the kitchen then,' Wharton said. 'You can tell that by the outside door.'

He opened the door and his hand went instinctively out to switch on the light. But the light was already on, and Travers, hard on his heels, collided with his back. Wharton had suddenly halted and was staring at a something that lay at his very feet, and Travers, peering over his shoulder, saw what it was, and slowly drew back. Wharton gave a grunt and then moved sideways into the room.

A man lay there, hands so outstretched that they reached to within a foot of the threshold. His knees were drawn up and by the knuckles of his right hand lay a glass that would have been smashed as he fell but for the wool rug that stretched across the nearer floor. He was a small, grey-haired man with the wizened face of an ancient ostler.

'Fred Ward,' said Wharton, and nodded down at the body.

Wharton got to his knees and, while the wincing Travers watched him, prised open the mouth and examined it, and drew back the eyelids. Then he slightly moved the whole body, and tried lifting an arm.

'Dead for hours,' he said, looking up at Travers. 'No smell in the glass though, and nothing spilled on the rug. Don't know, though. There's the faintest smell of whisky.'

The suit was well worn but tidy, and all at once, with a sideways cock of the head, Wharton began sliding his fingers into the breast pocket that was wedged down by the arm. The fingers went full home, then withdrew, and Wharton got to his feet.

'Papers of some sort in his pocket, but they'll keep.'

Once more he stood looking down and nodding at the dead man.

'What do you think it is? Suicide?'

'That's what it looks like to me,' Travers said, 'but suicide or not, it's all rather terrible.'

'The light was on,' Wharton said, and looked round the room.

'Therefore he did it last night. Blinds drawn too, and curtains and everything. And what was he trying to get to this door for? If he wanted an emetic he was going away from it.'

He shook his head again. 'Shall we telephone now or later?

That maid ought to be brought along here. Wait a minute though. Two people didn't turn up down there. Here's one of them. You thinking anything?'

'Yes,' said Travers. 'Probably what you are, that the other might be here too.'

'Come on,' said Wharton, and made for the dining-room and the outer hall again. His eye caught the telephone and he hesitated a moment, then he switched on the landing light and began mounting the stairs. The first door he tried was that on the right, above the dining-room.

'Ward's room, for a fiver,' he said, and gave a quick look round. Travers noticed the theatrical portraits and a couple of framed playbills, the tobacco pipes in a rack and the pair of trousers hung over a chair. There was something else that struck him too.

'Seems to have been a bit of a racing man,' he said.

Wharton glanced at the racing calendar on the wall, and the photographs of race horses that hung on each side of the dressing-table mirror.

'Plenty of time to get him taped. Let's try the other rooms.'

His voice was little more than a whisper – a clear enough indication that what the house might still hold was more in his mind than the dead man he had already seen. Travers, following at his heels, felt something oppressive and unnatural in the darkness of a strange house and the eerie switching on of lights in rooms that were silent and cold as death itself. Unlike Wharton, he had never grown indifferent, and the perfect murder for him would have been one with its twisted problem of death maybe, but no corpse and no final retribution in yet more death.

'The maid's bedroom,' whispered Wharton, turning off another light and moving back to the landing again. Another door was opened and he gave a sniff or two.

'A bit musty in here, don't you think? Why all the trunks and things?'

'Theatrical trunks and oddments,' Travers suggested. 'I'd say it's the lumber room of the house.'

Next came the lavatory and the bathroom, the latter undisturbed and tidy. Wharton opened a door at the far end and there was a large bedroom.

'Miss Legreye's own room?'

'Sure to be,' Travers said.

Wharton frowned as his eyes ran round. Then he moved across the carpet and opened the door to the left and there was the passage from the landing. He turned round again and gave another slow look round the bedroom.

'No untidiness. The bed's made.'

'You're wondering who made it?' Travers said.

'Well, presumably she slept here on Sunday night.'

'She might have made it herself,' Travers said. 'Or else Ward did.'

'But he was supposed to go away on Sunday afternoon. 'He shook his head. 'No bag here. Still, let's see what's in the next room.'

There was one room left and apparently it ran along the whole front of the house as if it had been converted from two bedrooms. Wharton opened the door, flashed his match and found the switch, then turned to survey the room. What he saw was the strangest sight of all his long career.

The general impression was of an immense room, at the right-hand end of which stood various pieces of furniture behind a long screen. A carpet was on the floor and there were pictures on the wall, while a sideboard and three or four chairs stood at the left end. But the real furnishing of that bare room was a single chair, high-backed and winged, in which a woman was seated.

'I beg your pardon.'

Wharton backed towards the door again, then halted and started. So natural had been the pose that he had assumed she was alive. With cautious steps, like a man who approaches some ambush or trap, he moved slowly across the room till he stood by her. His hand went out and his finger touched the cheek. Then gently he tried to lift the arm that lay along the chair.

'My God!' he said. 'Did you ever see anything like it?'

Travers shook his head, finding no words. Mary Legreye sat regally in that chair, arms along its arms and fingers hooked over its ends, like a queen posed to give audience. Her feet were on the hassock at the chair foot, and her eyes looked coldly towards the door across the room and beyond the screen that hid the piled furniture.

'Did you ever see anything like it?' Wharton said again. 'What'd she expect? The photographers to come?'

A side-table stood at her elbow and on it was an empty glass with an uncorked bottle by its side. Wharton sniffed at the glass, then lifted the small bottle with his handkerchief for a glove, and sniffed again.

'Like oxalic acid to me.'

In a moment he was trying to prise open the dead jaws and Travers again turned wincingly away. In a couple of minutes Wharton was wiping his fingers on the handkerchief and backing to the door, eyes on that chair as if it fascinated him.

'It's sheer lunacy,' he said. 'It doesn't make sense. How could she poison herself and then sit there and wait? Why'd she pose and who'd she pose for?' He clicked his tongue. 'If it was oxalic acid it'd have twisted her body up. She couldn't have sat there and suffered agonies and kept a pose like that. It'd be like holding your hands in a red-hot fire, and not batting an eyelid.'

'People have done such things,' Travers said.

Wharton glared. 'Indian fakirs and all that rubbish.' Another click of a switch and he was backing out of the door. 'Come on, let's phone. The sooner we get people here, the better.'

But down in the hall he was still overcome by the strangeness of the thing he had seen, and distance seemed to invest it with some new horror, for his eyes were puckering and he was shaking his head.

'I can't get over it. Fascinates you, doesn't it? Sitting there just like life, and been dead a day or two. And why was that room cleared like that and she sitting there as if she was having her photo taken?'

'Don't know,' said Travers, blinking away as he polished his glasses. 'All I do know is it's the most horrible thing I've ever seen. When you spoke to her and I realized she wasn't alive after all, I felt every hair stand up on my head.'

Wharton grunted. 'Well, it's no use talking. We've got to do something.' He thought for a moment, then produced his note-book. 'You try and get hold of that Arneford number, and if you can't, try the police-station there. Have that maid brought here as quick as hell's hammers, no matter what car they hire. And if you can, find out if anything else has been discovered at that end. I'll get off to the authorities here and do my phoning. This business is a bit too big for them to handle.'

He turned at the door.

'Leave these lights on and the door open. A man or two may be along before I am, but don't let anyone move anything – not even the doctor.'

Travers guessed that Wharton had meant those lights to be kept on as a kind of reassurance, and he was glad enough of it. It was preposterous to fear the dead; and yet as he noted down the numbers Wharton had given him, he would keep glancing apprehensively about him, and doing everything with bated breath as if at any moment some terrifying sound might set his hair rising again and his hand shaking. Even when he began to speak on the phone, he stood with his back to the stair cupboard, and his eyes on the open door and his ear always alert for a sound from the stairs that ran by his head.

A detective-sergeant was speaking at last from The Briars. Nothing had happened down there, and in his opinion the robbery was a genuine enough one, though all that was missing, as far as the maid could ascertain, were two miniatures that had hung in the sitting-room, and were supposed to be valuable.

Travers gave guarded instructions about the maid. All luggage was to be brought to Westmead with her, even if the station-master had to be waked up.

'You needn't say a word to Miss Bunce,' Travers told him, 'but there've been developments here. Find out from the railway people, if you can, whether Miss Legreye came down by train on Monday, and get hold of anybody in the village who saw her. Have somebody at The Briars to answer the phone to-night if necessary, and don't be surprised if Scotland Yard sends someone down by early morning.'

Travers hung up and for a moment or two stood irresolute by the phone. Then there was a sound on the gravel outside and two uniformed constables appeared. The local police-surgeon was due shortly, they said, and Travers put one man on guard at the front door and the other at the back.

But the two men somehow made all the difference. The house no longer seemed as clammy and deadly silent but was almost miraculously a mere building that held a grim, and even alluring, mystery. So Travers made his way upstairs again, putting on his gloves as he went, and it was the bedroom that he entered first.

What was in his mind was that if Mary Legreye had gone surreptitiously to Arneford on Monday, then she had probably intended to stay there till the maid and man arrived on Wednesday, and if so she would have taken a bag of the attaché-case kind with her to hold toilet articles and a night-dress. As far as he remembered there had been no mention of such a bag at the cottage, and she had therefore brought it with her back to town. If there were no such bag, then she had not intended to stay at the cottage but had made a sudden call.

He let his eye run round that bedroom. The bed was made but with no night-dress case upon the counterpane, and there was no sign that a living soul had entered the room since it was tidied on Sunday morning. Then on a sudden impulse he looked beneath the bed, and there was a small week-end case. In a flash he drew it out. It was light enough for a woman to carry, and it was unlocked. Its contents were a night-dress case and night-dress, a vanity set, enamel-backed mirror and brushes, three handkerchiefs and a pair of dark silk stockings. Travers closed the case and put it back.

But he was polishing his glasses nervously as he stood by the bed. The case was only a new complication, for why should she have brought it with her and yet have left behind her hat, gloves, and fur? If friends had called for her in a car, then surely she should have brought everything. If she had been terrified at something, it was easy enough to understand why she had picked up the case and fled, but why leave behind hat, fur, and gloves, all of which could be worn, and were therefore no encumbrance?

There was another sound outside, and voices, and he made his way downstairs again. It was the police-surgeon at the door, and Travers took him through to the kitchen.

'All that's required at the moment,' he told Travers, 'is to ascertain roughly the time of the deaths. I believe the Superintendent is hurrying his own man here from the Yard, and then we can discuss everything together.'

He raised his eyebrows and gave a nod or two at the sight of Ward.

'Suicide, eh?' He got down beside the body. Travers gave a little cough.

'If you don't mind, I'll leave you here for a minute. I shall be upstairs if you happen to want me.'

Now he made straight for that bare room where the dead actress sat, and as he switched on the light and stood by the door, he saw several things he had missed before. For one thing the blinds were not drawn, so that apparently she had died in the daylight. She was wearing, too, that smart black costume which the maid had described. A gold wrist-watch was on her left wrist and a ring on the finger of her right hand.

Then his eye caught something on the floor in a line between himself and the window at the far end of the room, but as he moved towards it he saw something else on the carpet by his foot, not two yards inside the door. He stooped and picked it up. It was a flake of green, like a tiny chipping of green paint. As he moved forward he realized he had forgotten the exact spot from which it had come, but he marked it as near as he could guess, and slipped the flake into the corner of an old envelope.

As for that larger thing on the carpet towards the window, it looked like a large crushed bead or ornament, and he left it where it was. Then as he turned he saw something both he and Wharton had missed – the little handbag, which was lying on the floor by the chair as if the dead woman had laid it there. It was of leather, black with neat repoussé work, and matched the costume she wore. But why she should have laid it on the floor when the table was at her elbow passed his comprehension, and then as he rose from his knees he heard a calling from downstairs.

The doctor was looking up from the hall as Travers came down.

'Finished with that fellow,' he said. 'I judge him to have been dead just about twenty-four hours. Suicide, almost certainly.'

'Know what it was?'

He shook his head. 'Oxalic acid, I thought at first. Probably something quicker, like amyscine. Now what about the other?'

Then once more there were voices outside, and in came Wharton, apparently on good terms with himself.

'Here you are then,' he said. 'Doctor Stott seen the bodies yet?'

Travers explained. Wharton sent the doctor up at the double. Travers waited for the confidences which Wharton was now prepared to impart.

'Everything fixed up at Arneford?'

Travers reported. Wharton nodded.

'An hour and a half and she ought to be here. Good idea that about the luggage and making inquiries.' He gave a wink. 'I've convinced the people here that this job's more than they can tackle. Any minute now and our own people ought to be here.' He cocked an ear at the sound of an approaching car. 'This might be some of them now.'

3
OVERTURE

THE NEW ARRIVAL was Menzies, the grizzled old police-surgeon from the Yard. It had taken Travers a good many years to discover that Menzies had a dour and ponderous sense of humour, and to appreciate the fact that corpses to a police-surgeon are merely raw material for the day's work. Now he and the old doctor exchanged smiles and nods, while Wharton received a grunt of recognition.

'What was all the hurry?' Menzies said.

'Got to have certain facts ready,' Wharton told him, and began the explaining as they went through to the kitchen. Menzies merely pursed his lips at the sight of Ward.

'Tried the glass for prints?'

'Not yet,' Wharton said. He had borrowed from somewhere a pair of rubber gloves, and now he took another glass from the dresser to replace the one by the dead man's hand, and stood the original out of the way on a shelf.

'Don't let anyone touch that. You'll find us upstairs when you've had a look here.'

As they stepped once more inside that long room – the drawing-room, as the maid was to describe it – Stott came to meet them, and his expression was that of a man who is glad to see someone with whom to ease his mind. Experienced though he was in the multitudinous forms of death and its innumerable backgrounds, something of horror must have seized him at the lifelike pose of the dead woman and the stark setting of the room.

'Extraordinary business, isn't it?' he said. 'If it weren't for various obvious things, you'd say she died of a heart attack sitting in that chair and waiting for someone to come through the door.'

'Yes,' Wharton said, and frowned. 'It's a queer business, as you say. But it was poison all right?'

'Oh, yes. The same stuff as that chap took downstairs.'

'How long's she been dead?'

'About two days.'

Wharton grunted. 'Monday night, eh? Sure it couldn't have been earlier? The afternoon, say?'

The doctor looked at him. 'Why do you ask that?'

Wharton waved a hand. 'The blinds aren't drawn, for one thing.'

'I see.' He shook his head. 'Of course what I estimate is merely approximate. She might have died as early as midday on Monday. Stomach content ought to tell us something.'

A step was heard in the hall. Wharton listened quickly as the steps sounded on the stairs.

'Menzies,' Wharton said. 'Come over here, doc, will you? I'd rather like to see what effect the sight of the room has on him.'

He opened the door and Menzies came in. One glance and he was staring, which was a noteworthy thing. He frowned as he fingered his chin, and his look round the room was a slow one.

'This how you found her?'

'Yes,' said Wharton laconically.

Menzies looked at the ceiling. 'Almost makes you expect to find a spotlight up there. She wasn't an actress, was she?'

'Mary Legreye,' Wharton said. 'If that conveys nothing to you, then I'll add that she was an actress.'

Menzies pursed his lips. 'Well, she certainly finished up like one.'

Wharton introduced Stott, and the two got to work. Travers drew Wharton's attention to the smashed bead on the floor. The General ran his glass over it.

'Doesn't look like a bead to me,' he said. 'More like an ear-ring. Wait a minute, though. I know what it is. It's the top of a fountain pen.'

His eye caught an ornamental bowl on a small table among the stored furniture at the end of the room, and he placed it above the fragments. Then Travers produced the flake of green enamel or paint, and indicated where it had been. Wharton ran his glass over it, frowned at it and gave it back.

'Looks like a paint chipping to me. You'd better hang on to it till we see if there's any green paintwork in the house.'

Menzies and Stott seemed to have finished the preliminaries and Wharton moved over to the chair.

'Any idea why she had that hassock?'

'None at all,' Menzies said, and gave Stott a look.

'Speaking purely personally,' Stott said, 'I'd say it almost looks as if she put the hassock there and her feet on it so as to be able to get a better bracing for her hands on the chair-arms. It sounds silly, I know, but it's rather as if she pressed her feet on the hassock and gripped the chair and made up her mind she wouldn't move a muscle while the poison worked. You know, a horrible sort of stoicism.'

'The nature of the poison ought to show that,' Wharton said. 'If it acted like blazes – well and good. If it acted slowly, and sort of twisted her up, then there's been some jiggery-pokery. What's your own idea, Menzies?'

'A damn sight sillier than Stott's,' Menzies said bluntly. 'She cleared this room, or had it cleared, didn't she? Well, then, she set a kind of stage. Either she wanted someone special to come through that door and see her as she is now, or else she want-ed the pictures in the papers after she'd gone.' He grunted, as if ashamed at that romantic outburst. 'Probably some perfect-ly prosaic explanation. Child's play to people like you and Mr Travers.' He paused to listen. 'Sounds like some more of the brains arriving.'

What Wharton was accustomed to call the circus was drawing up outside. Chief-Inspector Norris, so Detective-Sergeant Lewis reported, was well on his way to Arneford, and would ring from there. Flashlight and fingerprint men got to work, and Travers sent a message down to Palmer to go home with the Rolls.

But as Travers watched the same old routine work in the kitchen, his mind was busy with things from which, indeed, there was no escape. If there had been something strange and bizarre about the dead woman to workaday and unromantic minds like those of Wharton and Menzies, then to himself there had been something of the uncanny and the horrible. That pos-ing and the stoical wait for death was already the one vital thing in a case which had scarcely begun. So vividly was that room impressed on his mind's eye that it was as if he had stared for a long time at some yellow glare and could now see nothing but that same yellow colouring and background. Flashlights and fingerprints seemed like finding answers to questions that were red-tape and triviality compared with the one great question. Discover, in fact, just why she had staged that flamboyant death, and there, as Travers saw it, was a case completely solved.

And about that same posing in the chair, he had had a sud-den idea when Wharton had mentioned the hassock to Menzies.

Now, when Wharton came across to where he stood, he put the idea up to him, vague though it was.

'You remember that newspaper I brought from Arneford?' Wharton said. 'Well, her prints were on it all right. Ward's prints on his glass too.'

'Something I'd like to put up to you,' Travers said. 'You saw *Stony Heart*, didn't you?'

'Yes,' said Wharton. 'Why?'

'Remember that scene where Mary Tudor interviewed the ambassador of Philip of Spain? You know, all alone in that small room, when he gave her the miniature and she was pretending she wouldn't send one of herself.'

'Yes?' said Wharton slowly, and frowned.

'Recall anything to you, does it?'

Wharton frowned again, then all at once gave a nod.

'I've got you. That pose of hers upstairs! Why, it's the same kind of chair, now I come to think of it!'

'That's it,' Travers said. 'A high-backed oak chair – only the reproduction one upstairs has a soft seat. The way we found her upstairs was just how she sat in that scene in the play – imperious, regal, giving nothing away. There was a footstool too, if 1 remember rightly. I know there was exactly the same pose: the sitting body upright to make the most of her lack of height, and the arms along the arms of the chair.'

'Yes,' said Wharton, 'but how's it all help?'

'Don't know,' Travers told him, 'but I have a feeling in my bones that it's going to mean a good deal.'

Menzies called to them.

'Finished with him now if you want to move the body.'

'Right,' Wharton told Lewis. 'Go through his pockets.'

He resumed his talk with Travers, eyes casually on Lewis making the search of the dead man.

'Seems to me she adopted that pose for sentimental reasons, if it really was like that one in the play. But what about clearing the room? Why'd she do that? Pretty heavy work too for a slip of a thing like her.'

'Ward might have done it for her before he left,' suggested Travers.

'No use theorizing,' Wharton told him impatiently. Then all at once he was moving forward to Lewis. 'Hallo! what've you got there?'

'Looks like a couple of miniatures to me,' Lewis said.

Wharton flashed back a look at Travers. 'Now we're making a start. Let me have a look.'

The pair of miniatures had been folded up in a handkerchief in the fob pocket of Ward's trousers. According to Travers they were late eighteenth or early nineteenth century, in the original black frames with pinchbeck acorn ovals and rings.

'Ancestors of hers?' suggested Wharton.

'Maybe,' Travers said. 'Rather too well painted for ordinary decoration. More like some celebrated actor and actress of the period. Worth quite a bit.'

'Roughly how much?'

Travers frowned. 'Can't say but we could soon find out. Twenty guineas apiece, at the least. Depends on who they were.'

'Well, they give us a line on Ward and the burglary,' Wharton said. 'We know where he was either on Sunday evening or Monday morning.' He looked up. 'Don't we know a good deal more? Why shouldn't she have suspected Ward and followed him down to Arneford? She found the miniatures, and probably something else, gone, and came back here at once. Ward wasn't here and she committed suicide. Later on Ward returned and found her here, and did himself in out of remorse.'

He had been giving a look of somewhat humble inquiry while expounding that theory, and Travers had nodded with no particular enthusiasm.

'Attractive, George. I wish it explained just a few things more.'

'Plenty of time for that,' Wharton said, and took a look at his watch. 'That maid ought to be here at any time now. Anything else of importance in his pockets, Lewis?'

'Only these two race-cards, sir.'

'Race-cards!' Wharton said, and darted forward. 'What do you mean – only? Good God, these are what we're looking for!'

Travers saw the significance of the two cards. Ward had apparently spent the Monday and Tuesday of his holiday at Warwick races. Each card was laboriously marked, with non-runners carefully crossed out and the investment on each race noted in the margin, with initials which, as Wharton pointed out, probably represented the name of the bookmaker with whom the business had been transacted.

'Well,' said Wharton, but just a shade too confidently, 'that shows why she didn't find him when she got back here. And it proves why he didn't get back here himself till the time when he did himself in.'

Travers was shaking his head. 'All the same, George, I don't see where the miniatures fit in. You'd have thought he took them to sell or pawn, to raise money for the two days' racing. But we found them still in his pocket. And why'd he come back here at all? Didn't you understand from that maid that he'd left on Sunday for good, as it were? He wasn't to turn up again till this afternoon, and down at Arneford.'

Wharton tossed his head impatiently as he took another glance at his watch.

'Couldn't he have pawned the miniatures, raised the money and then got 'em out of pawn again last night? Still, that'll all be cleared up when she gets here. Nothing else of importance, Lewis?'

'Only this key, sir, that fits the front door, and this account from a bookmaker. And these other two or three keys on a ring.'

'Looks to me as if one might fit that lock at the Arneford cottage,' Wharton said. 'Still, let's have a look at the account.' He grunted as he ran his eye over it. 'Been going the pace, apparently. Owed six pounds odd, and I'll lay he didn't get much pay.' He glanced round the room. 'Might as well make a move upstairs. Soon as that maid gets here, you can get 'em both away, Menzies.'

The photographing was over and the fingerprint men were at work when the party entered the drawing-room again. The prints on the glass tallied all right, as did those on the poison bottle, which were Ward's above those of the dead actress.

'I like that remorse theory more and more,' Wharton said with a sideways nod. 'It certainly looks as if he got back here and found her dead, and knew himself responsible somehow. He saw she'd poisoned herself so he poured himself some out of the same bottle.'

He made an entry in his notebook at that, then moved nearer to the chair.

'Sallow complexion, hasn't she?'

'You mean, normally?' Menzies asked ironically.

Wharton waved his hand. 'Well, you and I've seen enough like her to know what she looked like when alive. 'He ran his glass over the grey cheeks. 'Been made up too, by the look of it.' He peered more closely. 'You have a look, Menzies, and you, doctor. Surely there's something wrong with her face?'

'She did have a sallow complexion,' Travers said. 'Perhaps I'd call it a saturnine or petulant expression. In my own mind I connected that with the suitability of the choice of her to play Mary Tudor. One rather imagines Mary to have had a pale and peevish face.'

He watched while the two examined the face of the dead woman, and the thoughts kept circling through his mind – pose in the play and pose in death; talk of miniatures and two stolen miniatures in a dead man's pocket; the make-up of the stage and the queerness which Wharton had discerned on the dead face. Then Menzies drew back.

'What do you think, Stott?'

Stott shrugged his shoulders. 'I'd say she made up, as usual, and then washed most of it off when she got indoors here. She didn't make any too good a job of it because she was upset.'

'Why did you say – as usual?' Wharton asked.

'Well, like any other woman then. If she had a naturally sallow complexion, all the more reason to disguise it when she went out.'

'The make-up was certainly removed,' Menzies said. 'She either washed in a hurry or else cried it off.'

'What's that?' Wharton was pricking his ears at once. 'You think that's likely? It fits in.'

Menzies gave a shrug of the shoulders. 'I can only say what I think. Tears don't come into my department.'

Wharton gave yet another glance at his watch.

'You can't move her till that maid arrives. She'll have to have a good look at her.' He fidgeted for a minute or two. 'If she isn't here soon, we'll have to find out what's happened. You get in that bag from under the bed, Lewis, and go through it and that handbag there. I'll have a look in Ward's room.'

The man in charge of the phone came up with a message. The car from Arneford had had a slight breakdown at Bagshot but would arrive in about a quarter of an hour. Wharton was cheerful once more, like a man who has waited for hours in a queue and at last moves towards the entrance. He lingered in the room for a minute or two and told Menzies all about the maid.

'Wonder if she'll be hysterical when we tell her about those two?'

'You're losing your nerve,' Menzies told him, and gave a kind of wink at Stott. 'The Superintendent is a great one with the ladies.'

Wharton moved off chuckling. It was always his boast that he could twist any woman witness round his little finger. Nature had endowed him, he would whimsically say, with some queer insight into their little tricks, their ostensible weaknesses and their subterfuges, all of which he could counter with stratagems and wheedlings and whatnots of his own. But his face straightened as he entered Ward's room and at once began opening drawers and turning over the contents.

'Not much here ... Those must be his best clothes he has on ... Uses his old pipes to keep moths away ... More theatrical keepsakes and rubbish ... Hallo! this drawer's locked.'

He went down to the kitchen for the keys which had been attached to the chain of the dead man's watch. Travers had a question for him when he came back.

'How much money was found on him, George?'

'Money?' said Wharton, and consulted his notebook. 'Two pounds eight and three. Why?'

'I just wondered if his financial position might have influenced his state of mind. If he'd had nothing, that might have contributed to suicide. I take it you're going into those race-cards to see how he got on at Warwick?'

'Lewis'll be the one for that,' Wharton said, unlocking the drawer. 'He's a great authority on racing.'

Travers had a look in that small drawer which Wharton had unlocked. Its contents were photographs tied neatly in various bundles, souvenirs of old music-hall times, envelopes full of press clippings, a cardboard box full of little personal knick-knacks such as a couple of old watches, pencils, oddments of make-up and a letter or two, and – something upon which Wharton at once pounced – a little diary book of the sort that sells for ninepence or a shilling. Wharton grunted as he turned over the pages.

'Racing tips and rubbish mostly. Catch-penny clippings about tipsters' letters and systems. Still' – he sighed hypocritically – 'I suppose the poor devil had to have a hobby.'

His eyebrows suddenly lifted, his finger went to a pencilled line and he held the diary towards Travers.

'See that? That'd be soon after that new maid got here. *Miss B. a nosy-parker.*'

Now he turned the leaves more carefully, reading extracts for Travers's benefit, his finger always dramatically pointing them out.

'*E n.p. again.* That'll be Edith up to her nosy-parkering. Row with Percy. Wonder who he is. *Quid Mr M.*'

He stopped there to consult his notebook.

'Those bookmakers of his are Lepper and Drive, so they can't be Mr M. Reckon he's someone Ward touched for a quid. Here it is again, only a week ago. We'll have to ask that maid who M. is. And look at this. Written only last Sunday. *Job for Mr M.* The last words he wrote.'

He was giving Travers an inquiring look. Travers frowned, and his fingers fumbled at his glasses.

'That book has his racing accounts in from the end of March, hasn't it, George?'

'Look for yourself,' Wharton said, and gave him the diary.

'Yes,' Travers said. 'Apparently he didn't back horses during the jumping season but made a start at the end of March at Lincoln, which means he's lost six pounds in three weeks or so. I see it's all down here – not the details of what he backed each day but the day's results and the full week's. We shall have to check that with the bookmakers.'

'I don't see what you're driving at,' Wharton said.

'That's because I haven't come to it,' Travers told him. 'And I don't know whether or not it's important when I do. What I want to point out is that he was mad about racing. He didn't take the book with him to Warwick but he'd have entered up the accounts for the two days as soon as he got home last night. But what happened when he returned here was so important that it kept him from making the entries.'

Wharton shook his head. 'You're looking at things from an angle I can't follow. Still, you take the book and see what you can make of it. Take these race-cards too.'

The remainder of the search produced nothing and they made their way to the drawing-room again. Menzies and Stott were chatting away and the fingerprint men were still at work.

'Anything else occurred to you two?' Wharton asked genially as he came towards the chair.

'As a matter of fact we were just discussing her,' Stott said. 'A bit of a spitfire, wasn't she? I mean, as I was telling Menzies here, I happened to hear my wife and daughter talking about some quarrel or other when she was supposed to have slapped some other actress's face.'

Wharton ran a critical eye over the dead woman.

'Well, there isn't much of her, and that kind's generally inclined to be quick-tempered. How old did you make her, by the way?'

The two came over. Menzies rubbed his lean chin.

'Nearer forty than thirty.'

'A bit younger, surely,' said Stott.

'What do you think, Mr Travers?' Wharton said.

But the last thing Travers wanted to do was to make another ghoulish examination of the dead woman's face.

'Let me see,' he said. 'Didn't she first come out with the London Repertory, just after the war? I seem to remember her as quite a young actress then, doing minor parts. That would make her about thirty-five.'

'The dangerous age,' said Wharton oracularly. 'That's why a woman hangs on to the early thirties for all she's worth. Soon as they get beyond her, then she takes a jump clean into middle age.'

'What do you mean by dangerous?' asked Stott.

'Well, in love affairs,' Wharton said, and waved airy hands while he hunted for more arguments. 'I mean, if she falls in love then, well, heaven help her.' He shrugged his shoulders. 'She knows it's the last chance. That's why she sticks this side of thirty-five as long as she can. Unless, of course, she's married already, or famous; then it doesn't matter a damn.'

'I hope you're taking all this down,' Menzies told Stott. 'We don't know a thing about women –'

The ponderous humour was interrupted by the sound of a car. Wharton hurried across to a window, opened it and leaned out.

'Here she is at last,' he said. 'Another ten minutes and you two can get to work. What about you, Lewis? Anything in the bag or handbag?'

Lewis gave a wry smile at the row of women's oddments of which he was trying to make an inventory.

'Not much in my line, sir.'

Wharton gave a nod and in a moment was pattering down the stairs. Travers, following more leisurely, saw below him in the hall the frightened face of the maid. Wharton's voice came unctuously.

'Ah! Miss Bunce, here we are then. Just come in here for a minute, will you, till you've got over your journey.'

Over his shoulder he made a quick sign to Travers, then with a fatherly touch of her arm, handed her over, and himself opened the sitting-room door.

'I'll just have a word with the driver,' he said, and Travers found himself alone in the room with the maid.

4
ACCORDING TO BUNCE

'Won't you sit down?' Travers said.

The room felt cold and damp and he stooped and lighted the gas fire. He heard her move behind him, while in the hall outside was the tramping of feet, which he guessed would be the men taking up the luggage.

'That looks much cosier already,' he told her, and smiled. 'Rather a shock for you, having to hurry all the way back here?'

Her look was watchful and strained, with something of apprehension, and, strangely enough, it softened her face and made her seem young and far from bad looking. She gave him a quick glance as she moistened her lips.

'Has anything happened?'

There was a slight cockney intonation that went perfectly with the look of her.

'I'm afraid there has,' he told her gravely. 'Ward has – well, he's committed suicide.'

'Oh!' Her mouth gaped, then as quickly the expression changed. 'In the gas-oven, was it?'

'You don't seem surprised,' Travers said, and then heard the telephone bell in the hall. That might be Norris, ringing from Arneford, and almost at once he could catch Wharton's quick impatient voice.

'I beg your pardon,' he said. 'You were asking if he used the gas-oven. Why did you ask that?'

'Well'- she tittered nervously – 'he was often talking like that. Used to say there wasn't anything worth living for.' A slight smile. 'Especially when his horses went wrong.'

'Ah, yes,' said Travers. 'We know all about the horses. Still, we'll wait a moment and then the Superintendent will be in.'

'The Superintendent?' She stared. 'You mean, the police?'

Travers smiled. 'Only the gentleman who was with me at Arneford.'

The door opened and Wharton stepped in. First he adjusted antiquated spectacles, which gave him that fatherly, understanding look, then he peered benignly over their tops.

'Here we are then, all nice and cosy. And how's Miss Bunce? Feeling not too tired?'

'I've told her about Ward,' Travers said. 'She was saying he often threatened to commit suicide.'

'Really,' said Wharton, as if shocked. He repeated the word to gain time, then gave a nod or two. 'But you haven't told Miss Bunce the other news. I'm afraid it's going to be a shock.'

Now she looked genuinely frightened. The words came stammeringly.

'Not – not anything to – to do with Miss Legreye?'

'I'm afraid so,' Wharton said. 'She's dead too … Suicide.'

She stared again, then all at once her handkerchief was out and she was sobbing. Wharton winked flagrantly at Travers and made his way over.

'There now,' he said, patting her back. 'There now, you must pull yourself together and be brave. I knew it'd be a shock to you but you mustn't let yourself give way. We've all got things to do. Besides, you've got all the pluck in the world –I know you have. I told Mr Travers here that we were lucky to have someone coming like you. Someone who'd just give a quick look at them both, so that we could be sure they *were* Ward and Miss Legreye.'

By the time the blandishments were over, she was sitting up and giving a last dab to her eyes. Wharton's hand went to her arm.

'Only a matter of two minutes and it'll be all over. You let me take your arm. There now, nothing to be frightened about. Nothing at all.'

The two moved off towards the kitchen and Travers stayed in the hall outside. Wharton was talking earnestly as the kitchen door was neared, then there was a gasp.

'It's Ward all right?' Wharton was asking.

'Yes,' she said feebly, and was feeling for her handkerchief again. Wharton began hustling her back to the foot of the stairs.

'There now, you see there wasn't anything at all.' He patted her shoulder.' Now I expect you'd like to see your mistress before she's taken away. Just a quick look.'

She gave a dab at her eyes, then let him lead her. At the door she seemed reasonably composed. Wharton whispered:

'Don't be alarmed at the men in the room. Two of them are the doctors.' A last reassuring pat. 'Now we'll go inside. Just a quick look before they take her away. She's sitting in her chair, looking ever so peaceful.'

He opened the door and drew her in. The room itself and its strange bareness seemed to catch her eyes first, then they fell on the chair and the seated figure. A queer little gasp, then her fingers went to her mouth and all at once she was slithering to the floor.

Menzies was over in a flash. Wharton drew aside till he looked up.

'Just a faint, that's all. She'll be all right in five minutes. There's some sal-volatile in my bag, Stott.'

'Just a minute,' Wharton said. 'Let Doctor Stott see to her in that bedroom and you get the bodies away. Have this one stripped and leave everything behind. Lend a hand there, quick, and have everything clear before she comes round. She's seen all I want her to see.'

Another moment and he was giving fresh orders. A man was to go to the local police-station to try to collect copies of any daily paper of Tuesday's and that day's date. Then he scribbled a brief announcement of the tragedies for the late press, and told Lewis to phone and collect in return any obituaries the press could supply.

'Get anything out of Bunce?' he asked Travers.

Travers told him the little he had learned. Wharton nodded.

'She was shocked all right. Never suspected a thing. Might as well see how she's getting on.'

He wreathed his face into suitable smiles as he entered the room, and his voice was rich with sympathy.

'How is she, doctor? Feeling better?'

'Much better,' Stott said breezily. 'Just a minute's fainting fit. Nothing to worry about at all. A few minutes and I'll send her something round.'

Wharton nodded to him to go, then approached the bed where she was now sitting.

'And how're you feeling now? Quite all right again?'

She smiled wanly.

'That's better,' Wharton said heartily. 'What you want is a real nice cup of tea. I think we could all do with one, Mr Travers, if you wouldn't mind seeing to it.'

It was a quarter of an hour later when Travers came in with the tray, and he found Wharton and the maid talking like old friends. Wharton breezily waved aside the regretful announcement that there was only tinned milk.

'Talking of food,' he said, 'did you find any in the kitchen?'

'Nothing but this slab of cake,' Travers said, 'and that was in a tin.'

Wharton thought for a moment, then manufactured a chuckle.

'Miss Bunce would make a good detective, so I've discovered.'

'Indeed?' said Travers politely.

'Yes,' Wharton went on. 'Take this slab of cake, for instance. Is it the same as you left it on Sunday?'

'I think it's smaller,' she said.

'There we are,' said Wharton triumphantly. 'Then Ward had some when he came in last night.'

She smiled. 'Oh, but he might have had some on Sunday.'

'And you can't tell us just how much of the cake is gone?'

She hesitated, then shook her head. Wharton cut in, still breezily,

'Well, no use talking and letting this tea get cold.' He began to pour out. 'By the way, Mr Travers, Miss Bunce tells me she made this bed. That means Miss Legreye didn't sleep here on Sunday. I suppose you haven't any idea where she did sleep?'

'I can't say,' she said. 'Sometimes she used to go to a hotel or to stay with friends and leave me and Fred here alone. That'd only be for a night, though.'

The talk slipped easily along as they sat there munching cake and drinking tea. Not only did Edith Bunce acquire a confidence but before long she was showing something of what would be a natural perkiness. She had a very poor opinion of playwrights, for instance, as was seen from her tone when she said that Miss Legreye had stayed on at Arden to read a play or two in manuscript.

'But you had the definite impression that she was going for a private holiday till she rejoined you and Ward at Arneford,' Wharton said. 'No idea at all where she was going, or to whom?'

'She just sort of hinted it was with friends.'

'I see, and Ward said he was doing what?'

She gave a superior kind of titter at that.

'Oh, him; he was going to the races. He didn't often get the chance.'

'Warwick's rather a long way,' Wharton said. 'How'd he raise the money?'

'He was paid on Saturday, same as me, and he'd been saving up. Oh, and he had a nephew at Warwick. That was why he wanted to go.'

Ward's hobby in the winter was apparently football pools and the tricky catch-penny competitions, but all that was only a kind of marking time for the opening of the flat racing season. His wages were a pound a week and his keep, and it appeared he was a very distant connexion of Miss Legreye's dead mother. He smoked about three ounces a week and every night he would spend an hour or so in the Three Bells, a public-house about four hundred yards away and just off the High Street. He appeared, in fact, to have been a steady goer, except in the matter of his racing hobby, when he was up in the clouds or deep in the depths according to the results of his betting.

'You didn't take him seriously when he used to talk about putting his head in a gas-oven?' Wharton said. 'It was merely blether, and you knew it.'

'I used to laugh at him,' she said. 'Then he used to get angry.' Her eyes narrowed. 'He told tales about me to Miss Legreye, I know that.'

'I know the type,' Wharton said sympathetically. 'But he got on well with Miss Legreye, did he?'

She sniffed. 'Couldn't do nothing wrong. I wouldn't have trusted no one same as she did him.'

'How do you mean?'

'Well, leaving him with the whole place when we were out, And letting him have the run of everywhere.'

All that turned out to mean that when Ward had a so-called holiday, he was at liberty to sleep out or use his Arden bed, a piece of information which Wharton was glad to have since it explained why Ward was in the house at all on Tuesday night.

'I know Ward's kind,' Wharton said, with a final summing up. 'Always harping on old times and the money they had. Still, we know most of what we want to know about him, thanks to you. And now yourself. What did you do when you left here on Sunday? Go for a nice time?'

At once something was wrong. She flushed slightly, opened her mouth, closed it again, then fidgeted nervously. When she did speak, the words came with a rush.

'I went with my sister, at Cadmarsh.'

'Cadmarsh?' said Wharton reflectively. 'Let me see now. Where's that?'

'It's near Cambridge.'

'Why, of course!' He clicked his tongue. 'And you stayed there all the time with your sister?'

'Well – yes. My sister-in-law she is, really.'

'Well, I hope you had a good time,' Wharton said, with a quick glance at his watch. 'You're not feeling too tired to go on? What about another cup of tea?'

The talk was resumed, and now Wharton came direct to the dead actress. Who were her friends – male friends in particular, and what men were frequent visitors?

'Oh, she wasn't that sort,' she said. 'She was ever so particular. You know, what they call prim and proper. She'd tick you off if you even so much as started talking about men.'

'Miss Legreye came of rather a good family, I believe,' said Travers, making one in the talk for the first time.

'Oh, yes. She told me about her father who was a vicar, somewhere in the country.'

'But who did actually come here?' asked Wharton.

The list was soon exhausted. There was Mr Frodling, the manager of the Odilon; Mr Quorne, who had been the Philip of Spain of the play *Stony Heart;* Mr Abney, who had been the Spanish ambassador, and Mr Martelle, who was the play's author. Wharton and Travers exchanged looks at that mention of a name beginning with M.

'Oh, yes; Mr Martelle,' Wharton said. 'He came here often, didn't he?'

'What, Mr Martelle?' She shook her head. 'He didn't come any different to anyone else.' A moment's thought. 'Twice he came, since I've been here.'

'A friend of Ward's, was he?'

Her lip curled slightly at that. 'Everyone used to be chipping Ward. He used to make out he was sort of like they was. You know, all mixed up with the theatre.'

'I get you,' Wharton said. 'And what about relatives?'

Again there was a peculiar hesitation as if she were afraid of using the wrong words.

'Well, there's her nephew.'

'A nephew, is there? And what's his name?'

She looked even more self-conscious. 'Well, Gray is his name, like hers. Legreye was her stage name.'

'Really,' said Wharton. 'That's news to me. And the Christian name of the nephew?'

'Well, Percy. I mean, she used to speak of him as Percy.'

There was another quick interchange of glances.

'You don't happen to know his address?'

She made rather too much effort to remember. 'I don't – not really. Lewisham, though, I believe. You see, he's Meerschaum, the one who gives impersonations on the wireless.'

'Oh, yes,' said Wharton. 'I've heard him. Gives impersonations of the stage and screen stars. Calls himself Meerschaum, and his name's Percy Gray. Any other relative?'

'Well, there's her husband.'

'Husband?' said Wharton, startled. 'I hadn't the faintest idea she was married. Just shows you, Mr Travers, how little we know about the private affairs of some public people.'

She was bursting to cut in with the story.

'He's not really her husband, not now. She got a divorce last November, well, not a real divorce. I mean, she isn't free from him till the end of this month.'

'I get you,' Wharton said. 'She obtained a decree nisi, as they call it, and she had to wait six months for it to be made absolute.' He pursed his lips, then had an idea. 'I suppose she wasn't intending to marry again?'

'Well,' – she tittered – 'I'm not supposed to tell you, but I said to her one night when she was in a good mood – which she wasn't sometimes – about getting married again, and she snapped my head off with why shouldn't she. I said she ought to – you know, putting her in a good humour again – and she said some people might be surprised. She sort of smiled to herself – you know, all girlish like – and said if she did it would be something romantic, like the play.'

She paused triumphantly. Wharton made a wry face.

'Like the play? I don't get you.'

'Well, that was what she said. Like in the play. You know, the play she was in – *Stony Heart*.'

Wharton looked at Travers. Travers shrugged his shoulders.

'We'll talk about that some other time,' Wharton said, then gave a roguish look. 'But I suppose a clever young lady like you had her own ideas who the gentleman was?'

'Well'– another titter – 'I used to think it was the one who telephoned sometimes.'

'Now we're coming to it. And who was the gentleman who telephoned?'

'I don't know,' she said. 'He had a deep bass voice – ever so deep.'

Wharton grunted. 'Well, that helps a bit. Anything else you can remember?'

'I only heard him two or three times,' she said. 'He used to ask if Miss Legreye was in and wouldn't give no name.' She'll know who it is, 'he used to say. When I used to tell her the gentleman with the bass voice was on the phone, she used to flush and look all silly.'

'And you never met anybody, here or elsewhere, who had that voice?'

'Well, no – I didn't.'

'Do you mind telling us the husband's name?' Travers asked.

'Certainly,' she said. 'Wolters. Mr Alfred Wolters. Fred told me all about him, how he used to come round kicking up rows and how she got a separation.'

Wharton took a quick look at his watch, then got to his feet.

'Good heavens! Gone twelve o'clock. Time you were in bed, young woman. Just one little question and then off you go. Didn't you tell us that during the month you've been here, there was a holiday down at Arneford?'

'That's right,' she said. 'Soon as I got here, it was. We went down last thing on Saturday and back Sunday night because Miss Legreye was playing.'

'And what did everybody do there?'

She frowned in thought. 'Let me see. Miss Legreye went to see some friends at Southampton. She went by bus in the morning and didn't get back till after tea. I tidied the place up and Fred did a lot to the garden. A rare old state they were both in, because she'd only bought it in November.'

'Right,' said Wharton alertly. 'Now just a peep in the drawing-room and then – bed. You needn't be alarmed. There's no one there now but a nice young police-sergeant.'

She smiled saucily at that but the self-possession went as she neared the door. Wharton led her in and had a quick word with Lewis to clear the air.

'Well, Lewis, finished that inventory? If not, here's Miss Bunce to lend you a hand. You might go through that heap of clothes, for instance, Miss Bunce, and see if everything's all right.'

'Why have they been altering the room?'

The question was unexpected and there was fright behind it. Wharton smiled.

'Oh, that's nothing at all. Time enough to-morrow to talk about that.' The look became crafty 'Unless you can tell us about it?'

She shook her head and said nothing, but her eyes were still searching the room.

'Was this the original chair used in the play?' Travers asked.

'Oh, yes,' she told him. 'She bought it as a keepsake – you know, when the run ended.'

'Seen these before?'

She stared at the miniatures which Wharton had suddenly produced.

'Why, they're the ones that were stolen!'

'That's right,' Wharton said. 'But we'll talk about them in the morning. The clothes all right?'

'I think so,' she said, then frowned. 'I don't remember these, though.'

'Which?' Wharton said, and came nearer to relieve the embarrassment. 'I see. Cami-knickers. What's wrong with them?'

'Well' – she flushed slightly – 'they're out of date. And she wouldn't have had artificial silk, like this. All her things are crepe de chine.'

'But she might have had them, unknown to you?'

'Well, she might. But they look almost new.'

'Ah, well,' said Wharton, 'we'll leave them here and they won't run away. What about her jewellery? Where's that kept?'

'In the bank, except what she used to call the little things.'

'Various items here, sir,' cut in Lewis.

'Right,' said Wharton. 'That sleeping draught that Doctor Stott sent is in Miss Bunce's room? Good, then it's time for bed.' He moved off through the door with her, still talking. The door closed. Lewis gave a wink.

'Not a bad little piece that, sir?'

'I'm no judge,' Travers said, 'but I won't disagree.'

'The General playing up to her, sir?'

Travers smiled. 'Well, I gather we're all expected to be polite to her till further orders. Where are the print men, by the way?'

'Doing Ward's room,' Lewis said, and made a quick motion to indicate that Wharton was coming back.

He came in, watch in hand.

'I've arranged to have a talk with Norris at one. He's had all the prints by now. What'd you think of our friend who's just gone to bed?'

'Quite a good witness,' said Travers, careful not to catch Lewis's eye.

'A cheap little hussy – that's what she is,' Wharton told him. 'Two lies at least she told us. First thing in the morning we're checking up on her alibi.'

'We'd have been in Queer Street without her,' Travers said.

Wharton shrugged his shoulders. 'Well, what are witnesses for? Mind you, though, she hasn't even begun to tell us all the things I want to know. However, let's get on with it. Lewis, you go through two race-cards Mr Travers will give you and check the figures with the reports of racing at Warwick last Monday and Tuesday. You'll find the racing results in those two newspapers, and Mr Travers will explain anything you want to know. Take into account the fare, admission to the cheap ring, and nothing else. And if you'll go through that diary of Ward's, Mr Travers, I shall be obliged. I'll go through those press obituaries till it's time for Norris, then we'll have a look at all her private papers.'

He was turning away, and then he suddenly gave Travers a queer look.

'By the way, you were remarkably quiet all through that interview. You must have been doing the devil of a lot of thinking?'

Travers smiled. 'I don't know that I wasn't.'

'Any ideas?'

'Not particularly.' He was giving his horn-rims a polish and blinking away in the light. 'I did wonder why such great ones as you and Norris should be busy digging yourselves well into this case if it's nothing more serious that a double suicide.'

'Oh?' He shot a quick look. 'They're curious suicides, aren't they? And weren't you and me pitch-forked into the whole thing?'

Travers gave a shrug of the shoulders. 'It's not my affair, George. But when are you handing over again to the local people?'

Wharton glared. 'Who says I am?'

Travers smiled. 'Then you're not satisfied they are suicides.'

'Are you?'

Travers shook a whimsical head at him. 'You and I know each other too well to bluff. You're positive there's something fishy and so am I.'

'Have it your own way,' said Wharton, always grudging of information. 'But why do you think they're not suicides?'

'I'm pretty sure one isn't suicide,' Travers said.

'Which one?'

'You begin,' Travers insisted politely.

'I talk when I'm sure,' Wharton said. 'There's a time when theorizing's all to the good and a time when it's no damn good at all.'

Travers took a coin from his pocket and clapped it on the back of his hand.

'What is it, George? Head or tail?'

'Woman,' said Wharton, and, quickly, 'Why?'

'It's head and you've lost,' Travers told him. 'Your turn to say why you think the suicides or suicide is faked.'

'I'm saying nothing,' Wharton told him. 'Except perhaps this. Ward didn't commit suicide, or my name's Smith.'

'That's what I think about Mary Legreye,' Travers said.

'Oh?' said Wharton, and shot another look. 'How do you know?'

'You told me,' Travers said suavely.

'I told you? When?'

Travers shook his head. 'No use theorizing, George. It mayn't even be a theory – only a hunch.'

Wharton grunted an inaudible something and went off to his obituaries. Lewis caught Travers's eye and gave an almost imperceptible wink.

5

THE LONG NIGHT

WHARTON CAME BACK from his telephoning at a quarter past one and he was in reminiscent vein.

'You wouldn't think it was only eight hours ago all this started.' He got out his pipe. 'Sandwiches and hot coffee due at any time now, and I know someone who won't be sorry.'

'What's Norris up to?' Travers asked.

'Just looking round,' Wharton told him. 'He's had all the prints and he's got a couple of men with him. How're you getting on, Lewis? Worked it all out?'

'Yes, sir,' Lewis said. 'Me and Mr Travers between us. We reckon he cleared himself and just a few bob over. Can't say how much because we don't know what he spent on little things. That's allowing cheap excursion fare and seven and six for the ring, and two bob a day for oddments. We didn't pay any attention to his night's expenses.'

'Here's the address of his nephew, at Warwick,' Wharton said. 'I found it among the things in his room. And I've got a man going down there by the first train to get all the dope he can. Which reminds me. Soon as the pubs open in the morning, I want you to go yourself to his pub and pick up a bit more. What about you, Mr Travers? Got hold of anything out of that book?'

'Not a great deal,' Travers said, and showed him a small list of extracts. 'Here's confirmation of that first visit to Arneford the maid mentioned, when he did the garden. It refers to a tip given him by the local landlord of the Hare and Hounds. Here's one other reference to Percy, or I think so. It simply says – *P here*. But what about this? Lewis found it in his waistcoat pocket.'

It was a small paragraph torn quite neatly from a newspaper, and evidently from a column of theatrical chit-chat.

Martin J. Kevstein, President of Kevstein Incorporated, is due in London on Monday. Rumour has it that he is interested in Stony Heart, for which an offer by English Associated Motions, we understand, has already been turned down. In view of the present craze in America for British historical plays, Kevstein may be the big business with whom the Odilon interests have been waiting to deal.

Wharton merely pursed his lips when he had read it.

'You don't think it's important?' Travers said.

'Well, why should it be?' Wharton challenged him. 'Ward saw this in some paper, and as he was naturally interested in the play, he tore it out.'

'Exactly!' said Travers. 'He tore it out. If he had seen it in a paper in this house, or where he could bring that paper home here, he would have cut it out neatly and doubtless put it among the clippings in his private drawer. Also it's a spotlessly clean piece of paper, and therefore I'd say he tore it out of a paper he was reading on his way to Warwick on Monday.'

'Perfectly sound reasoning,' said Wharton, and ironically: 'I might say a model for comparative beginners like Lewis here. But what's its immediate value?'

'Frankly I don't know,' Travers told him, 'except that it's the last known link in the connexion between him and Miss Legr-eye.'

'Links!' He grunted. 'We're as bung full of links as a chain factory. Still, make a note, Lewis, to send a man first thing to find out what paper and issue the cutting came from.'

Suddenly he caught sight of that bowl that covered the broken top of a fountain pen, and at once he was grabbing an envelope and getting down to his hands and knees and picking up the broken pieces.

'I must ask that maid in the morning if her mistress had a fountain pen like this. By the way, you'd have thought that anyone who trod on it would have known it and picked the pieces up. Just look here a minute.'

The two went over. Wharton explained.

'Looks a certainty that Ward trod on it. See the softness of the carpet, and the thickness of this knobbly bit at the end of the pen? What'd Miss Legreye weigh? Eight stone, or eight and a quarter at the most. Ward may look skinny but he's best part of ten stone and his boots were pretty solid.'

He got to his feet with his envelope.

'In the morning we'll send out and get a top as near to this as we can and make experiments. We've got to be sure that Ward actually did come into this room.' He thought of something. 'By the way, Mr Travers, show Lewis that speck of green you put in the envelope.'

Lewis had a look.

'What is it, sir? Paint or enamel?'

'Whichever it is,' Wharton said, 'the house must be looked through for paint or enamel like it.' He listened. 'This sounds like food coming. Better knock everyone off for a quarter of an hour.'

Lewis and Travers fed upstairs but Wharton had his quick meal at the telephone, and came up ready to go on till breakfast.

'I've arranged for a man to go down to Cadmarsh, where Bunce said she spent her little holiday,' he announced. 'He'll be there by breakfast-time.'

A tap at the door and the phone man came in.

'Doctor Stott would like a word with you, sir.'

'Then why couldn't he have rung when I was down there?' Wharton said snappily as off he went. And it turned out to be nothing in particular after all, merely the wonder if Wharton knew that Ward had a twisted arm.

'What the devil difference does it make?' Wharton asked plaintively when he came back. 'I didn't spot it but I knew he'd had a stroke or something that put him out of the juggling business. The worst of these damn doctors is they have no sense of proportion.'

The muttering died away as he got out his pipe again. By the time it was lighted he was quite affable.

'Well, no rest for the wicked, they say, nor yet the ungodly. What's the next item on the programme? I think perhaps, Lewis, you'd better make an exact plan of that collection of furniture behind that screen so as to supplement the photos. In the morning we'll get that maid to have the room put as it was when she left it. If that produces ideas, we'll put everything back as it is now. After that you'd better go through all the luggage that was brought from Arneford, make an inventory and replace. Get what help you want.'

The pipe had gone out and he lit it again.

'What about you and me going through that bureau and any other drawers in here and her bedroom, Mr Travers? I expect these keys will be all we want. Better have a print man with us as we go along.'

But Wharton and Travers were soon in each other's way and it ended by Wharton taking over the bedroom search. Travers began on the drawing-room bureau, with Cowper, whom he knew well, for print man.

The bureau drawers were all open and held nothing of moment. But when the top was unlocked, the first things to be seen were a couple of manuscript plays.

'These will be the ones she told the maid she was staying on to read,' Travers told Cowper. 'What's this one? *Host of Heaven,* by Julian Corte. Never heard of him, though that's nothing against him. "Act One. Scene One. A Labour Exchange".' He turned the pages quickly. 'Another play about the dole. Try it. Cowper, will you? Take pages here and there to see if she read it right through.'

He picked up the other, and at once noticed it was a far less ornate affair; evidently typed quickly and only casually bound with brown paper. *Unwritten Diary,* by P. Martelle, it said on that cover, and beneath it – 'Tentative title and rough draft.'

'This is by the chap who wrote the play she was in last,' Travers said, and began dipping into it. It turned out to be a play about Pepys, and ingenious enough. The play began where the famous Diary ended. A skilful young continental expert had apparently put Pepys's eyes right and had then begun an intrigue with Mrs Pepys, who did a considerable deal of paying back her husband in his own coin.

'Her prints are all over this first one,' Cowper reported, 'so it looks as if she read it. Pretty light, though, towards the end.'

Travers smiled. 'Which might mean she got a bit bored and skipped the last pages. Try this one the same, will you?'

He watched the powder blown. In ten minutes it was clear that the play had not been read or even looked through. On the cover were unknown prints – presumably the author's – and hers superimposed.

'So much for that,' Travers said, and paused to write down his report.

Next came the small drawers inside the bureau, some locked and some not. An address book was hailed with delight.

'This'll save quite a lot of bother,' Travers said. 'So will this letter from her solicitors. About an investment apparently. Here's another, something to do with her divorce. And what's this? Curious. A receipt from a firm of private inquiry agents for thirty-two pounds.'

'Probably something to do with her divorce,' Cowper suggested. 'There's usually a lot of keyhole work wanted.'

'You're right, I expect,' Travers said. 'It's dated last October. Now what's in this one? A cheque book. Only four cheques left. Let's have a look at the counterfoils.'

In a minute or two he was looking for used cheque books and going through their counterfoils too.

'Found something, sir?' Cowper said.

'I don't know that I haven't,' Travers said. 'Perhaps you wouldn't mind asking the Superintendent to spare us a minute.'

There was nothing blase or superior about Wharton as he saw what the counterfoils told. Travers had four in all, and the two oldest showed no payments to Percy Gray. But the one beginning in the October had such payments, as did the current book. Most significant were the actual figures:

December	£10
December	£10

January	£20
January	£20
February	£10
March	£20
April	£20
April	£50
Total	£165–0–0

'It can't be an allowance she was paying him,' Wharton said. 'The figures are too erratic. It's blackmail. wouldn't you think so?'

'I certainly do think so,' Travers said. 'There's quite a story in those figures, if we could only read it. It's as if he was feeling his way till March, then had a setback. Then he was able to put on pressure and he finally got fifty pounds just before she died.'

'I'm beginning to see that story all right,' Wharton said grimly. 'A few hours' time and we'll prove it up to the hilt. If she was waiting for a decree absolute and was in love with some other man, as that Bunce woman told us, then she might have compromised herself and laid herself open to blackmail.' He frowned. 'I'm beginning to see a whole lot of things.'

Travers had been looking through that address book.

'Here's his headquarters,' he said. 'Twelve A, Tower Walk, Lewisham. Looks like a flat.'

'Right,' said Wharton, and ran a quick eye over the book. 'He'll be telling us a few things shortly or I'll have his liver out and slide on it.'

That room produced nothing else of consequence. Wharton had discovered nothing in the bedroom, but when he came back to the drawing-room, Travers was just closing the doors of the sideboard that stood by the far wall.

'Anything in there?'

'Drinks, and what look like the upstairs glasses,' Travers said.

'What's that?' He came over and had a look for himself. A decanter of whisky was there, a small quantity of brandy in another decanter, and partly used bottles of ready-mixed cocktail and creme de menthe, with two unopened bottles of port.

'The doors were locked?'

'No,' Travers said, but showed the key.

Wharton grunted. 'Then there was something she trusted Ward with, that I wouldn't myself.' He took bottles and decanters out. 'Go over these quickly for prints.'

All showed prints, some unknown, but the significant thing was that the neck of the whisky decanter had a beautiful set of Ward's, and the cocktail bottle quite a good set of hers.

'Right,' said Wharton, putting everything back again. 'If the post-mortem showed he took the poison in whisky and she took hers in the cocktail, well and good.' He suddenly looked round. 'But he couldn't have trodden on that pen-top on his way to this sideboard. It's nearer the window and clean off the line. And another remarkably funny thing. He couldn't have got back here till after dark. If he came up here, then why didn't he draw the blinds?'

'There're two things about that,' Travers said. 'In the first place he might have reached here before dark. The race-card shows that he didn't back anything on the last two races at Warwick, which hints that he took an early train home. Also, even if it was dark when he got here, what he saw in this room would have given him a shock big enough to have made his actions abnormal.'

'The whole thing's uncanny to me,' Wharton said, and grunted. 'I can't help thinking that Norris is where the truth is. Why did she bolt from Arneford and why did Ward presumably commit suicide – or do all these abnormal things – when he found her dead? Answer me those two things and there's nothing left to ask.'

He got down on his knees and had a look through the other compartment of the sideboard, which contained glasses as Travers had said.

'You've seen all these?' he asked.

'As a whole but not in detail.'

Wharton got to his feet. 'Well, tell me this. You saw the glass that stood on this table by the chair – the one out of which she is supposed to have drunk the poison. It was a glass just like the one Ward used. Now then. Why did she go to the kitchen and get a kitchen glass when she could have taken out of here one of the glasses of the kind she was accustomed to use herself?'

Travers smiled dryly. 'Why not look at it the other way? Why not say she did get a glass from the kitchen and therefore she went to the kitchen before she came up here?'

'Leave it, leave it.' He waved an impatient hand. 'No use magnifying little pieces of evidence. But just a minute, though. Hasn't the time come for you to say why you thought hers wasn't a case of suicide?'

'Frankly,' said Travers, 'my ideas were based on what you said about the nature of the poison. If it acted quickly, then the muscles would have been violently contracted – some muscles, shall we say. Now except for that gape of her mouth, which gave that dreadful look of expectancy – her whole pose was serene. Regal, I called it. On the other hand, if the poison was slow working, then she couldn't have timed her death so as to have left herself in a placid pose after enduring a long agony. What, in fact, I seemed almost to deduce was this. Someone found her here soon after she was dead, and that someone placed her in the chair where and as she was found.'

'She must have been in the chair before rigor mortis set in, because she fitted it like a glove.' He looked up. 'But that doesn't say she didn't commit suicide?'

'I know it doesn't,' Travers said. 'But follow this. Admit someone found her dead and placed her in that special pose in the chair. The same person must have also placed the side-table right against the chair and put the glass and poison bottle on it.'

'Why?' He smiled dryly. 'Because he had a particularly neat and orderly mind and wanted everything to match? Or to give the impression of a dramatic suicide when it wasn't suicide after all?'

Wharton frowned, then shook his head. 'The funny thing about your theories is that you wrap them up in such highly coloured paper that I buy 'em before I know what's inside.'

'It's a good theory,' Travers said doggedly. 'They say money talks, and I'd be prepared to bet a goodish sum it contains a thundering big percentage of truth.'

'Well, let's have a look in the kitchen,' Wharton said. 'You've been frank with me and now I'll give you my ideas about Ward.'

Down in the hall he opened the front door and took a look out. The first faint streaks of dawn were in the sky, and he gave a gratified nod as he closed the door again.

'Another hour or two and this damn night'll be over. Nothing like daylight for taking the romance out of theories.'

'You stay there by the door,' he said when they came to the kitchen. 'There's the marked outline of Ward's body. I go to the table, where the chair was. Did he drink the poison here? Was he standing or sitting?'

'Does it matter?'

'It doesn't,' Wharton said, 'provided you agree he wouldn't have taken it by the door. Now, I try not to be self-conscious and I take this glass, put some water in it, and stand here holding it. Say I'm plucking up courage. Then I gulp it down, and what's the instinctive thing to do? Why, to set the glass down.'

Travers gave a shake of the head. 'If he had had a shock, he mightn't do the normal thing.'

'very well,' said Wharton patiently. 'Would he have wandered about holding the glass in his hand, waiting for the poison to work? However quick it was, it would have been minutes rather than seconds. Yet he died by the door and he'd been holding the glass till the last moment because it was found by his hand!'

Travers nodded.

'He's been crawling towards the door, still holding the glass! In heaven's name, why? If he'd repented of trying to poison himself and was making for the phone and to call a doctor, why clutch the glass?'

'Perfectly sound,' Travers said. 'In other words, the glass might have been put there afterwards.' He smiled. 'In still more words, your theory is a complement to mine. If the glass was placed there, it was to give the appearance of suicide to what wasn't anything of the kind, and by the same person who placed Mary Legreye in the chair.'

'That's it,' said Wharton largely. 'Now have a look what's in this dresser drawer.'

Travers admitted that in his search for food he had not thought of that dresser, since the only drawer in which he had looked contained cutlery and napkins. But in the right-hand top drawer was a small paper bag, and it contained a strip of bacon and two eggs.

'There you are,' Wharton said. 'I found that when I was down here earlier. It's what Ward bought on his way home on Tuesday night, ready for his breakfast on Wednesday morning. That shows he didn't come here with the idea of committing suicide. Also we ought to be able to trace where and when he bought the things, which will tell us when he arrived here.'

Travers was shaking his head.

'There's something desperate behind all this, George. He came home with his next day's breakfast; perfectly normal, as you might say. Then in less than no time he was dead. And if our two theories are right, *then nothing fits.*"

'Why not?'

'Well, whoever put Mary Legreye in the chair did it before rigor mortis had set in. But Ward wasn't presumably anywhere near the house till hours after that. Therefore, if the glass was placed at his dead hand, it was by another person, or else the same person paid a second visit.'

Wharton let out a breath. 'This is getting on my nerves. Dammit, I'm getting so I can't think.' He clicked his tongue. 'Let's leave it till we've had an early breakfast and a wash and tidy up. There's that spare room upstairs I want to look at.'

He made for the maid's room at the landing top, and listened outside the door.

'Right and tight in there,' he whispered. 'I hope she wakes up fresh as a daisy. Before the day's out she's going to get one or two nasty shocks.'

With that enigmatical threat he moved off to the spare room. There was no question of going inside it, so full was it of every kind of white elephant, discarded bags and cases, and everything, in fact, from an old settee to an umbrella stand.

'Smells a bit mouldy,' he said. 'And look at the dust. Someone's been in recently, though. Look at that.'

'That'was a disturbance of the dust for about a yard from the threshold. Wharton, on closer examination, thought the space had been wiped over with a cloth. Then he got down to the job, sniffed the floor boards and ran his glass across while Travers held matches close above it.

'Nothing you can see,' he said, and got to his feet. 'I'll make a note to ask that maid if anything was spilt here and wiped up just before she left. Of course it may have been Ward, looking for something he wanted.'

But he seemed loath to leave that doorway till he was positive the dust had not been disturbed inside the room. Then as he closed the door he gave a little anxious grunt.

'That's the very devil in our job. You never know what's a clue and what's not. I wouldn't mind betting there's something sitting right under our noses in this house that'd save us the hell of a lot of trouble if we only knew it when we saw it.'

Lewis reported his job as practically over. Wharton took a look through the window and then drew the blinds. Morning was at hand and already a sparrow or two was cheeping in the shrubbery.

'In about a quarter of an hour,' Wharton said, 'I'll get the cameras here to do that drawing-room. That'll mean an hour's time before we begin, so give that maid another half hour, then tap on her door and say the bathroom's clear. Later on I may want you to go to Lewisham. In the meanwhile you might look the house through for green paint.'

He nodded back at Travers and moved out to the landing again. The phone man called from the hall.

'You're wanted on the phone, sir. Doctor Menzies.'

'Ah!' said Wharton, and hurried down the stairs. He was already talking when Travers got there.

'Just a minute and I'll write it down ... Right. I'm ready ... Both poisons show same reactions. Oxalate group, but you'd like another opinion. You've only to call in Sir Barnabas; you know that as well as I do.' A grunt and he was going on. 'Yes, I'm ready. Poison quick in action. In woman's case about three minutes; in man's, slightly more ... Yes, I've got that ... Woman's taken in mixed alcoholic drink of cocktail variety ... about four hours after breakfast. Man's taken in whisky about half an hour after consuming tea and what may be cake. Time eight to ten p.m. Tuesday night.'

Wharton paused long enough to give a triumphant glance in the direction of Travers, then he licked the end of his pencil and was ready again.

'Got something else, have you? Going to surprise me? I very much doubt it ... Well, out with it.'

And then Wharton was dramatically quiet. Travers saw his eyes open wide. When he did speak, his voice was strangely mild.

'That's all? ... . Right. Goodbye.'

He hung up, then stood there shaking his head. A deep breath and he was spilling the beans.

'Well, the fat's in the fire now, with a vengeance. What do you think's happened?'

Travers shook his head.

'You'd never guess in a hundred years. She was pregnant, that's all. Two months gone.'

6

WHARTON SMILES

TRAVERS WAS BUSY polishing his glasses, and wondering how to reassemble the scattered pieces which had begun to form at least a corner of the intricate puzzle.

'Would you mind slipping upstairs and doing a couple of things for me?' Wharton said. 'Write a brief description for the press of those two miniatures, and bring down some of those stage photos of Mary Legreye from the bureau.'

The next quarter of an hour was spent at the phone. The man for Warwick was not starting till eight o'clock and his inquiries were widened to include a tour of any pawnshops to see if Ward had raised money on the miniatures. Travers's description of the miniatures was also sent to the morning papers, with the statement that the police were anxious to be informed if any pawnbroker had handled them. Then three photographs of the dead woman were rushed down to Norris to facilitate inquiries outside the village.

'The camera-men ought to be here soon,' Wharton said. 'Let's adjourn for a breather.'

He chose the downstairs sitting-room and lighted the gas fire.

'What'd you think about that Legreye news?' he said.

'It knocked all my ideas endways,' Travers told him. 'From what the maid told us, and various other things, I had the idea that she was starched and straitlaced. A charming woman, no doubt, but not the publicity-seeking, darling-to-everybody kind.'

'What various things?'

'Well, her name wasn't too well known. I admit it was better known after the run of *Stony Heart* began. Also she'd put in most of her time at repertory work, which isn't exactly the kind that gets all the headlines. The papers didn't even consider her divorce front-page stuff, or you and I must have seen it.'

'That's right,' Wharton said. 'Those obituaries from the press were very brief and stodgy. By the way, that husband of hers is, or was, a wine-merchant in Calcutta Street.' He paused in the act of lighting his pipe. 'But it was a shock to your morals – that news?'

'Heavens, no!' said Travers. 'My tastes don't happen to lie that particular way – sex, and all that, I mean – but I daresay I'm perfectly liable to break loose. The shock was finding myself completely off what was beginning to be a well-known road.'

'You don't know women,' Wharton said, with a self-congratulatory nod. 'When the straitlaced ones do go off the rails, they go clean off.'

A tap at the door and Lewis looked in.

'Excuse me, sir, but that maid's getting up of her own accord. I can hear her moving about the room.'

'Then take a look in her room when she goes to the bathroom,' Wharton told him.

He lighted his pipe again. 'I've been doing a lot of thinking these last few minutes, and I'd like to tell you how I'm beginning to see things. I don't claim I'm right; in fact, all I want to do is make a kind of rough sketch of what may have happened in the light of what we know – and don't know. We'll begin at last November when the six months' waiting period began for the decree absolute. Since she was already separated from her husband, we may assume that the reason she hadn't got a divorce before was either disinclination or because one go was enough. But she fell in love with another man – X, we'll call him – and that was why she wanted to be free from Wolters. You agree?'

'So far, absolutely.'

'Well, during those six months she had to act circumspectly. But she slipped, and Percy got to know it. He didn't know a lot but enough to draw cash for his knowledge. So right on to the events in which you and I got mixed up. As time went on – say, when she knew she was pregnant – she noticed a cooling off on the part of X. It had been decided that this last week-end she should get rid of the servants and meet X at the cottage, so she went down there on the Monday morning. When she got there she had a most terrible shock. Something compromising herself up to the neck had been stolen, but, worse than that, X didn't turn up. What was there was a farewell letter.'

'Ingenious,' said Travers to his inquiring look.

'Well, that brought on an absolute brainstorm. She knew no more till she found herself back here. Then she cried a bit, maybe washed her face in the downstairs cloak-room where we found the damp towel, and then went upstairs. There I'd say the brain-storm came on again, and she began to clear the room for her final stage. The last thing she did was to pour a tot of that cocktail stuff to hide the poison taste. Later that day, X – who had his own key – had reason to come here, and he put her in the chair.'

'It explains a lot of things,' Travers said. 'In fact it's a good theory, as far as it goes.'

'Don't I know it?' Wharton rounded on him. 'I know it leaves out Ward, but I do put it to you that all Ward's actions may be perfectly natural. She may have left him the miniatures, with a note here. He found the note and burned it, and then did himself in, knowing that his income had gone for good, and, unless she'd left him some money, he'd have to spend his days in some institution.'

'The whole thing's attractive, and I like it.' He smiled dryly. 'All we have to do is to be satisfied in our minds that the whole thing is merely a disastrous love affair and a double suicide, and then we can hand back to the local police after all.'

'Oh, no,' Wharton told him grimly. 'Even if we do have to swing right round and admit the suicides were genuine, I'm sticking on here. This case has got hold of me. When I hand over it will be when I know the right answer to every damn question – '

Another tap at the door and Lewis slipped in.

'That maid's got her hat on and is going out. I told her she couldn't and she said she only wanted to post a letter. I've sent a man ready to be on her tail.'

'A letter,' said Wharton reflectively.

'I've seen it, sir,' Lewis said. 'It was lying on her bed while she was in the bathroom. Addressed to a Mrs Bunce, Cadmarsh, Cambridge.'

'Splendid, splendid!' said Wharton, and chuckled. 'Let me know when she comes back, if I don't hear her.'

He knocked out his pipe and began filling it again.

'Smart chap, Lewis – sometimes.' A sideways nod. 'I told you Bunce was due for a shock or two. Writing to her sister-in-law to fake an alibi. By the way, what are the vital times for an alibi. assuming the suicide was faked?'

'If the suicides weren't suicides, but murders, then the times of death.'

'Of course, of course.' He frowned. 'Pity we can't be a bit more exact as to times. Still, we'll want to know the whereabouts of X, or anyone likely, at round about midday on Monday and round about eight o'clock on Tuesday night.'

He listened. 'Sounds like her. If so, she's soon back.'

Lewis was waiting near the door. Travers smiled a good morning. Wharton was positively effusive.

'Ah! Miss Bunce, out bright and early, I see. And how'd you sleep?'

'Very well, thank you,' she said. She regarded it as no bad thing, apparently, to be the centre of attraction, and as she stood there smiling with the morning freshness on her, she looked decidedly pretty.

'Well, you must spare us a moment,' Wharton said regretfully. 'Shan't keep you long. Then if you'll brew us all a big pot of tea, we'll be remarkably obliged. In the sitting-room here, I think.'

He hung back for a word with Lewis, who whispered that she had popped into a telephone booth, had apparently not been able to get the number she wanted, and had then turned straight back for home.

'Now then,' said Wharton as he came bustling in. On went the antiquated spectacles. 'Just a quick question or two. That sideboard upstairs with the drinks and glasses in. Was it kept open, or locked?'

'Oh, locked,' she said. 'Miss Legreye wouldn't have left it open, not with Ward about.' She proceeded to qualify the innuendo. 'I don't mean he drank a lot, because he didn't, but Miss Legreye said he wouldn't – well, have the temptation, see?'

'So I guessed.' He took out the envelope with the pieces of pen top. 'Have you ever seen Miss Legreye with a fountain pen to match this?'

'Yes,' she said at once. 'She had one just like it. I saw her using it Sunday.'

'And the spare room upstairs,' Wharton went on. 'Just inside the door is a mark as if someone had spilt something and then wiped it off. It wasn't you?'

She looked genuinely surprised. 'No, it wasn't me. I haven't looked inside there, not for days. We were going to give it a good clean up, but not till we got back.'

'Then where did the trunks or bags come from in which the Arneford luggage was put on Sunday?'

'They were down in the cloak-room.'

'I see. And now about Miss Legreye. Was she unwell at all this last month or so?'

'Oh, yes,' she said, as if delighted to give the details. 'She wouldn't have a doctor, though. Said it was indigestion and biliousness.'

'I see. And what were your days off? Sundays?'

She showed the first hesitation, or perhaps apprehension. Wharton nodded pleasantly in encouragement.

'Well, Sunday afternoons. Fred used to get off then as well, if he liked.'

'I see. And now the last question. Something that's puzzled us very much since you first told us. Will you try to explain more about what Miss Legreye meant when she told you that if she married it would be just like the play?'

She frowned in thought. 'Well, it wasn't that – not really. I said to her – no, she said to me – it'd be funny if it was like in the play.'

'And you can't tell us precisely what she meant? I mean, in the play she married a king and was very much in love with him, as they say. But I don't see how that helps to explain; do you?'

'That was what she said.'

'Well, we must leave it.' He got to his feet, then sat down and pulled out his notebook. 'Just a formality I was forgetting. Very silly of me. I might have got myself into trouble.' He peered whimsically over his spectacle tops. 'Do you know I've never taken down your particulars? Still, no time like the present. Full name?'

Her eyes narrowed and she was very much on the alert.

'Bunce. Edith May Bunce.'

'Age?'

'Twenty-four last January.'

'Date of coming here, we have – near enough.'

'The fourteenth of March, it was.'

'Good. And your previous employer, and her address?'

'Mrs Quorne, Hilltop, Highgate. Her husband is the brother of Wilfred Quorne who was Philip in the play, and she recommended me, see?'

'I understand. And you don't happen to know the name and address of your predecessor here?'

'Oh, yes. Janet Stone, her name was. Somewhere in the country she came from. Somewhere St Albans way.'

Wharton closed the book with a snap and got to his feet.

'Well, that's all, and as I was saying to Mr Travers here, what we should be doing without you I don't know. And now you'll make that tea for us?'

Out she went and Wharton nodded at the closing door.

'She's useful, I'll say that for her. But what was that hint about the play? She couldn't have meant marrying the actor who took the part of Philip, could she? Wilfred Quorne, wasn't he?'

'I rather think Quorne is married,' Travers said, then smiled. 'At least, I know he is. A daughter of his was taking part in some wireless show or other not so many nights ago.'

Wharton put away his pipe and stretched himself. Then he made for the outer door and took a deep breath or two of honest morning air.

'Looks like being a fine day for a change. Did you ever know anything like the weather we've had?'

Travers was pointing to something on the gravel drive some seven feet from the door.

'Isn't that an oil spot there? As if a car drew up not too long ago?'

'Maybe one of our own cars came right in,' Wharton said, and called back to Lewis who was coming downstairs.

'Any of our cars draw in here by the door?'

Lewis shook his head. All the official cars had drawn up at the kerb outside.

Wharton pursed his lips for a moment, then made for the kitchen.

'Get the men for tea,' he told Lewis, 'then stand by for moving the upstairs furniture back.'

In the kitchen the kettle was boiling. Edith Bunce greeted the great man with the smile of an old friend.

'I was just going to send for you. You didn't say how many I was to make for.'

* Make as much as all the pots will hold and you won't go far wrong,' he told her jocularly. 'And while we're here, will you clear up just one little point? How was the luggage to go from here to the railway station?'

'The last time,' she said, 'there wasn't much, and Fred took it himself. This time I heard him told to take it in a taxi.'

It was getting on the way for ten o'clock when that long business of the drawing-room was over. Bunce, who supervised the restoration of the room, seemed to have no ideas at all, till Wharton tackled her about the ability of her mistress to have moved certain heavy pieces. That appeared to give her inspiration, and she produced an idea which intrigued Wharton very much – that Miss Legreye had been struck by some scene or other in a script she was reading, and had had the room cleared accordingly by Ward before he left, in order to see how the author's manipulation of his cast worked out in practice.

'What do you think, Mr Travers?' Wharton asked.

Travers could not say. He was inclined to think an actress of Miss Legreye's experience would have been able to visualize any situation without going to such drastic measures as upsetting her drawing-room. All the same, he was not prepared to disagree with the suggestion.

'Right,' said Wharton. 'You camera-men finished? Then put everything back and check with the original photos to make sure. Miss Bunce, if you'd like to go out and get something for your lunch, you can most certainly do so.'

He made a sign to Lewis to get a man out ready, then went off for more phoning. Stephen Frodling, manager of the Odilon, was run to earth at that theatre; Wilfred Quorne at his home; Charles Abney was not found but Quorne said he might be able to get hold of him; and Martelle, the playwright, was found through his club to be staying at the Golden Bow, just off Manchester Square.

Up Wharton went again and found both Travers and Lewis waiting for him.

'I've found a scene at the beginning of that script she read which would suit the comparatively intimate interior she made of this room,' Travers reported.

Lewis said he had gone right through the house for green paint and hadn't found any.

'But I did find this, sir. Just happened to see it, outside the door of that spare room.'

It was another chipping of the same green paint, slightly larger than the first. Wharton frowned.

'Hard to see, was it?'

'Only sheer luck I happened to spot it, sir. Stooped down to tie my shoe-lace and there it was. Couldn't find any more, though.'

'Then if it was hard to find,' Wharton said, 'it may have been there for days or weeks. Still, let Mr Travers put it with the other piece. Those people are due here at twelve o'clock. Lewis, you be in the Three Bells as soon as it opens.'

Then the outside news began to come in. The first was from Cadmarsh. The Yard man had inquired at Mrs Bunce's house for Miss Edith Bunce, and had been greeted with surprise. His reply had been that he had understood she was there. The sister-in-law said she had not seen Edith for best part of a month, and had had only one letter, and that a fortnight ago. So much for the main gist of the report.

Wharton smiled to himself at that – and the smile was what Travers once said would have been the smile of a lion who sees approaching in the arena a particularly plump and succulent Christian. But when the second piece of news came there was no smiling.

It was Chief-Inspector Norris, ringing up from Arneford. Nobody in the village had seen Miss Legreye on Sunday or Monday, and she had not come off the local train.

'Have you had a house-to-house visit?' Wharton asked.

'Inquired at the whole twenty-three of 'em,' Norris told him dryly. 'Besides, she's Arneford's most famous character, as you might say. All that's left to try is the bus, and that's a local one, so it won't be difficult.'

'Hang on as long as you think necessary,' Wharton said. 'I've got various people connected with her theatre coming here shortly, so ring me up again at about two.'

'I've got one piece of news,' Norris said, 'and the local man is trying to follow it up. On Sunday night a youngish man asked a man here where Miss Legreye's cottage was. He was a smart, town-looking young man, driving a small car, and he had one of those little thin moustaches like a smear. He'd gone right by it and when he was told so he said it didn't matter.'

'Follow that up,' Wharton said anxiously. 'If you want an extra man, let me know and I'll buzz one down.'

The third report was from Lewisham. The Yard man there said Percy Gray's flat was empty, and the tenant of the upstairs flat said he had seen nothing of him for a week and more, and he believed he was away on a music-hall engagement. What was to be done? Wait, or report back?

'Ring in an hour's time, unless anything happens,' Wharton told him, 'then I'll give you final orders.'

Travers had been out for a scratch meal. Wharton did some quick thinking, then asked him to get hold of Portland Place and see if the B.B.C. knew anything of Meerschaum's whereabouts.

'You might try the office of *Variety* as well,' he said. 'I'll be back in ten minutes. Just nipping out for a bite.'

Over a plate of cold ham and a pot of tea, Wharton looked through the current issues of the *Radio Times* and *Wireless Pictures*. He was luckier than he had dared hope. Meerschaum was appearing in the Saturday night variety programme and his picture was among those of the artists. But the luck lay in the quick identification with the youngish man who had inquired at Arneford for Miss Legreye's cottage, for Meerschaum – described as 'the man who makes you see stars' – had a streak of black along his upper lip.

But the other periodical supplemented the information. It gave pictures of practically every person in the week's programmes, including Meerschaum, but added the additional news that that week he was appearing at the Bioscopic, Portsmouth. Wharton's early-Christian smile came again.

The pieces, he told himself as he walked back to Arden, were beginning to dovetail in. Percy, the blackmailing nephew, had gone to Portsmouth on the Sunday, ready for his week's engagement, and had fitted in a visit to Arneford. He had doubtless returned to the cottage, after showing indifference as to over-shooting it, and had committed the burglary. What other things he had done, and just where Ward fitted into the scheme, remained to be seen.

Travers had succeeded in obtaining most of the same in-formation, and could add that the previous week Meerschaum had been appearing at Reading. Nothing could have fitted better, as Wharton saw it. Meerschaum had delayed leaving Reading till the Sunday, and then had called at Arneford on his way to Portsmouth.

The man who had been on Bunce's tail reported that she had gone to the post-office and had been in a telephone booth for a good fifteen minutes. Then she had done some shopping, and had come straight home.

'I must write up some notes,' Wharton told Travers. 'What I'd like you to try to do for me is to get hold of that man Kevstein, and find out if by any chance he saw Miss Legreye, either here or elsewhere. This paper says he's staying at the Florid, in Carlton Square.'

Wharton retired to the downstairs sitting-room. Travers got hold of the Florid, and Kevstein's secretary.

'Mary Legreye?' he said, as if the name were strange. 'Oh, yes, wait a moment, Mr Travers, will you?'

Travers visualized him sitting at an enormous desk, papers a foot deep all round him, for there was a muttering and rustling before he spoke again.

'You there, Mr Travers? ... Nothing about Miss Legreye at all. No correspondence or anything.'

'Has Mr Kevstein seen her by any chance?'

More muttering and rustling, then: 'I have every detail of Mr Kevstein's movements since he's been here, and his arrangements for the next two days, and there's no mention of Miss Legreye.'

'Then just one final question,' Travers said. 'Is Mr Kevstein negotiating for *Stony Heart*?'

A suspicious silence, then: 'But Miss Legreye wouldn't be concerned in that? That would be a matter for the author, or his agents.'

'Exactly,' said Travers. 'Sorry to have taken up your valuable time. Goodbye, and thank you very much.'

Then in came Lewis, bursting with news. Wharton put aside his pen and lighted his pipe instead.

'Not many there when I got in,' Lewis said, with reference to the Three Bells, 'but the landlord was and I sprang the news about Ward. He hadn't seen anything in the stop-press or the early papers, and you ought to have seen his face when I told him. Then him and me adjourned to his private room and had a couple of beers while he pumped me and I did the same to him. And this is the important thing, sir. Ward was a steady old cuss, like that maid said, and he was in for his usual glass on Saturday night. The landlord asked him how things were and he said okay, and then a voice said, "Glad to hear it. About time you paid up something on account." That was a chap named Swallow, who's agent for Ward's bookmakers. Ward sort of sneered at him and laughed, from what I can make out, you know, sir: "You and your six pounds! what's a measly six pounds? Wednesday morning you can have your six pounds, and I'm finding another bookmaker." There was a lot more backchat and then Swallow sheered off. When he'd gone the landlord asked Ward if he'd been kidding him and Ward was highly indignant. I should have told you, sir, the landlord knew he was going to Warwick races, and he wanted to know if he had any good tips. Ward said he might have a bit of luck at Warwick, but if he hadn't, it *wouldn't make any difference*. On Wednesday morning the bookie would have his money *and there'd be some left over*.'

Wharton proceeded to cross-examine Lewis but could elicit nothing further. The landlord had tried to pump Ward and had not succeeded. Wherever Ward was getting his money, he was keeping it to himself.

'I still think Ward may have been bragging,' Wharton said. 'Did you ever know a punter who hadn't faith enough to move not mountains but whole damn continents? I know he expressly denied he was relying on the Warwick visit, but that doesn't make me change my mind. Do you know when I will change it? When we can prove that he pawned those two miniatures.'

But even while he was speaking he was thinking of something else: what a pity it was that Ward had not mentioned his windfall as for Monday. That would have implied collaboration with Percy Gray, and a reward for assisting in the Arneford burglary on Sunday night.

The phone man looked in.

'Inspector Norris, sir.'

Wharton got up at once. 'Still, there's a lot in what you've got, Lewis. Arrange to be there when the pub closes this afternoon, and take the landlord's statement. If he's on the phone, you might get that man Swallow there too.'

Norris's news was of such importance that he wished Wharton to have it at once. It now appeared that the young man in the small car had met the 7.15 local, which had connected with the London train. Off that same train had got a young woman who was a stranger to the clerk, but it was not known if she had gone off with the young man in the car. What was known was that at about seven-twenty that same night, a small car, with a woman in it, had remained for a few minutes drawn up on the verge about a hundred yards beyond The Briars in the Southampton direction, and then it had been driven away at a fast pace. That news had been given by a courting couple.

Wharton was positively in ecstasies. Two young and plump Christians were coming his way. A minute's thought and he rang the Yard. If all went well, Percy Gray should be up on the Arden carpet at about half-past two that afternoon, but only after Edith Bunce had been made to reveal a few things with which to confront him.

Then a private car drew up outside. Wharton, still chuckling, took a look out, then nodded back at Travers.

'Here come some of the nobs. When we all get in there, I'd like you to sit alongside me. You know all the patter.'

7

ALIBIS

QUORNE WAS a distinguished-looking man of fifty; of medium height, dark almost to swarthiness, and with a rich, deep voice. His Philip in the play had been hailed by the critics as his best performance of thirty years on the stage.

Abney, the ambassador of *Stony Heart,* was a pleasant young fellow of thirty: well built, dark, thin-faced and with the manners and simple courtesies of a gentleman. Frodling was quite another type: blond, burly, jovial, beefy and exuding satisfaction with life. A man of the world and a man's man, might have described him.

Martelle was tall, dark, and wiry, with the quick nervous motions that one associates with men of frailer and more scholarly build. The other three were clean-shaven but he wore a closely clipped moustache, which gave him the look of an army man. His age was thirty-eight, and in looks at least, he was the most distinguished of the four. He spoke rather quickly but his voice had a likeable resonance.

Wharton, chastely subdued as became the sorrowful occasion, introduced Travers, and uttered about the dead actress a few pious platitudes which were remarkably well received. Then he ushered the four into the sitting-room.

'Sit down, gentlemen, please; and do regard all this as nothing but a helpful and informal chat.' On went his spectacles and he peered benignly over their tops, and decided apparently the time had come for a gentle unbending.

'I expect you'll be surprised, gentlemen, to hear the precise reason why I've asked you to be good enough to come here. It's not entirely because you were colleagues, in a way, of the unfortunate lady on whose case Mr Travers here and I are engaged. It's also because you knew her, and, as I'm informed, are the only people to have been on terms of sufficient intimacy to have – well, come here to tea.'

There was a faint smile at that. Wharton consulted his notes and resumed.

'But to be serious. Do any of you know if the dead lady had any reasons whatever for committing suicide?'

There was a general shaking of heads. Quorne's voice emerged from the murmur.

'The last thing I'd have thought she'd have done.'

'Me too,' said Frodling. 'Mind you, she never said a lot about her private affairs, but I saw her only last week and she was just the same as she always was. She was looking forward to going on tour.'

'Ah!' said Wharton, 'that brings me to my next question. But before we go any further, do please remember that everything is implicitly confidential. Never a word of what's said here ever reaches the press or the public. Now the question. What were her plans?'

Frodling looked at Quorne, and Quorne at Martelle.

'In the ordinary way she'd have gone on tour in about three weeks' time,' Frodling said. 'On the other hand – well, Mr Martelle knows more about that.'

'If you mean the next play,' Martelle said, 'I thought it was agreed production couldn't be before September? I mean, if the play was – well, the right play.'

'What we're driving at,' Wharton said, 'is simply at finding out whether she had any financial fears for the immediate future.'

The smiles answered him. Abney's smile was rather diffident as became much the youngest of the men.

'She was very comfortably off,' Quorne said.

'And very careful,' added Frodling.

'Yes, perhaps she was. Generous too, when the cause was good.'

'It may interest you to know that her will of last year left a considerable deal to theatrical charities,' Wharton said. 'That will she destroyed in January last, and – unfortunately – put off making another.'

'The nephew inherits?' asked Frodling quickly.

'The husband, surely,' Quorne said. 'The decree isn't absolute.'

'It's a ticklish point in law,' Travers said. 'I wouldn't care to express an opinion. There was a judicial separation, which may make a difference.'

'I'd rather like to hear about the divorce,' Wharton put in, and fixed his eye on Frodling. 'How did it arise?

'He was a swine,' Frodling said promptly. 'Don't you agree, Wilfred?'

'A very bad egg,' Quorne said.

'After the separation he made himself very objectionable,' Frodling went on. 'He used to pester her one way and another and once he actually assaulted her. I don't mind saying it was I who put her on the right lines to getting rid of him. She had him watched and caught him red-handed. He called it a dirty trick – in court, that was – and said he'd get even. Mouthing, of course; nothing else.'

'A monied man, is he?'

'My God! no. He got to lifting his elbow a bit too much and lost his business. He's now a traveller for a firm of wine merchants. Spends a lot of time on the Continent, I believe.'

Wharton nodded magisterially. 'And any chance of the lady getting married again?'

It was at Quorne that he looked this time. Quorne shook his head and smiled dryly.

'I wouldn't call her the marrying sort. I was in New York when I heard she'd married Wolters – I've known her for the last twelve years, by the way – and I was pretty well surprised.'

'You didn't consider her the marrying sort?'

'Well, she wasn't a woman with what they call sex appeal. Quite good-looking, of course, and a real good sort at heart, mind you –'

'One of the best,' chipped in Frodling.

'Glad to hear it,' said Wharton. 'But any faults?'

'Who hasn't?' asked Quorne. 'She was a bit of a shrew, I admit, and a bit of a prude – though that's refreshing these days.'

'What do you think, Mr Martelle?'

'I?' He smiled. 'I'm afraid I never was really close enough to her to express an opinion. I liked her – as she was, if you understand me – and I liked being in her company. She was genuine, and gave that impression from the start. I may put it tritely, she was a lady in every conceivable way.'

'Well, I'm very grateful to you, gentlemen,' Wharton said. 'Now a very foolish question, which I must ask you nevertheless to consider highly confidential. Suppose she didn't commit suicide –'

He broke off to regard with a patient amusement the stares of incredulity.

'Supposition, gentlemen, and for the purpose of obtaining certain information in a roundabout way. Suppose, bluntly, she had been murdered. Who was a likely one to have done it?'

He leaned back in his chair, peering over his spectacle tops. Heads were shaken.

'Wolters wouldn't,' Frodling said emphatically. 'He was all froth and bluster.'

'Well,' said Wharton, after a silence. 'I must confide in you, gentlemen, to this extent, that if we get no further we shall never know why she did what she did. She was reasonably well off, her future was assured, she was just about to get rid of an undesirable husband, she had some very good friends, and yet – well, there we are. But about poor Ward. What can you tell me about him?'

There were quiet smiles at the first mention of Ward's name.

'He was a character,' Frodling said, with a sideways nod. 'Many a half-crown he's touched me for in my time. Not that I ever grudged it.'

'He had an artful knack,' Martelle said. 'He never actually begged but he had a way of bringing himself forward till you simply had to fork out. The last twice I saw him, I remember I subscribed. And I passed him on a racing tip.'

'Honest, was he?'

'What, Ward?' said Frodling indignantly. 'I'd have trusted him with anything.'

Wharton smiled. 'Yet Miss Legreye used to keep the sideboard locked.'

'Now you're talking,' Frodling said. 'Honesty and helping yourself to a drink – well, they're not the same thing.'

'She always spoke very highly of him,' Quorne said.

'I'm glad to hear that too,' said Wharton. 'And none of you gentlemen ever heard him threaten to do himself in?'

Martelle had to laugh. 'Sorry, sir, but that was a standing joke. That was always his gambit when he was about to qualify for a loan.'

'Just one other question,' Travers suddenly said. 'I think I may divulge the fact that Miss Legreye was found dead in her drawing-room – a room which you all know – but some of the furniture had been cleared away as if to make a large open space. She'd been reading the manuscript of a play –'

'Pardon me,' broke in Martelle, 'but I left a play here with her on Sunday.'

Wharton concealed his surprise. Travers went on.

'I'm afraid there were two plays: yours, Mr Martelle, and another. But the point is this. Could she have been so intrigued by a certain scene in that play as to have tried to see how it acted? I mean, would she actually have set the scene as near as she could?'

There was a general pursing of lips and a shaking of heads.

'Sounds unnecessary,' Frodling said.

'Yes, 'said Quorne, 'it's a thing I'd never have done myself. One ought to be able to visualize a scene with comparative ease.'

'Thank you, gentlemen,' said Travers. Wharton cut in at once.

'You were probably the last person, Mr Martelle, to see Miss Legreye alive.'

Martelle flushed.

'Nothing to be alarmed about,' Wharton told him hastily. 'You won't have to attend any inquest. But would you mind telling me what happened on Sunday?'

'Well, I was up in town for two or three days, seeing my agent about a play of mine in which a certain American gentleman may be interested. I managed to get my new play down in a kind of rough draft and I'd promised to let Miss Legreye read it. I rang her up on Sunday morning and said I'd bring it in during the afternoon. She said she'd be alone, and could I post it?' He smiled tentatively at that. Quorne came to the rescue.

'You'll pardon me, sir, but that was rather typical of Miss Legreye. Incredible as it may sound in this year of grace, she wouldn't have thought it quite the thing to have Martelle here if she was alone.'

'And there was the question of avoiding talk, in view of the divorce — so I understand.' That was Abney, coming in for the first time.

'I understand,' Wharton said. 'Go on, Mr Martelle.'

'I said I'd drop the manuscript in at about three then, and I did. Ward was here and I spent about — well, ten minutes or a quarter of an hour upstairs, and she told me she'd take the play into the country and read it there, and I said I'd come over and hear what she had to say, seeing I was so close —'

'You mean, you were staying somewhere close to Arneford?'

Martelle smiled. 'I live at Arnemouth — I mean, I spend a lot of time there.'

Wharton fingered his papers to conceal his interest. Martelle gave him an inquiring look and then went on.

'You see, I'd never actually been to her Arneford cottage. Oh, and I also said she'd have to let me know before Tuesday night because I'd be in town again on Wednesday morning, and I mightn't be down that way again for days.' He smiled diffidently. 'That was all, really. Except that I saw old Ward and gave him a ride to the railway station with some luggage.'

'Nothing queer about Miss Legreye's manner?'

'Nothing at all. She was very charming, and quiet, and looking forward to her stay in the country.'

Wharton got to his feet and began putting away his spectacles. His manner was dignified and gravely judicial.

'You're busy people and I won't take any more of your time, except for one thing. People of less standing would be very annoyed at what I'm about to say, but here we're all men of sense and goodwill. I may say that every person who in our opinion was at all known to the late Miss Legreye will be asked to give an account of his or her whereabouts at certain times.' He saw the looks of bewilderment. 'You see, there're all sorts of things outside the actual suicides which we're not at the moment at liberty to divulge. But what all you gentlemen will particularly appreciate is the fact that once I have the particulars I'm requesting, then you cease to be worried in any way by the law. Not that we may not have to ask you certain questions – the kind I've been asking this morning, and which you've been good enough to answer.'

There was more blether and blarney, and the upshot was that the four adjourned to the scullery and were called out one at a time.

Abney was the first. He was playing golf on Monday on the Winstonly course for the Actors against the Old Halfordians, and made a night of it down there. He returned to town about midday on Tuesday, and in the afternoon had a free seat at a trade show of a picture. The whole evening he spent with two friends whose names he gave, and it was almost midnight when he left them. Wharton smiled graciously, gave copious thanks and more apologies, shook hands and Abney was ushered out.

Frodling spent the whole of Monday and Tuesday, from nine in the morning of each day till ten o'clock at night, at the Odilon, where the new Fletcher lighting was being hurriedly installed. He gave the assistant stage-manager as reference, and he and Wharton parted apparently pals for life.

Wilfred Quorne had spent the whole of Monday's daylight working in the garden of his Hampstead house, though he was alone at the job from about three o'clock till five. The evening was spent with his young daughter at a picture house, and on Tuesday he took her back to school at Brighton and remained there till after tea, when he returned to town and spent a domestic evening in the house. He gave ample references.

With a man like Quorne, Wharton's thanks were less flamboyant and more sincere.

'No offence whatever,' Quorne smiled, 'I'm happy to have been of service, though I may say I've spent a wretched half-hour here in her house.'

'Would you mind telling us just one thing in confidence' Travers said. 'What was her age?'

'Mary's age?' He frowned. 'Thirty-three or four. Yes, it would be thirty-four.'

'A fine fellow, that,' Wharton said as the door closed on him. 'Now for the last, and I may say I meant him to be the last.'

But he was all apologies when Martelle came in.

'It's absolutely all right,' Martelle said. 'Someone has to be last.'

His movements were really interesting. He had gone straight down to Arnemouth, where he had a bungalow. He liked working there, he said, and he also had a tiny yacht and a small motorboat.

'A great spot for that kind of sport,' smiled Travers.

Martelle agreed. He had had a big racing-boat up to a few months before but had sold it on account of losing his nerve after a very narrow escape from disaster.

On Monday he overhauled the baby yacht and at about ten o'clock was going by the rough jetty when a young woman hailed him and asked if he would take her over to Beachington.

'I think she took me for a pro,' he said. 'But I was going over in any case. Her name was Dolly, that's all I know. I rather think she was a factory wench, or something like that.'

There was something droll about the way he spoke of her, and Wharton had to smile dryly.

'And what happened then?'

'Well, I did some shopping at Beachington and then I ran across her again. I slipped into the Grapes to get out of her way and then she came in the saloon bar where I stood her a port. She was going on to Portsmouth later, and that's all I know. Then in the afternoon I played golf and then I went home. On Tuesday I looked over my car in the morning and got the local garage to see to a thing or two and after lunch I went to Southampton and got a wireless off to the *Princesse Louise* to tell Miss Wain – Coralie Wain – I'd be meeting her at Plymouth next morning at six.'

There was something in the way he mentioned the name that prompted Wharton's question.

'Your fiancée, is she?'

'Well' – he blushed slightly – 'she wasn't then but she is now.'

'What charming news!' Travers said. 'Miss Wain is a very important, and, I'm sure, a very delightful person.'

He smiled. 'She has done rather well, hasn't she? But as I was saying, I got my wireless off and was back at Arnemouth at about four. I practised a hole or two, had a meal and started off for Plymouth at about nine or so.' He smiled. 'I'm rather a slow driver and I wanted to get to Plymouth early enough to try to get breakfast and have a general clean-up before the boat docked.' The smile became rueful. 'Which I didn't.'

'A breakdown?'

'Not quite. You see, the roads in Somerset had been badly affected by the floods, and I tried to avoid a certain way and then wandered about, so to speak, and finally ran out of petrol. Then I had to walk two miles back to a village called – called? – oh, yes, Hamsie, where I knocked up the proprietor of a one-eyed garage. After that –'

Wharton waved his hand. 'Ample, Mr Martelle. Sorry to have had to trouble you at all. Most good of you to come here. And if we should want you for any information, you'll be at the same hotel?'

'For some days at least,' he said. 'I'm selling my place at Arnemouth, by the way, because I may go back with Miss Wain to Hollywood,' He gave that delightfully diffident smile of his. 'I mean when she isn't Miss Wain.'

'Good luck to you,' Wharton said, and shot out a hand. 'I suppose, by the way, it was that extraordinary prudishness on the part of Miss Legreye that kept you from calling on her at Arneford?'

'I don't think she'd been there long,' he said. 'Besides, to tell you the truth, from what poor Ward told me, I didn't like the sound of the place.'

'Yes, Ward,' said Wharton reflectively. 'He kept a kind of notebook diary, by the way.'

Martelle stared.

'Oh, yes,' Wharton went on. 'It wasn't highly literary; just a few notes now and again.' He chuckled. 'He put down the day when you gave him a quid.'

Then Wharton looked concernedly at Travers. 'What was that entry in the diary I was to ask Mr Martelle about? Oh, yes; about the job for Tuesday.'

'The job for Tuesday?' Martelle said, staring again.

Wharton had the diary out and found the entry. Martelle had a look, then smiled.

'That'd be when I gave him the racing tip. I said he was to put ten bob on for himself and ten for me. He knew I'd never collect my end, even if it won, so really he ought to have entered the item as a quid to him.'

'That clears up that then,' Wharton said and, all smiles and blether again, accompanied him to the door.

'Interesting collection of people,' he remarked to Travers when he came back. 'None of them at all stand-offish. I did think our friend Martelle a bit nervy, didn't you?'

'I thought he was extraordinarily taken aback when you mentioned that diary,' Travers said.

'What's that?' Wharton gave him a look, then smiled. 'I reckon you and me'd be if we thought people'd been writing things about us. What we do know is why Martelle is mentioned at all and not Frodling, for instance. Frodling only tipped in half-crowns; Martelle in quids.' He frowned. 'Which reminds me. Why was Percy mentioned? Perhaps when we come to get some truth out of him we'll learn that he tipped in quids too.'

'Martelle's a lucky fellow,' Travers said. 'I believe Coralie Wain is a charming person, and what she makes per picture takes one's breath away.'

'English, is she?'

'Didn't I say it took one's breath away?' smiled Travers. 'But it was curious Martelle and Mary Legreye should have been so near last Monday and yet so far?'

'Yes,' said Wharton, and frowned. 'I must get out an SOS for any friends of hers with whom she stayed or lunched that last time she was down there. You know that country he was talking about? Arnemouth's the Southampton side of the mouth of the Arne and Beachington's the Portsmouth side.' He sighed. 'Well, still no rest for the wicked. I think I'll write up those alibis, then do some phoning. We've got to make some sort of showing to the powers that be.'

'I suppose Norris will do Martelle's as he's down there?'

'That's right. He's ringing me at two.' On went the spectacles again. 'You might give Bunce a look, will you? She's been checking her late mistress's belongings.'

'When's she for the balloon ascent?'

'As soon as I've spoken to Norris,' Wharton told him. 'Oh, before you go, didn't it strike you that Quorne had rather a fine bass voice?'

'Quorne?' He shook his head. 'A man like Quorne wouldn't go in for the sort of things we're inquiring into. Besides, won't there be time to talk of that when his alibi's been tested? But talking of Mary Legreye and the SOS; you'll be inquiring at the same time about friends in town whom she used to visit on Sundays? I know you're bearing it in mind, but the fact remains she didn't sleep here on Sunday.'

'I know,' Wharton said. 'I've also remembered that individual who called at the house on Wednesday and bolted. Still, we've got our hands full for a bit. After Bunce comes Percy – at least, I'm hoping so – then I want to get hold of Wolters, the husband.' He nodded to himself. 'We mayn't have a lot to show but you've got to remember that it's still a goodish way off twenty-four hours since you and I blundered into this case.'

Travers found Edith Bunce in her mistress's bedroom and one of Wharton's men helping her. Lewis had departed for the Three Bells to take the statements.

'I was to say if anything was missing,' Bunce said to Travers, 'and I can't find anything except a brooch. A cameo brooch, it was.'

'Just what was it like?'

'It was big, and like a gold frame all round it, and sort of coral colour. A woman's head was on it, sort of carved out. She promised it to me. That's how I know it's gone.'

'Perhaps it will turn up,' said Travers, not particularly interested.

There was a tap at the door and in walked Menzies. He and Travers adjourned to the drawing-room.

'Wharton said I'd find you up here,' Menzies said. 'He's nearly as busy as he thinks he is. Find anything special?'

'I don't know that we're a single idea wiser than we were before,' Travers told him cheerfully enough. 'You people found the poison yet?'

'Sir Barnabas is pretty sure,' Menzies said. 'One of the oxalate family, as Stott and I guessed, only we can't carry about with us names as long as your arm.'

'Difficult to procure?'

'It's being used in the latest processes for rubber,' Menzies said. 'Anybody can get hold of enough poison to do in a suburb if he knows the ropes. A bad business about that pregnancy, didn't you think?'

'I'm afraid it hasn't helped us much so far,' Travers said, answering the implied question. 'If it ever got known there'd be a good many disbelievers. Everyone regarded her as the strait-laced sort.'

'I know,' Menzies said. 'That's why I sprang it as a surprise on Wharton. Tell him from me, by the way, the formal inquests are to-morrow. I must be pushing off. As much to do as Wharton thinks he has.'

Travers secured the phone in one of Wharton's intervals and told Palmer he hoped to see St Martin's Chambers again one day before he died. Then Lewis came in with the statements and Wharton's stenographer arrived. Lewis and Travers killed time by searching, without result, for more chippings of green paint. Then Wharton's voice was heard in the hall and down they went.

'Percy's due very shortly,' Wharton told them. 'And I've had some news about Wolters. He was sacked on Saturday and has been on the booze ever since.'

A quick listen from the foot of the stairs.

'Tell that maid to come down here, Lewis. As Mr Travers would say, the balloon's about to ascend.'

8
TRAVERS IS RESIGNED

EDITH BUNCE was the least bit nervous, probably on account of the two strange faces. Wharton explained the stenographer and the nature of an official statement, though she was still somewhat ill at ease.

But the recital of happenings went on smoothly enough till she came to the time when she left the house with her personal bag. Wharton put in a question there.

'And you never saw Miss Legreye alive again?'

'No,' she said. 'I didn't.'

'Well, go on. And after you left the house?'

'I went to my sister's.'

Wharton gave Travers a most comical look over the tops of the spectacles. Travers knew the old threat of a coroner's court was coming, and it came.

'Suppose our friend Miss Bunce told that to the coroner, on oath, and suppose the coroner knew what you and I do. Perjury – isn't that the word for it?'

Her face coloured slightly.

'I don't know what you mean.'

Wharton shrugged his shoulders. 'It's perfectly easy to get at what I mean. Tell us where you really were.'

Her face crimsoned. She licked her lips but the words refused to come.

'I could tell you myself of course.' Another careless shrug of the shoulders. 'But it's you who're making the statement, not I. I could tell you what train you took, to where, who met you – everything. Still, you tell me instead.'

'There wasn't anything wrong.'

The remark was so extraordinary that Wharton and Travers both stared.

'You mean?' Wharton said, and: 'All this is highly confidential, as I told you. Everybody here has ears but no tongue.'

'Well' – she was casting quick looks about the room – 'we had separate rooms.'

'At the hotel, you mean?'

'Yes; where I was staying.'

'Well, get on,' Wharton told her impatiently. 'We'll say you got to the station. What happened then?'

'We just went to Portsmouth.'

'Oh, no. There was something else first. What did you do in Arneford?'

There was a hesitation and her brain could be seen working. Wharton leaned forward, wagging his head.

'If you're thinking of concocting anything in the nature of an untruth, take my advice and don't. I'm a patient man but my time's valuable. Get on with what happened at Arneford.'

'Well,' she said nervously, 'Mr Gray hadn't seen Miss Legreye's cottage so I showed it to him.'

'You saw it together?'

She gave him a quick look. 'Well, I stayed in the car and he looked at it.'

Wharton leaned forward again. 'It wasn't he, by any chance, who was responsible for that burglary?'

'He wouldn't do a thing like that,' she said indignantly.

'Very well,' said Wharton. 'Only I had the idea that that was perhaps the reason why you were scared down there that evening. And how long did you stay at Portsmouth?'

'Till Wednesday afternoon. I came straight on from there.'

'I see. And how long has the acquaintance been going on between you and Mr Gray?'

Her cheeks crimsoned again.

'Only recent – really.'

'And yet you trusted him sufficiently to spend three days and nights with him in a hotel. Who paid? He?'

Another quick look, then: 'Yes, he paid – really. It was a sort of a holiday.'

'So I gather,' Wharton said dryly. He leaned forward once more. 'But I'm putting it to you that the holiday, as you call it, was payment.'

She gave another indignant look. 'Mr Gray never paid me for anything.'

'Not for spying on his aunt?'

That struck home and Wharton followed up the blow.

'Do you think we haven't found out things? We know his aunt gave him money. If I was to tell you half what we know, you'd be shaking in your shoes. I say you spied on your mistress.'

She shook her head. 'I didn't. I never did anything. He asked me –'

She stopped short.

'Yes?' said Wharton, as if hard of hearing. 'He asked you what?'

'Well, who came here. There wasn't any harm, really. I just told him who came.'

Wharton got dramatically to his feet.

'Well, if you're not going to tell us the truth, we must have you taken where you will.'

'All right. But –'

'No buts,' Wharton told her. 'Either we hear the whole story now or the matter's out of my hands.'

'Well' – she fidgeted nervously – 'I did tell him about the man, the one with the bass voice.'

Wharton sat down again. 'I see. And did he know who the man with the bass voice was?'

'He didn't. Really he didn't.'

'But he was trying to find out?'

'Yes.'

'And who did you both think he was?'

'Once I thought it was Mr Frodling having a joke – the first time that was. Then I thought it was Mr Quorne, but I knew it wasn't him.'

'Why?'

'I don't know. I sort of knew it wasn't.'

'I see. And you and Mr Gray went to Arneford to spy on Miss Legreye because you thought she'd gone down there on Sunday night. That's why you took a late train.'

She said nothing but the answer was plain on her face. Wharton glanced at his notebook as if to resume, when there was a tap at the door.

'Mr Gray here, sir. Says he's in a hurry, sir. Wants to get back to Portsmouth.'

'Does he?' said Wharton curtly, and then with heavy irony: 'Well, we'll see if we can oblige him. Ask him to wait a couple of minutes.'

'Mr Gray here,' he said, and peered over his glasses at Bunce.

'Well, take Miss Bunce to the kitchen and see she's comfortable till she's wanted again. Lewis, ask Mr Gray to be so good as to step in here.'

His eyes watched the door close on Bunce. His lip drooped.

'No harm done, eh? I'll lay a fiver she wouldn't like to go before a panel of matrons.'

The phone man popped in again.

'Message from Warwick, sir. Just starting back and there's little to report.'

'Right,' said Wharton. 'Ring through to the Yard and say I'll be seeing Wolters in about an hour.'

Then the door opened and Lewis was ushering in Percy Gray.

Gray looked a very young man, and much less presentable and glamorous than his portrait had shown him. That streak of moustache, so popular in the dance band and film worlds, gave him an air that was more tawdry than exotic, and altogether, in spite of a voice that showed traces of education and even breeding, he was none too likeable a specimen. Wharton did the usual apologizing, thanking, and explaining.

'Your age?' he asked.

'Twenty-three.'

'And when did you first hear of this terrible affair?'

'This morning,' he said. 'I saw it in one of the London newspapers.'

'You didn't think of coming here?'

'No,' he said. 'I didn't see what I could do, and I had to go on again this evening.'

Wharton was already thinking him a cool customer, and somewhat swollen headed. His own tone became more dry and monitory.

'I understand you want to get back to Portsmouth for the first house this evening, Mr Gray. Whether or not you do will depend entirely on yourself. And one other thing. I don't want to lay traps for you and catch you out in possible untruths, so I'll tell you at once that Edith Bunce has made a very full confession.'

If ever a man looked a fool, it was Gray. Then he pulled himself together and tried what dignity could do.

'She couldn't tell you anything about me.'

'You think not?' said Wharton, and: 'Well, I've warned you. Now look at this list of monies paid to you by your aunt. We'd be glad if you'd explain.'

But after that one quick shock, he was more sure of himself and was giving nothing away, though he took quite long enough scanning Wharton's sheet.

'That's right,' he said. 'She gave me the money.'

'Look at me,' Wharton said. 'We know all about what you tried to find out, and that sheet of paper tells some of the answers. Now you tell us what you did find out. Here's what you got. Now tell us what you sold.'

'I didn't sell anything,' he said aggrievedly, then, strange to say, smiled. 'It all began as a joke. I came here one day when 1 happened to be hard up and we happened to be talking about

Wolters, and how he might be having her watched the same as she'd had him. You know all about it?'

'My dear sir,' Wharton told him grimly, 'you've no idea how many things we do know.'

That put him out of his smooth stride for a moment or so, but no more.

'Well, that's what we were talking about, and I happened to say what wouldn't he give to find something out about her. Then I saw her stare at me, just as if there was something, but I didn't say anything, only when I came to ask her if she'd help me out, she wanted to know what I meant.' He smiled lamely. 'That's how it began. I mean, I never did say I knew anything, but she always thought I did.'

'And you encouraged that belief?'

'I didn't do anything either way.'

'I see. And why did the payments decrease so badly at this one period here?'

'Well, I think she'd begun to rumble me. She guessed I didn't know anything.'

'I see. She tried you out. And as the new maid came at about that time, you got her on your side and induced her to spy –'

'She didn't want much inducing.'

'So I gathered,' Wharton said. 'And she discovered the man with the bass voice. You hinted to your aunt that you knew who he was and the payments began again. What was the fifty pounds for, by the way? Anything special or a tightening of the rack?'

'It wasn't blackmail, if that's what you think.'

'My dear sir!' Wharton raised his hands in pious horror. 'For goodness' sake, don't mention the word. But what was the money for?'

'For my car. I told her I had to have a car and she gave me the money.'

'I see. The same car in which you met Edith Bunce on Sunday night?'

'There wasn't any harm in that?'

'So she's been telling us,' Wharton said dryly. 'But you had a look at that cottage alone. Curious time to inspect a cottage from the outside – I mean, waiting till it's dark.'

He gave a quick look, wondering just how much Wharton knew.

'Well, tell us. Why were you so interested?'

'Well, I hadn't seen it before. Besides, I'd come from Reading and I fitted in with the train.'

'Why shouldn't she have gone straight to Portsmouth?'

'I wanted her to ride in the car.'

Wharton gave one of his quaint looks at Travers over the tops of his spectacles.

'Mr Gray has the answers ready before we can think of the questions.' The tone changed. 'Now listen to me. What happens to you to-night, Mr Gray, depends entirely upon the answer you give to the question I'll now put. What did you find out about your aunt?'

He shook his head. 'Nothing. I swear I didn't.'

'What you were doing all the time was preying on her fears?'

'I wasn't preying. I mean – well, she gave me the money and I wouldn't have asked her if I hadn't wanted it.'

Wharton grunted. 'But you used to quarrel with her.'

'I never did. Who told you that?'

'Who told me?' He was feeling in his breast pocket for Ward's diary, then apparently changed his mind. 'That I'm not prepared to tell you, but I have written evidence.'

'Whoever told you, it was a lie. We used to talk but we never had any real row, as you might say.'

'I see. And now about Ward. You knew him well?'

'Yes.'

'Did you try to get him on your side, the same as you did Edith Bunce?'

'I wouldn't trust him and never did. He was just a cadger and a whiner.'

'Did Bunce like him?'

'I don't see why she should. He was always trying to make mischief – so she said.'

'That's all about that,' Wharton said. 'You any questions, Mr Travers?'

'Only about the various times,' Travers said. 'Mr Gray might give an account of his movements from Monday morning after breakfast till bedtime on Tuesday night.'

Those took a considerable time and there was a difficulty in giving the names of witnesses other than Bunce. The two houses at the Bioscopic were a help, and the times of his appearances – 7.10 and 9.15. Then Wharton suddenly produced the two miniatures.

'Seen these before?'

It was reasonably certain that he had not. Wharton put them away again and got to his feet, wagging a finger in his best judicial style.

'I suppose you're aware of the fact, young man, that you're in none too happy a position. Blackmail's a nasty word, and I hate it, as you know, but here are certain figures and your own statement. Now write down the address where you can be found this week, and see you're available if we should want you. When you're sent for, come at the double. And just a minute. Seen Wolters lately?'

Gray stared. 'No. Why should I?'

Wharton gave a shrug of the shoulders and nodded over to Lewis to show him out.

'A nasty little specimen,' Wharton said to Travers. 'He and Bunce are two of a kind. That stage name of his begins with M, by the way. I suppose Ward couldn't have been referring to him, by any chance.' He answered his own question. 'Couldn't be, though. He mentions him as Percy.'

He had been feeling for Ward's diary again, and now his look was most comical.

'That's funny. I could have sworn I had it in my hand just before he came in, then I remember slipping it in my pocket. Or didn't I?'

'I remember seeing it on this table,' Travers said. 'There, where Bunce was sitting.'

Lewis came in then.

'Got the car number, sir.'

'These are his prints,' Wharton said, indicating the paper on which Gray had written the address. Then he dashed into the kitchen, Travers hard behind.

Bunce was not there but the Ideal stove was alight, and he whipped off the top. Then out to the hall again, with Bunce coming downstairs.

'You haven't by any chance seen a small book?' Wharton said, and began describing it.

'No,' she said, and it looked as if she were telling the truth.

Wharton pursed his lips. 'All right. We shan't want you again for a bit. You can go out to the pictures if you want to, and buy yourself some food.'

He nodded to the man in attendance, then stalked off to the sitting-room again.

'Funny about that book, not that it's all that important. You'd better have a man hunt the house for it, Lewis. I don't think I'll send you to Portsmouth to do Gray's alibi; I'll get a spare man. Keep an eye on that maid and when the Warwick man gets here, take his report if I'm not back. If you want me, I'll be either at the Yard or this number.'

Out went Lewis. Wharton gave a shake or two of the head.

'Damn funny about that diary, you know. I'll swear I had it in this room. I had it when Martelle was here, and I had it just before Bunce came in. Or hadn't I?'

'It'll turn up,' Travers said.

Wharton began getting his things together. Travers was given the miniatures and asked to get them valued. Wharton took over one of the paint chippings for analysis, and then remembered he had done nothing about testing the weight required to smash the top of the fountain pen. Lewis received instructions accordingly.

'We'll go by Underground, I think,' Wharton said. 'I'm making for the Yard. You coming, or going home?'

'Home,' Travers told him promptly. 'You've had a shave, George, and I haven't. And I'd like a bath and a real meal again.'

'You're one of these powder and puff detectives,' Wharton said in his best he-man manner. 'I've gone without a bite for more than a day before now. Wouldn't mind a glass of beer, though. Which reminds me of Wolters. They told me he'd been on the booze till turning-out time this afternoon, and then he was followed home, and there's a bloke sitting on the doorstep still. Hope Wolters'll have slept it off by the time I see him. Not that he'll tell us much.'

And there, though he was unaware of it, Wharton said two things which were far nearer the truth than he could ever have suspected.

Palmer welcomed Travers as if the two had been parted for years. A change of undergarments and a grey suit were laid out after the bath, and then came the question of tea.

'You'd like something extra, sir. There's a very nice York ham, sir, I can recommend.'

'Ham?' said Travers. 'I seem to have been living on ham for days. Just have tea-cake, and I'll save up for dinner.'

Before the meal he had an idea and rang up Lorn and Brook of Piccadilly, the Fine Art dealers. Harry Lorn was in and was vastly intrigued by Travers's descriptions of the miniatures, which was what Travers intended. He would be round inside ten minutes, he said.

Travers consumed the tea-cake with a good conscience. What-ever happened, he told himself, he would stir from the flat no more that night, and he would be in bed by nine. Harry Lorn arrived just as the table was being cleared.

'Let me get you some tea,' Travers said.

'Not for me,' Lorn said. 'I'm a busy man. Where're the min-iatures?'

Travers produced them and he took a quick look. He was obviously interested.

'Where'd you buy 'em?'

'I didn't,' Travers said. 'At the moment they're in the posses-sion of the law, which wants them valued.'

Lorn took them to the window.

'Mind if I take them out of their frames?'

'Go ahead,' Travers said, and watched the show.

It was five minutes before Lorn was prepared to give an opinion, then it was a tentative and wily one, as if he still hoped to purchase.

'I think the man's David Garrick, just before his death. The woman's probably Mrs Sherwood.'

'An actress?'

He smiled. 'An actress, my dear Travers, but not necessarily a lady.'

'The miniaturist?'

'I think, Maria Hadfield, the wife of Cosway. Garrick, I'd give you two hundred guineas for; the lady, fifty, seeing it's you.'

'Wish I could take it,' Travers said. 'Still, if there's any chance of their being sold, I'll do my best to give you the first chance.'

'You'll let me see them again some time?'

'If I can,' Travers told him.

So Lorn departed and Travers drew in a chair to the fire and puffed luxuriously at his pipe. Soon his thoughts were running back to that extraordinary case, and distance, he was somehow finding, was lending a strange clarity to the view. All the hampering details seemed to disappear of themselves, and all that was left was the outstretched arms of a dead man on a kitchen floor, and a dead woman who sat in a regal chair with staring eyes and parted lips.

Combine those two figures, he suddenly thought, and it was like some grim conversation piece, with the furniture of the room and its colourful gewgaws to be wholly disregarded. She had befriended Ward and he must have thought a tremendous deal of her, and it was curiously apt that they had met the same end by the same means in the same house. Clues and theories seemed to be nothing as against that stark fact.

As for Mary Legreye, Wharton was probably right. Two months gone in pregnancy, and the time coming when her state could scarcely be concealed, seeing what her profession was. If X was cooling off, then she must have been getting desperate. She had gone to Arneford to meet him, and, as Wharton said she had met nothing but the chilling letter that told her plainly that as far as he was concerned the affair was ended.

Then the brainstorm. She had snatched up the bag and the attaché case and had next found herself back at her house. There the partial madness had persisted and she had prepared for death. As for moving the heavy furniture, was there not some theory that madness gave incredible strength? The same strength of purpose had made her grip the arms of that chair till her mouth gaped and her eyes stared with the pain.

As for Ward, he had almost certainly gone down to Arneford and taken the miniatures to pawn or sell in view of the book-maker's demand and the fact that he might need money at War-wick. But he must have been far more serious about suicide than people gave him credit for. He had gone to Warwick and had not found it necessary after all to do any pawning, and he had come home to find Mary Legreye dead, and by what means had been only too obvious. Remorse had made him kill himself with the miniatures still on him.

Those facts now seemed to stand clear, and the difficulties were trifling. Naturally Mary Legreye had taken care that no one should see her on the way to the cottage that Monday morning, and with regard to getting home, some cunning of brain might have prompted her to try the same means for returning. She might even have wandered for a time and then have been given a lift by some motorist. After all, in these modern days, there was nothing odd about a woman either distraught or without a hat – and the day had been a sunny one. It was only the evening that had turned misty.

Then with regard to the glass that had been found by Ward's hand, Travers had an idea. Once during the war he had been instructing some men of a labour battalion in throwing live Mills bombs. Many of them, once the pin was out, had been seized by sudden fright which had made the throwing exceedingly dangerous for the instructor, because their fingers would somehow refuse to give way, and when they finally relaxed, the bomb would be thrown with no more strength than was needed to clear the parapet.

So with Ward, thought Travers. He drank the poison, then suddenly said to himself: 'Oh, my God! What have I done? I'm going to die. In horrible agony. I can feel it already.' And so on, but always clutching the glass, till he finally fell and tried to crawl to the door and the telephone.

Then Travers ruefully recognized that if the surmise was fact that was the end of what had promised to be as unusual a case as he and Wharton had ever known. The local people would take over again ...

The phone bell rang then and Travers rose to answer it, waving a lazy hand at the quickly-entering Palmer.

'Yes?' he said.

'Is that Mr Travers?' The voice was a strange one.

'Speaking.'

'This is Detective-Sergeant Applebed, sir, speaking from Aldgate. Superintendent Wharton says will you come along, sir.'

'Where to?'

'Summery Street, sir. The street going north from the Blue Feather. Number thirty-one, sir, about a hundred yards along.'

Travers frowned. 'Anything important, is it?'

'I think it's about a certain party, sir. He's done himself in.'

Travers hung up with no goodbye, and, his resolutions gone, made for his overcoat and hat.

9
VOICES

THE YARD HAD picked up Wolters through a not unusual channel – the anonymous informer. At about twenty minutes past two someone had rung up with the information that a man was talking big in the Blue Feather at Aldgate, about the Westmead suicides, and saying he could tell a lot if he opened his mouth. He also claimed to be the husband of Mary Legreye.

The detective-sergeant arrived within ten minutes, just on turning-out time, and found a constable having trouble with a man, who happened to be the one the Yard wanted. But the man was obviously in a bad way, for his speech – vehement enough –was blurred and thick, and his legs were none too steady. The constable indeed was on the point of taking him away when the Yard man had a word with him and followed the man to his lodgings, from which he had not since stirred.

Wharton timed that call of his to be well before opening time at the local pubs, for if Wolters needed a hair of the dog that bit him, he would be at the Blue Feather again and unfit for talk in no time. Applebed, the detective-sergeant, was waiting in Summery Street, and reported that he had a man at the back.

'Why didn't you go to the pub and try to get hold of a witness or two?' Wharton asked him.

'There was a bit of a shindy going on,' Applebed said. 'The one I wanted, sir, was the barmaid, but when I'd seen Wolters safe here and had got back, the barmaid had gone. Her afternoon off and she'd gone to the pictures. She'll be in when they open, sir.'

'Come on then,' said Wharton. 'You and I'll have a little preliminary talk with Wolters. What sort of man is he?'

'Looked to me to be ripe for d.t.'s,' Applebed said. 'Fat red face, all purple-veined; you know the sort, sir.'

Wharton knocked at the door. It was a dingy but tidy enough house in a drab, monotonous street, and the oldish woman who opened the door looked a cut above the neighbourhood.

'May I see Mr Wolters?' Wharton asked.

'He's in his room,' she said. 'What name, please?'

'Just say, an old friend,' Wharton told her.

She left them on the doorstep with the door ajar, and they could hear the knock when she reached Wolters' room. The knock was repeated, and then in a minute she was at the front door again.

'I can't make him answer. He must be too sound asleep.'

Wharton nodded. 'Came home in rather a bad way, didn't he?'

Her old eyes had more sorrow in them than anger.

'He's been a lot like that lately.'

'Well, if you don't mind,' Wharton said, 'I and my friend will see if we can wake him. It's a matter of tremendous importance, and for him too.'

She was all at once frightened. Wharton patted her skinny shoulder.

'Nothing for you to get alarmed about. You come up with us too.'

The door of the room faced the stairs at the top of the landing, and it was locked. Wharton knocked, rattled the door, called, knocked again loud enough to waken the heaviest sleeper, then stepped back with narrowing eyes.

'Something fishy about this, ma'am. What's your name, by the way?'

'Frid,' she said. 'Mrs Frid.'

'Well, Mrs Frid,' Wharton said, 'I'll tell you now that we're two police officers. No need to get alarmed. He hasn't done anything. All we want to do is speak to him, so we must break down this door.'

He gave a nod to Applebed; two shoulders went back together, then met the door, and the lock burst at the first thrust. Wharton blundered inside with the impetus, then his hand was holding the woman back.

'You go downstairs now, Mrs Frid. There's another police officer outside your back door, and you might ask him to step up here.'

A chair had been wedged between the top of a tall wardrobe and the ceiling, with a rope tied to it, to give the height. Wharton slashed the rope through and lowered Wolters' body to the ground.

'Been dead a couple of hours at the least,' he said. 'Send that man of yours to find a doctor, then let him get divisional headquarters.' He scribbled something on a sheet from his notebook. 'You ring this number and ask Mr Travers to come along if he can.'

He closed the door and propped a chair against it, then had a look round. On a table by the bed, wedged between a water carafe and its glass, was a note.

Goodbye all. Everyone has been doing the dirty so here goes like they both did at Westmead. Mrs Frid is to have everything there is. Signed in his right mind by ALFRED WOLTERS. May the Lord have mercy on his soul.

The writing staggered like the legs of a drunken man, but it was legible and still had a fluency and a character. Wharton puffed it for prints, then took a pressure of the dead man's and found they agreed. Then he made no bones whatever about going through his pockets, and found nothing that seemed to have the slightest bearing on the case.

Voices were heard downstairs and he looked down to see the doctor. Mrs Frid was wiping her eyes on her apron. Wharton and the doctor exchanged credentials on the stairs, and Wharton went down to the landlady.

'A bad business, Mrs Frid,' he said, 'and very upsetting for you. He'd been with you a long while, had he?'

'Over a year,' she said, 'and a better lodger no one wanted. No matter how he came home he never said an angry word to me.'

'I wonder why I didn't run across him on Monday?' Wharton said reflectively.

'He started the drinking on Monday,' she said. 'He came home and slept, the same as he did to-day, and then went out again and didn't come in till closing time, and I had to get him upstairs myself.'

Wharton clicked his tongue. 'You've certainly looked after him well. Now you go and make yourself a nice cup of tea and cheer yourself up. Fretting doesn't do any good to anybody.'

He saw her through, then nipped up the stairs again. The doctor had apparently finished the preliminaries.

'Dead about two hours?' Wharton said.

'Nearer three,' the doctor told him. 'Mind you, I don't think he'd have lasted much longer, the way he was going. I attended him about a month ago and I warned him. What's interesting you?'

'There's something about him that sets me thinking,' Wharton said. He stooped down and held the lolling head between his hands, turning it this way and that. Then he let it relax again, and he was smiling grimly as he straightened himself.

'Curious, isn't it? I've been looking for him and wondered if I'd ever find him, and here he is and can't tell me a thing.'

'Really? And have you searched him?'

'That sort of thing has to be done officially,' Wharton said with pious dignity. 'I suppose you can't hang on for a few minutes till the local people get here? They're on the way. Don't think me callous but I'm after bigger game than this, and I've a most urgent appointment.'

So Applebed's man was left with a report for the local police and a message for Travers, and Wharton and the detective-sergeant made their way towards the Blue Feather. A few minutes later Travers joined them, and he was interested enough to hear that Wolters was the man who had been at Arden on Wednesday night.

'Come on,' said Wharton, glancing at his watch. 'They're just opening the doors and we want to be first in.'

The proprietor turned out to be an ex-boxing-champion whom Wharton had met before.

'Tell you what, Super,' he said, 'I'll get my wife to relieve Alice for a bit, and you and her can have my room.'

Wharton had expected to meet a piano-fronted, platinum blonde, but found Alice to be a little dark girl, cockney, thoroughly self-possessed, quiet in manner, and obviously competent. She owned up to being well on the way towards thirty, and had known Wolters, off and on, for years.

'Oh, no,' she said, at Wharton's instinctive look: 'I'm not the one he did his carrying-on with in that divorce case. I'm married, and got a couple of kids of my own, though you wouldn't think it. I knew him as a customer.'

'You're going to be a great help to us,' Wharton told her. 'And what we want you to do is to go back to this morning, or early afternoon, and tell us just what he was talking about. Word for word, if you can. We don't mind how long we're here.'

'Well,' she began, 'he'd been in since opening time this morning and I was thinking of speaking to the guv'nor about not serving him any more, when he started talking about the suicides what've been in the papers. The first I really heard was when he said Miss Legreye was his wife. You see, I'd read about his divorce in the papers but I'd sort of forgot about him and Miss Legreye being the ones. Then he started swearing about her; you never heard such language as he was using. "Mr Wolters," I said, "either you stop using language like that or I'll speak to someone who'll make you." That shut him up. Oh, I ought to have said how that when he said he was Miss Legreye's husband, everyone sort of crowded round to listen.'

'Sensation in court, in other words,' said Wharton.

She smiled at that. 'That's right. Then he said he could tell the police a thing or two if he opened his mouth. Then someone gave him a drink – doubles, he'd been having – and he said only last night before the police found out what was in the house, he was there himself!'

Wharton was suitably surprised.

'Yes, and he said he was asked to go there by that man Ward who was found dead the same time as Miss Legreye. He said he rang him up on the telephone at where he worked – used to work, I should say, and didn't he start off using the foulest language again, all about how they'd done the dirty on him, and I really was going to call the guv'nor when he stopped the swearing. Some of them were arguing with him, see? – and then he started explaining how Ward had told him to go round to the house last night, and how he said, "Why not now?" and how Ward said they were all going away and there wouldn't be anyone there, but he was to come last night and how he'd be sorry for himself if he didn't. Oh, and Ward asked if there'd be a quid or two for himself if everything was okay.'

Wharton had given more than one glance up at Travers. Now he made Alice go over her statements again, though it had been plain from the start that, like the rest of the saloon bar, she had missed no word of Wolters' revelations.

'Now,' he said, 'listen to this and see if I've got it right. On Saturday morning last, just before he was sacked, Wolters was rung up by Ward who told him it would be to his advantage to come round to Miss Legreye's house last – that is, Wednesday – night –'

'Oh, at nine o'clock, it was, and it wasn't to be before.'

'That's interesting,' Wharton said. 'And Wolters wasn't to go before Wednesday as Ward and the others would be away. Ward also hinted that Wolters was to make some sort of a good thing out of the visit as he asked for a tip for himself.'

That seemed to be all that Alice could remember, except that Wolters began arguing and then quarrelling, and then it was closing time, and she understood he picked a quarrel with a man and there was trouble outside.

'He didn't say if he actually entered the house last night?'

She shook her head.

'He didn't express any surprise at Ward ringing him? I don't mind telling you that he and Ward weren't the best of friends.'

'Let me see,' she said. Then she nodded. 'I remember now. You don't mind me using the words he did? – because I remember he said he wondered what that bastard wanted. That was what he said. "I wondered what the bastard wanted, but I thought I'd better go, then I found he'd only been making a fool of me." Only he said it worse than that.'

And that was the full extent of the information that Alice could supply, though she volunteered to find at least two customers of the saloon bar who had been present. Her peep into the bar showed one there already, and Wharton asked him to step inside the private room, but he could add nothing to Alice's version, though his account confirmed hers.

Alice went back to her job and Wharton and Travers stayed on with a couple of drinks, talking things over. Applebed was given a report for the local police.

'The place to test out what we've just heard is Westmead,' Wharton said, and finished his drink. 'I don't think we can do any more good here. If anything does happen to turn up at his lodgings, we shall be told.'

'I'd like to put forward a suggestion,' Travers said. 'If Wolters was a frequent visitor to the Continent, is it unlikely that Ward wanted to let him have the miniatures so that he could sell them abroad?'

Wharton frowned in thought.

'And might not Ward have got confused in the dates?' went on Travers. 'He rang Wolters and mentioned Wednesday, then made a mistake and thought it was Tuesday. Or, more feasible, he told Wolters Wednesday when he ought to have said Tuesday. He'd forgotten that he'd be at Arneford on Wednesday.'

'But he didn't forget it,' Wharton said. 'He expressly told Wolters that everybody would be in the country.' He shook his head. 'The whole damn thing's crazy. It doesn't hold together anywhere. All our evidence is that Ward and Wolters hadn't a thing to do with each other. Either Ward was on the side of the wife or the husband. There aren't any half measures about a situation like that. If Ward was on Miss Legreye's side, then he hated Wolters like hell. And didn't Wolters call him a bastard?'

'On the other hand,' Travers said, 'Ward might have been playing some double game and with Wolters. She might have discovered it, and the discovery might have contributed to the brainstorm and the suicide – always supposing it was suicide.'

'My brain's going round as if I'd been playing chess for twenty-four hours on end,' Wharton said, 'and I have been, if it comes to that. But remember something else. If Wolters was coming to Arden to collect the miniatures, why should Ward ask for a percentage on the transaction? It'd have been the other way about! Again, if Wolters was coming to Arden for any reason at all, it would have been an event. Why didn't Ward make an entry in that diary of his – if you can call it a diary?' He clicked his tongue. 'Where the devil could that book have got to? Still, perhaps Lewis will have found it by the time we get there.'

Then he suddenly stared, like a man who sees an unexpected daylight.

'Wait a minute. Was it Ward who rang up Wolters? All our evidence says it wasn't.'

'You mean, someone using Ward's voice?'

'What else should I mean?' Wharton told him. 'Come on. The quicker we get back to that Bunce woman, the better I'll like it.'

The Yard man who had been at Warwick was waiting when they reached the house, and Wharton kept him waiting still longer. Bunce was sent for at once, and her manner was extraordinarily subdued. Wharton donned no spectacles and tried no tricks, but he did expend a little preliminary graciousness.

'And now, Miss Bunce,' he went on, 'we want you to think very carefully and be sure of the answers you give us. If there's any idea in your mind about giving us the sort of answers you think we'd like, then cut it right out. Tell us the facts as you know them. About Ward, for instance. Where was he all Saturday morning?'

'He was here.'

'You look surprised,' he told her. 'Think again. Did he go out of the house at all?'

She shook her head. 'He didn't, not so far as I know.'

'Go over the events of the morning,' Wharton said, and after some false starts, she was able to give them.

'That's all right as far as you yourself are concerned,' Wharton said. 'But where were you from, say, eleven o'clock till lunch? Upstairs, or down?'

'I was in the kitchen nearly all the time,' she said. 'I didn't go upstairs at all. Miss Legreye was out for a walk and didn't come in till nearly lunch time, and Ward was helping me and doing the downstairs rooms.'

'Now we come to the real point,' Wharton said. 'Did he use the telephone?'

She stared. 'The telephone? No. I never did know him use the telephone, not once a week. He never touched it except when I had to ring up some tradesman or get a number for Miss Legreye and I was busy and had to ask him.'

Wharton spent another five minutes, exhausting the same one point, and could get no further.

'What kind of voice had Ward?' he asked next.

It was noteworthy that she gave a faint smile.

'Oh, a sort of – well, high-pitched, as they call it. Sort of through the nose.'

'Try and show us,' he said.

She giggled. 'Oh, but I couldn't.'

'Try,' Wharton told her. 'Just say, "Good morning, Mr Smith, and how are you?" just as Ward would have said it.'

She made an attempt or two, and Wharton was apparently satisfied.

'That's capital,' he said, and then gave a private sort of nod. 'I can't help thinking that your friend Mr Gray could have done it better, though.'

She was suddenly self-conscious at the mention of Gray's name. Wharton eased off into by-paths for a minute or two, then gently steered the conversation back. Bunce admitted that Gray had more than once imitated Ward successfully. Then she relaxed sufficiently to relate a specific incident.

'He made his aunt ever so angry once. Last April Fool's Day it was, and he was here. She told me all this afterwards. He made out he was having an argument with Ward outside the drawing-room, and he was making Ward be ever so rude, and she came out to see what was going on, and it was only Mr Gray all the time.'

'Very clever; very clever indeed,' commented Wharton. 'But just one last question. Think very carefully. What were your own ideas about how Ward was going to spend his time between, say, when he left the house on Sunday, and Monday morning? I'm assuming you knew he was going to Warwick races by a Monday morning train.'

'He had the luggage to take to the station.'

'And after that?'

'I think he'd have gone to the pictures,' she said. 'He might have taken up Miss Legreye's tea, if he was here, and then he'd have gone to the pictures. When we were at the theatre he used to go some nights and have a fourpenny seat and sit everything right through twice.'

'Pretty good value for money,' Wharton said. 'A comfortable seat in the warm and dry for a whole evening, and all for fourpence. And you can't think of anything else he could have done with himself?'

Bunce had no ideas.

'And he'd have come back here to sleep in any case?'

'Well,' she said, 'I don't see where else he could have gone. He hadn't no relations, only that one at Warwick.'

Wharton nodded. 'Well, there I'm afraid we must leave it. 'Poor Ward's gone, and all his faults with him, and that seems to be the end of it. Was he ever a pal of Wolters', by the way?'

'I don't know,' she said. 'I don't know how they was before I got here; you know, before the divorce and all that upset there was. He used to say some awful things about him, though, to me.'

'Didn't like Wolters, eh?'

'That he didn't,' she said. 'I had to tick him off sometimes, he used such language about him.'

That concluded the latest talk with Bunce. Wharton turned mild eyes on Travers when she had gone.

'Well, now where are we? Back where we started from, or I'm a Dutchman. If we'd never seen Wolters at all, we'd be just where we are now.'

Travers shook his head.

'You're being despondent, George. What's the sense of playing chess and having the other fellow presenting you with all his pieces?'

'What other fellow? Is this sort of metaphorical?'

'Oh, no,' Travers said. 'If Ward didn't do the phoning, then someone else did.'

'Or Wolters was a liar and made up the whole thing.'

'But he came here, George. We saw him here last night.'

'That doesn't affect the argument,' Wharton said obstinately. 'He was here for other reasons and for other causes. He knew he had been seen, and he thought the police would be after him. That may have been why he did himself in.'

Travers was hooking off his glasses preparatory to a polish.

'Then where might our friend Meerschaum, *alias* Gray, come in?'

Wharton stared. 'What was he to get out of bringing Wolters round here last night?'

'That's what we might have to find out,' Travers told him gently. 'In the same way it might have been Meerschaum who created a wholly fictitious character with a bass voice, and used him for purposes of blackmail.' He smiled to himself, warming to the theory. 'We've heard of love affairs conducted through the post, and parties marrying who've never seen each other till they stood at the altar. Why not a phone courtship?'

Wharton uttered an indignant snort. 'Pregnant, wasn't she? I suppose that was done over the phone too?'

Travers had to chuckle. 'Good for you, George. But demolition of a theory isn't necessarily grubbing up the foundations. I'm convinced there's a lot in what I've said. And it has a basis in fact. Unless Wolters was a liar, for some reason quite unknown to ourselves, then he *was* rung up by someone using Ward's voice, and he was lured round here last night.'

'Well,' said Wharton, and with finality, 'I'm making a concentrated effort to find out just where Ward spent that Sunday.

'If I can't find anything – pictures or anywhere – then I'll think he was at Arneford, doing that burglary. It doesn't make sense. but I'll try to believe it. Why a man like Ward who had the free run of this house at all times should have gone down there, when he could have helped himself to plenty of pawnable articles here, beats me entirely.'

'I've seen nothing in this house which might be described as of real value,' Travers said. 'There isn't a thing in it that I covet. There isn't a portable article that's worth the taking. But those miniatures were worth a tremendous lot of money to a man like Ward.'

Wharton called Bunce in again.

'Did Miss Legreye ever mention those miniatures to you?'

He had to repeat the question and amplify it before the answer came. It appeared that Miss Legreye had had the miniatures in a drawer for some years, and had rediscovered them. There was something about them that seemed to her to suggest the wall of the Arneford cottage as a suitable hanging place, so she took them down there that first time Bunce had gone down, about a month previously. Miss Legreye had also said that some time she would have to get them valued as they looked old and out of the way.

Wharton next had in the Warwick man, and this was the gist of his report.

A. No miniatures had been pawned.

B. Ward spoke contentedly of himself to his nephew, and mentioned another visit as possible later in the year.

C. He gave the impression of being in funds, and took the whole family to the pictures on Monday night, and to the second-best seats.

D. He passed on a racing tip to the nephew and said it had been given him by 'one of us', by which the nephew understood a member of the theatrical profession.

E. The nephew accompanied him to the races on Monday but not on Tuesday. Ward parted from the family after the midday meal on Tuesday and mentioned that he would have to leave early as he had to get back to town on business. There was no mention of the word 'job'.

The Yard man's own impressions were that Ward had done a considerable deal of spreading himself. The nephew was not aware of the real position Ward occupied in Miss Legreye's house, and he actually imagined that at any time his uncle was likely to take up work on the halls again.

Wharton congratulated him on a good job, and the Yard man left. Wharton got out a pipe, slumped into a chair, and gave a shake of the head.

'Well, this case and I part company for a bit. I'm going to get something like a night's rest, if the telephone'll let me, and take it easy till the alibis get in, and that ought to be by midday to-morrow. Then there'll almost certainly be a conference here in the early evening. You'll have to be at it.'

'Then I'll get away for some sleep too,' Travers said. 'You coming now?'

'Coming?' He glared. 'Who said anything about coming? I'm dossing down here.'

So Travers said good night and left for town again. As the outer door closed on him he could hear Wharton asking Lewis if anything had been discovered about that diary.

10

ALIBIS AGAIN

THE FOLLOWING are synopses of the reports furnished by various officers of the Yard who inquired into the whereabouts of those people whom Wharton considered might be even remotely concerned with the deaths of Mary Legreye and Fred Ward. The reports lay emphasis upon what Wharton had considered the vital times:

a. From midday on Monday, the approximate hour when Mary Legreye took the poison, to 10 p.m. that same night, after which rigor mortis had set in and made impossible the placing of her in the chair.

b. From 7.30 p.m. on Tuesday night, which a study of trains and traffic showed as the earliest time of Ward's arrival at Arden, to 9.30 the same night, which was the latest hour at which, according to the expert opinion of Sir Barnabas Craig, he could have taken the poison.

CHARLES ABNEY. Travelled to Winstonly in the car of Bernard Prene, the actor-manager, and arrived at 9.40 on Monday morning. Presence on the course or in the clubhouse vouched for by secretary. Slept at Dormy House and left for town next morning by the 10.55. Movements on Tuesday vouched for from 6.30 to 11.30 p.m. by the references given.

STEPHEN FRODLING. Lunch brought in at 12.30 from Frangini's and eaten in the Odilon. In the theatre then till 4.35, when took ten minutes out for tea, and then remained in the theatre till 10.05 p.m. On Tuesday took lunch out and not back till 3.00, and remained in the theatre after that till 9.35. Tea was brought in from Frangini's at 5.00.

WILFRED QUORNE. The maid proved work in garden from 9.30 on Monday morning till 12.30, and when she went out at 3.00 p.m., he was still there. Usually there are two maids but one is away on holiday, and Quorne is a widower. Mr Quorne, who offered every facility, called in his daughter and said, 'What time did you get home, darling, and what was I doing?' She replied, 'Just after five, daddy, and you were still gardening.' Then they had tea together and went to the pictures at 6.15, returning at 9.10, at which time the maid was home.

On Tuesday, movements at Brighton duly certified by references, and Mr Quorne reached home at 6.30. The maid, questioned by him, said that she saw him then, when he said he would have only a light supper at 9.00; saw him again at 9.00 when she announced supper, and finally at 9.20 when she took coffee into the study. She then went to bed and heard no further movements.

PERCIVAL GRAY. (Known professionally as Meerschaum.) Breakfasted Monday upstairs, room 32; room of Edith Bunce, 33. Both seen down at 11.00 a.m., when Gray went to theatre. In for lunch at 1.00 and out again at 2.35, then going – according to later talk with chambermaid – to the pictures. Tuesday morning movements approximately the same. Tea at 4.45 and then in lounge till 6.00, and left 6.45, presumably for show. Returned at 7.35 when had dinner, and out again at 8.50. In finally at 9.10.

ALFRED WOLTERS. Movements through whole necessary period vouched for by landlady and the proprietor of the Blue Feather, Aldgate.

EDITH BUNCE. See under Gray.

Martelle, in the opinion of Wharton when talking with Chief-Inspector Norris over the phone, needed most careful inquiry.

'Not that I see anything fishy myself,' Wharton said, 'but the powers that be are bound to go into his whereabouts very closely on account of his living down that way, and because he was the last person, as far as we know, who saw her alive. Ward probably saw her later, but he can't talk.'

It is as well to state that Wharton was hurried over those instructions to Norris, and forgot to put any limit to times. Since therefore Martelle himself had gone on till the hour when he knocked up the proprietor of that village garage, Norris proceeded as far as that point too.

Norris was a product of the old school, and an excellent product at that. He might be slow but his grip was tenacious as a bulldog's, and he was a tireless, patient worker. Wharton, in a moment of irritation, once said of him that if he had had a moustache he would have waxed the ends, by which he doubtless meant that the ramrod back and the steady head proclaimed too much the policeman in him. But he was more like an old army warrant officer than a policeman; quiet and watchful in manner, and with a natural dignity and a simple courtesy that always made inquiry easy. Ludovic Travers had an enormous affection for George Wharton, and could smile only too readily at his eccentricities and likeable failings; but for Norris, Travers had a profound respect.

It was towards tea-time that Norris left Arneford for Arnemouth and his first inquiry was for Martelle's house. It turned out to be a bungalow of superior quality, lying on the bank that overlooked the estuary, and about four hundred yards from the tiny village. A wall surrounded it but it had practically no garden, though the trees and the undulations of the country made it secluded. A nice spot, Norris decided, and one in which he would have been perfectly content to end his own days.

The estuary bank had been cut away and shored up to make a roomy boathouse, quite capable of housing both the small yacht and the motorboat which Martelle had mentioned. And since there was a rising covered way that led from the far end to what looked from the bank to be a side door, Norris concluded that there was an entrance from the boathouse to the bungalow itself. Quite a large garage was built into the bungalow end, and that apparently had also its entry to the bungalow.

Having seen that much, Norris moved off towards the small village. A somewhat tottery landing-stage was on the miniature cape that jutted out into the estuary, and across the water he could easily see the larger village of Beachington, about three hundred yards away. The tide was out and a man was working at the keel of an upturned boat.

'I suppose Mr Martelle hasn't been along today?' Norris asked.

The man shook his head. 'Haven't seen him since Tuesday,' he said. 'They was telling me he'd gone away.'

'Tuesday,' said Norris, and rubbed his chin. 'I know he was here Monday.'

'Monday,' echoed the man, and laughed. Then he gave Norris a look. 'You're one o'them London friends of his, I reckon.'

Norris nodded an assent.

'You can have a rare laugh on him, if you are,' the other went on.

'Good,' said Norris. 'You tell me the tale.'

The tale was the one Wharton had already heard, with minor amplifications. A bus ran at longish intervals between South-ampton and Arnemouth, and during Monday morning a young woman got off it and made her way to the river.

'I see her myself,' he said, 'but I didn't pay no heed and then all at once I heard her hollering to Mr Martelle, who was draw-ing alongside in that little yacht of his. Thought he was a boat-man or ferryman or something, on account of that peaked cap he wear, and asked him to take her across and how much would it be. Regular knocked of a heap, he was, then I winked at him, and I said to her, "He'll take you Miss, and he won't charge you no more than a shilling." Rare smart little piece she was. Rigged up to the nines. Regular cockney too, by the sound of her.'

Norris had heard enough, and duly noted down the joke.

'I'll pull his leg about that,' he said. 'And now I want to go across myself. What about you taking me?'

No sooner said than done. Another boat was taken and Norris was rowed across and charged sixpence, so that the shilling had apparently been part of the joke. On the Beachington side was another landing-stage with a handy pub, called the Grapes. A man who looked as if he might be the landlord was taking ad-vantage of the spring evening to use the time before the opening of the pub to put in an hour or so on his garden. Norris leaned on the fence and made a remark about the wet season, and in two minutes the landlord was leaning on his spade.

'I just came from Mr Martelle's,' Norris said,' but he happens to be away.'

'Yes,' the other said reflectively. 'I haven't seen him for a day or two. He's usually up and down the river or out at sea various times of the day. Monday was the last time I actually saw him. He came over in the morning and stayed about a half hour in the bar.'

There had been a kind of reminiscent smile.

'They were telling me about some young woman taking him for a ferryman,' Norris said. 'I must pull his leg about it when I see him.'

The other nodded. 'A flashy bit of goods. One of these good-hearted kind, so my missus said. They had quite a talk. Worked in some big factory in Bristol, so my missus reckoned, but cockney as they make 'em.' He winked. 'Here, you tell Mr Martelle this, and don't let on who told you. This young woman came in the bar, see? Going on to Portsmouth, she was, after some bloke of hers, so I reckoned, and Mr Martelle asked her what she'd have, seeing as how he'd brought her across. "What are *you* having?" she says. "Gin-and-It," he says. "That's what I've got," she says, "so they tell me." "What's that?" he says. "You haven't got anything" – meaning she hadn't got a drink. "Not 'arf I haven't!" she says, just like that. '*It*'s what I've got.' Then she started singing some song about she'd got *It;* you know, a song you may have heard on the wireless.'

'I get you now,' Norris said. 'What they call sex-appeal.'

'That's right. What I reckon we used to call fast in my young time. And she was – take it from me. Not that that'd worry Mr Martelle. He was a regular one for the ladies – so they reckoned.'

So much for Martelle's movements till about twelve-fifteen on the Monday. Norris had a look round the village, and at some distance from the inn hired a man to take him across the estuary again. His next inquiries were at the local garage, which lay at the Southampton end of the village.

'I really came down to see Mr Martelle,' he told a man who appeared to be the head mechanic, but was boss as well.

'He's up in London,' the man said. 'Tuesday night he left for Plymouth to meet some ship or other.'

'I know that,' Norris said. 'By the way, is he still driving the same car?'

'The same old Dawburn thirty,' the man said, and then smiled. 'If you call it driving. That car can do ninety – you know that – and I'll lay a fiver no one ever sees him go faster than thirty-five.'

'Really?'

'Lost his nerve over that accident he nearly had in that big speedboat of his.' He nodded confidentially. 'I don't mind telling you he'd have given up driving a car at all if I hadn't talked him out of it.'

'Now I'll tell you a funny thing,' Norris said, and related how Martelle had run out of petrol, and his various adventures. The other laughed.

'Just the sort of damn muddle he would get himself into. I remember he asked me – no, I asked him – when his car was in here, whether he'd got enough in the tank and he reckoned he had seven or eight gallons.'

'That wouldn't take him far,' Norris said.

'Take him best part of a hundred miles. He can get fifteen out of her on a steady run.'

'That's just about what he did do,' Norris said. 'What time did he leave here?'

He thought. 'Leave here? About nine, I'd say it was. He rang up about half-past eight to see if I had in a new indicator I was getting and I told him it hadn't come so he said he'd manage.'

Everything so far was perfectly smooth running and Norris's last trip before dusk was to the inland golf course where he again inquired for Mr Martelle.

'I haven't seen him the last day or two,' the caddie-master said. 'He was playing here Monday afternoon, though.' He called to some unknown inside the hut. 'Wasn't Mr Martelle practising some shots after tea on Tuesday?'

The answer apparently was in the affirmative, and Norris moved on again. Now he was beginning to wonder just what point there could be in making that long trip to the west. Still, he supposed Wharton knew better than himself and so he pushed his car on that same night as far as Dorchester. There he wrote his notes and, with the aid of a large-scale map, worked out the details of the morning's trip.

He was away and gone by seven o'clock, and by nine he thought he had identified the fork where Martelle had turned to the left to avoid the undermined road and one-way traffic on the right. So he took the left himself and sure enough soon found himself considerably entangled. Several times he had to ask his way or consult his map and it was ten o'clock when he was back again at the fork.

Now he made straight for the village of Hamsie, coming in from the south, which was the way Martelle must have come on foot. The garage lay at the entrance to the village and the owner remembered only too well having been knocked up in the early hours of the Wednesday morning. Moreover he described the affair as perfectly natural. On most English roads or even lanes one expects nowadays to meet lorries even in the small hours; indeed, those are the hours when most distance travelling of heavy traffic is done, and the gentleman was not to know that he had blundered into a maze of lanes where it would be hard enough for two baby cars to pass each other, and where there weren't likely to be lorries from which one could beg a part can of juice.

There was no doubt about the make of car or the identity of its driver. Norris, with the satisfaction of having done a job thoroughly, if a trifle too easily, turned his own car towards town. Trouble with a petrol feed delayed him or he would have reached Westmead for tea. As it was he arrived about five minutes after the departure of Ludovic Travers, and he found Wharton raving about the loss of Ward's diary. Loss it certainly seemed, for Lewis said he had gone through the house with a small-toothed comb, and had seen never a sign of it.

The dining-room had been made Wharton's new headquarters, with the sitting-room for Bunce till such time as she could leave for Cadmarsh, which Wharton had promised as likely the following evening. Once more he tackled her about that book of Ward's.

'Are you sure you never saw it?' he said, putting the question as bluntly as he dared. 'It's a curious thing to me but it was on the table in here one minute and gone the next.'

'If you're accusing me of stealing a book, I don't see why I should take it. I never even knew there was a book.'

'Who's accusing you of anything?' glared Wharton. 'But you've got eyes in your head, haven't you?'

Out he went, muttering to himself. Then he tackled Lewis.

'I'll lay anything you like she took it and whipped it in that kitchen boiler. Why, I don't know, and I shan't know, but I'd give the very devil of a lot to find out.'

The sight of Norris calmed him down and he was his best cooing self again.

'Ah! here you are, Norris. Got all you wanted?'

'Here's the report, sir,' Norris said, 'and I think you'll find everything okay.'

Wharton waved it aside. 'The alibi was all right?'

'Word for word correct, sir. He was never within miles of Arneford on Monday and he didn't stir far from his bungalow all Monday and Tuesday, right up to nine o'clock on Tuesday night.'

'That settles that then,' Wharton said. 'Find anything else down there?'

'You mean at Arneford?' He shook his head. 'I think I told you everything over the phone. She bought that little property last November; gave four hundred for it furnished. Answered the usual advertisement the house agents put in the papers. That's all I didn't tell you, I think.'

'The burglary all in order?'

'The local people were satisfied,' Norris said. 'They checked up with the maid before she left and couldn't find anything missing, except a couple of miniatures. Looked to me as if whoever broke in was after papers or documents or something like that, though why she should keep any such things down there is something I can't quite get at.'

'Well, you know one end of the story,' Wharton said. 'Now you'd better go through the house here with me and hear the rest.'

Half an hour later they reached the drawing-room and found Lewis there with several tops of fountain pens.

'Didn't have time to do the job before, sir 'he said. 'Got most of these at Woolworth's, just before they closed.'

Wharton took an immediate interest, explaining all about the test to Norris.

'The idea is this,' he said. 'First of all, here're the broken pieces of the top that was trodden on just there, where that mark is. Bunce knew the pen the top came from but we haven't found a sign of it, so we can't make out why she had a top but no pen. You see the point? – and that makes the top interesting from the start. The next thing to remember is that she was here in broad daylight, and apparently took the poison at somewhere about midday. Very well then. The top ought to have been plain to see, so why didn't she pick it up? The third point is that we don't think her weight would have broken it, even if she did tread full on it; and if she did tread on it – and if she broke it, if you like – then why didn't she still feel she'd done it and pick the pieces up?'

'Would she trouble about a trifle like that when she was about to do herself in?' Norris asked.

'There's a lot in that,' admitted Wharton. 'But another question. If she came this way at all it was to get that cocktail mixture from the sideboard here. She didn't have to step where the pen top lay. It's right off the line. It's dead in line with the door and the window.'

'Perhaps she expected someone to come after all,' Norris said. 'You said she sat in that chair, sort of staring at the door. Why shouldn't she have had a last look out of the window before she took the last step?'

Wharton nodded. 'That's a remarkably sensible suggestion. Still, let's try what weight breaks the pen tops.'

Bunce was called up first. Wharton told her to tread full on the object but without pausing. One try out and Bunce did as directed.

'There we are!' said Wharton triumphantly. 'It isn't smashed at all. It's merely pressed into the carpet, so to speak. And what's your weight, Miss Bunce?'

'Just nine stone,' she said.

'There we are then,' Wharton said. 'Miss Legreye weighed pounds less.'

Bunce was thanked and dismissed, then Lewis walked across. The effect on the top was about the same as that on the one in Wharton's envelope.

'And you're what, Lewis?'

'Twelve stone ten, sir – or was when I weighed a week ago.'

'And were you actually conscious that you'd trod on something?'

'I think perhaps I was, sir. But only because I knew it was there.'

The phone man came up then and the experiment was delayed. Mr Martelle wished to speak to Wharton direct. What he wanted was that manuscript he had left with Miss Legreye, if the police could release it.

'In any hurry?' Wharton asked.

'Well,' he said, 'what I was thinking is this. I have to be your way in about half an hour's time so I wondered if I might call and collect it.'

'Call in any case,' Wharton told him. 'I'm almost certain you can have it. I've only got to make an inquiry or two.'

It was Travers he rang up, but Palmer reported that Travers was in bed and asleep.

'Don't disturb him,' Wharton said, and did a bit of quick thinking. But there seemed no reason whatever why Martelle should not have his own property back, especially as the dead actress had apparently done no more than lay it in her bureau, so upstairs he went again.

'Now,' he said, 'we'll try a last experiment. Norris, you blindfold Lewis and lead him gently about the room. I'll take two pen tops and slip them where he walks, and I want him to say if he feels anything.'

It was like Wharton to try some knavery, and Lewis, ears alert, heard him move where he squatted.

'I thought I trod on something then, sir.'

'That's where you were wrong,' Wharton said. 'Carry on, Norris.'

Then Lewis's foot went full on a top and smashed it, but he felt nothing. Wharton was satisfied.

'Well,' he said, 'I'm still to be satisfied that she trod on a top and broke it. Besides that, look at the thickness of your shoes, Lewis, and think of the thickness of hers. There's not a lot of wonder you didn't feel anything.'

'Then what about Ward, sir?' Lewis said. 'Why couldn't he have trod on the pen top?'

'He was the very one who'd have picked it up, if he did,' Wharton said. 'Still, there we are. As Mr Travers says, you've got to take notice of so many things that look unusual that it's ten to one you miss the very thing you ought to see.'

So Wharton resumed that initiating of Norris into the intricacies of the Arden end of the case, and then Martelle arrived, and a lady with him.

'This is Miss Wain,' he said. 'She was dreadfully worried whether you'd think her a sensation-monger for coming with me, but she knew Mary Legreye, though she'd never been here to her house.'

'I'm delighted you did bring Miss Wain,' Wharton said. 'Old fogies like me never get the chance of seeing stars in the flesh, as they say.'

She smiled at that. A most attractive-looking young woman. Wharton thought her; and quiet, almost gentle, in manner.

'Not a very bright star,' she said. 'But I did feel I'd like to come here, just for a moment. Poor darling! It was a dreadful end, wasn't it?'

'A bad business,' Wharton said, and introduced Norris. 'I have to fetch the manuscript upstairs, by the way, so if you care to see the actual room, you may come up now.'

She looked at Martelle rather nervously. He smiled reassuringly, but his face straightened as he turned to Wharton.

'I think perhaps we would like to see the room. I was telling Coralie how I was the last to see her alive.' He paused with foot on the stair. 'There's nothing there that – er –'

'Nothing to alarm anybody,' Wharton said. 'Merely a room.'

'I've thought so much about her since I heard,' Coralie Wain said wistfully. 'And that poor man Ward too. I never knew him, but it was dreadful.'

The, door opened and Wharton stepped in, holding out a hand as if to lead in Coralie Wain. Martelle entered soberly, then all at once was staring.

'I say, what's happened?'

'The room you mean?' Wharton said. 'That, in strict confidence, is one of the mysteries – I might say, the mystery – of what happened here. I shan't upset you, Miss Wain, but here's how Miss Legreye was found.'

He seated himself in the chair.

'My God!' said Martelle. 'How ghastly!'

'It's awful to think of,' she said. 'I can't bear to look.'

'It gave me a shock, I can tell you,' Wharton said, 'walking right in here and switching on the light and seeing her, just as if she were alive.'

'Just a minute,' said Martelle, brows puckering. 'Didn't you mention something about moving the furniture when Quorne and we others were here?'

'That's right,' Wharton told him.

'Well'- he frowned again – 'I don't want to suggest anything at all personal, but if she sat as you did just now, isn't that rather like a scene from my play? You didn't see the play, I suppose?'

'I did,' said Wharton. 'So did Mr Ludovic Travers, and he happened to draw my attention to the same thing.' He gave a shrewd look. 'Does it suggest anything further to you?'

'Well – no. Except perhaps that Mary Tudor was the sort of climax to her career, and that particular scene was the big moment. I mean, what I wondered was if she had it on her mind, poor soul. I mean, well, one assumes there's something in the verdicts the coroners' juries always bring in, about being of unsound mind. Sorry if I don't make myself clear.'

'But you do,' Wharton said, 'and I may say it's something that occurred to us straight away. But while you're here there is one little point on which you might shed some light, as the author of the play. Perhaps we might go downstairs now, by the way.

'The point is this,' he said, when they were down in the dining-room again. 'We have a witness who says Miss Legreye was talking about the divorce being made absolute – you know the business – and Miss Legreye was asked tactfully if she would marry again some time. The answer – a guarded answer, I take it – was that if she did it would be like the play. She meant, I gather, a marriage like that in the play.'

Martelle was looking blank.

'But you saw the play,' he said to Wharton. 'In it she married a man she hadn't seen, except through the eyes of his ambassador and through the miniature.' He smiled in a puzzled way. 'What on earth could she have meant?'

'Perhaps someone who hadn't asked her,' suggested Coralie Wain.

'Ah, well,' said Wharton resignedly. 'I suppose it will go down in the records as an enigma. Here's the manuscript, Mr Martelle, and may I wish it luck.' Then an arch look. 'By the way, when's the wedding?'

She smiled. 'That would be telling.'

'No one's to know,' Martelle said, smiling too. 'But we're due in Hollywood inside two months.'

She pouted. 'And we shall miss the Coronation.'

'You'll have something better than the Coronation,' Wharton told her roguishly. 'But about your play, Mr Martelle – did Kevstein buy it?'

'Kevstein?'

Wharton chuckled. 'We old stick-in-the-muds get to know a few things.'

'Well, I have sold it,' Martelle said. 'And to tell you the truth, that's what's made me feel so miserable in this house. Mary Legreye'd have loved playing Mary Tudor in New York.'

'Poor darling!' said Coralie Wain.

Martelle shook his head, then pulled himself together.

'Better be moving along. If you should want me, sir, I shall be at the same hotel.'

'Just a minute,' Wharton said, fluttering round for paper. 'If Miss Wain would be so good as to give me her autograph.' He explained. 'For my wife, really. She'd never forgive me if I'd missed the chance.'

Another minute and they had gone. Wharton, who had seen them off at the gate, came back to claim his autograph. He looked at the sheet of paper with longing eyes.

'Lovely set of prints she's left here, Norris. A pity we'll never be able to use them.'

11
THE END IN SIGHT

JUST WHEN Wharton was thinking seriously of dossing down, as he called it, on the dining-room couch, he had a sudden rush of ideas. First he rang Wilfred Quorne, and was lucky enough to find him in. He was never early to bed, he said, and would be delighted to see Wharton at any time.

'You'd better take over here tonight,' Wharton told Norris. 'First thing in the morning, if I'm not here, get in touch with the local post-office and find out if, and when, they received any instructions about re-addressing any letters to Arneford. There weren't any letters down there, so if any came here I'd like to know what happened to them.' He came a little nearer to the point. 'She might have got some letter here on Monday early that made her hurry down there.'

He gave Quorne's number and said that unless Norris heard anything to the contrary he would not be back till towards noon next day. Lewis would do what was necessary at the formal inquest.

In a minute or two he was driving his own car townwards. Quorne was waiting for him.

'I don't even think I'll take my coat off,' Wharton told him. 'It was just something I wanted to ask you about, and I thought I'd rather do it here than over the phone.'

But he did take off the coat after all, and he drank the hot toddy Quorne made.

'Good stuff, this,' he said. 'A ground frost tonight, or my name's Smith. And now about this business of mine. I'd like to see any relatives of Miss Legreye's former dresser, if there are any.'

'You mean Jennie Stone?' He thought for a moment, then shook his head. 'Jennie was getting on, you know. She was over seventy. Wait a minute, though. There was a sister. That's right, a sister just a bit younger than herself. I remember some talk about it when she died.'

'You don't remember her address, I suppose. If it's any help to your memory, I'm told that Jennie's own home was St Albans.'

Quorne shook his head. 'I seem to remember something but I can't be certain. But why not go down there? It isn't so far.'

'Maybe I will,' said Wharton, who had had that intention in his mind all the while. 'And now about another little matter. You were an old friend of Miss Legreye's –"

Quorne broke in there with a necessary caution.

'I hope you people outside the theatre – you'll understand my calling you that? – won't bring any misconceptions to bear on your inquiries. I've been thinking that ever since yesterday. Theatre people are all working people. We arrive at our dressing-rooms, we go through the show and we go home.' He smiled. 'No orgies, no gossip, and sometimes not even a good evening. An occasional five-minute conference, perhaps, with the producer in the chair.'

'You mean, there wasn't any real friendliness between her and you four people.'

'Yes, and no. Outside the theatre, and even connected with the theatre, Mary and I had common interests. We'd played together years before, and we'd toured together, which is always different. But there was only the barest connexion between, say, her and Abney, or even Frodling.'

'And Martelle?'

'Most certainly. Martelle had a hand in what I might call agreeing to her taking the big part in his play, but I don't think he came to town more than once a month.'

'I'm glad you told me that,' Wharton said. 'I admit I'd got the idea you were all what they call one big happy family. Still, all the better for the question. Why did she buy that Arneford cottage? One had the idea she was a Londoner dyed in the wool, so to speak.'

Quorne rubbed his chin. 'Well,' he said slowly, 'I think I can give you no end of reasons. She never did like London after that trouble with Wolters. She'd inherited the Westmead house from her mother and when it fell vacant she moved into it, and I think she'd have gone further out still if it hadn't meant long travelling at night. And about the cottage, I suppose you know her father had a living somewhere down that way a good many years ago? She had a sentimental interest in the district.'

'Now I'm beginning to understand,' Wharton said. 'She studied the local advertisements till something turned up.'

'I thing that's about right,' Quorne said. 'I remember she came to me in great excitement when she thought of buying the property. I had a private word with Martelle some time later, and he told me it was a dead-and-alive sort of place which he wouldn't live in for a pension. I didn't tell her what he'd said about the village because I didn't want to spoil her pleasure.'

Wharton had need of no further information, and he thanked Quorne warmly, and left. He arrived towards midnight at his own house, bearing one autograph in an envelope as a present for his wife. He slept untroubled by the phone, was up at six next morning, and by eight o'clock was at St Albans.

On account of Janet Stone there had been some minor local interest in the death of Mary Legreye, and he had very little difficulty in running the sister to earth.

Maggie Stone, now pensioned off and living in a small bungalow on the town's outskirts, had been a housekeeper for the last forty years of her life, and Wharton found her an ideal witness. The trouble was that she had so little to relate. She and her sister had written to one another only at Christmas and on their birthdays, and the last time Maggie had seen Janet was a year before the sudden death of that sister from heart failure.

'Oh, yes,' she said, in answer to Wharton's question. 'I know where Mr Gray was. I ought to, seeing I was born there, and my poor dear sister was there till he died.'

The Rev. Henry Gray had been vicar of Cheney Magna, and Wharton pricked his ears when he learned that the village was not far from Southampton on the Arneford side. Since Maggie Stone's account was obviously correct, it might mean that when Miss Legreye had spoken of Southampton, and visiting there, she had really meant Cheney Magna.

'I suppose you didn't keep any of your sister's letters?' Wharton asked.

She said she had not been long in the bungalow and had not properly unpacked, but she would look. One letter only was forthcoming.

'It's lucky I didn't burn it,' she said. 'I remember now, it came last Christmas just as I was going away, and that's why I happened to keep it, to read again.'

Wharton read it carefully, and in the middle came to something.

'Keep it to yourself but I should not be surprised if there were changes here when all this trouble is over, which it will be in April, please God. Better luck next time, I say, but not a word to nobody about it.'

'May I have the letter?' Wharton asked.

'Well,' she said,' it's the last my poor sister ever wrote.'

So Wharton contented himself with a copy and asked her to keep the original in a safe place. If any other letters did turn up, he was not anxious to see them, since the one previous to this would have been in the April before. Wharton put a final question when he rose to go.

'Anybody at Cheney Magna whom Miss Legreye would be likely to visit still?'

'Visit there?' she said, and shook her head. 'There's nobody, only the vicarage, and I don't think she knew them. My sister never went there with her, or mentioned it to me.'

Better luck next time, and that repeated request for secrecy seemed to Wharton to establish beyond doubt that however careful Mary Legreye had been, the shrewd eyes of her old dresser had seen below the surface. 'And yet,' said Wharton to himself, 'where's the value of the letter? It merely proves that there was a man in Mary Legreye's mind last Christmas, and we know that well enough from the pregnancy. A woman like her wouldn't have let a man go so far if she hadn't been sure of marriage once the decree was absolute.'

But he did get in touch with the Yard at once and had a man sent to Cheney Magna. Something might emerge from the inquiry, and whatever that something was it would be hailed with considerable relief. For what was worrying Wharton was that every oracle seemed dumb. Of all the inquiries that had been made, none had produced an answer. No one had seen Ward on Sunday after his trip to the station; or Mary Legreye on her way to Arneford, or back. No hotel claimed to have housed her, and no friends recalled a visit, while no pawnbroker had handled the miniatures.

What this damn case amounts to,' Wharton said to himself again, 'is that it's so ruddy simple. We keep trying to put into it what wasn't there. What it looks like coming to is a couple of honest-to-God suicides, and if I'm still hanging about Westmead this time next week, then my name's not what it is.' He shook his head. 'What got me was going into that room and seeing her sitting there and thinking she was still alive. If she'd had the sense to lie on the floor, I'd have known it was suicide. Too much of Mr Travers's damn romance – that's what's been cluttering up this case.'

The conference was at Arden, and at two o'clock. Ludovic Travers arrived well in time.

'Have a good night, George?' he said.

'But for two things,' Wharton said. 'It began too late and ended too early.'

Then, being in a mood of self-pity, he reeled off the list of what had been done, including the St Albans visit.

'There weren't any letters here,' he said, 'because she went to the post-office herself on Saturday morning when she was out shopping and filled in the usual form to have everything sent to Arneford till further notice. We've also got another inquiry on at all rubber works where the poison might have been obtained. Sir Barnabas Craig was here for half an hour having a look round in view of the conference, and a man's on his way to that Cheney Magna place where her father was vicar.'

'And who's coming at two o'clock?'

'The usual,' Wharton said. 'The Assistant Commissioner and the Chief, and Sir Barnabas.'

The surgeon was the first to arrive: a quiet, unobtrusive, tactful man, no more conspicuous than a city clerk. Menzies and he were soon in talk and then came the Assistant Commissioner, Colonel Aston, and Daniel Woodland, the Chief Constable. The usual greetings, and some banter, and then the tour of inspection began at the kitchen. Bunce had been sent to the pictures, but in any case she had never complained about that chalk outline of Ward's body that still lay clearly on the kitchen floor.

Travers could not help smiling to himself as that procession made its slow way around the house, reminding him as it did of those general inspections of the war, with a staff trailing and inarticulate, till summoned all at once to answer some question. There was much consulting of notes and photographs, but nothing new for the trailing Travers till the paint chipping was mentioned.

'This where the piece of green paint was found?' the Chief Constable said, and regarded the spot with a mild interest. 'The analysis, by the way, says it's a chipping from a tin, and merely paint and not enamel. I don't know if that gives you any ideas. It's very inconclusive to me.'

Wharton agreed that the paint might have come from anything. Then he was called on to sit in the chair, while the company regarded him.

'Very theatrical, to say the least of it,' the A.C. said.

'Well, she was theatrical, wasn't she?' smiled Woodland.

'I suppose she was.' He turned to Craig. 'Could she have died like that or was she placed there?'

Sir Barnabas shrugged his shoulders. 'I'm of the opinion that she died inside three minutes, and I think we should do well to look at it from the end, rather than the beginning. I mean this. Don't think she adopted that posture and made up her mind to stick it out. My opinion is she couldn't have done it. But let's say she took the poison and waited till the effects began to be felt. The last phase was when she sank back into the chair; the position, in fact, in which Superintendent Wharton finds himself at this moment. Call it, in layman's language, the final relaxation.'

'Might I ask a question?' said Travers.

'Do, please.'

'Why was the death placed at about midday?'

'Four hours after breakfast,' Craig said. 'A good breakfast, by the way. That would make the time between twelve and one.'

'And if the breakfast was as late as ten?'

'Then four hours later.'

'My point is this,' Travers said. 'It was a warm day and she was in this room that catches the sun. If she were placed in the chair, what was the latest hour when it could have been done, assuming death at two, and not at midday?'

'The shoulders and arms would have been affected early,' Craig said. 'To come to the point, I should say she could not have been moved after ten o'clock.'

'That's all,' said Travers. 'The alibis, I believe, have been tested to cover that time. Had you said midnight, they'd have had to be tested all over again, which would have been a very tricky business.'

The move down to the dining-room came at last. The A.C. took the chair.

'Smoke if you wish to, gentlemen,' he said. 'I don't think we shall be very long, however. In fact, I'm wondering whether or not Superintendent Wharton has changed his mind.'

'To be perfectly frank, I have, sir,' Wharton said. 'You'll admit there was justification ...'

'Every time,' he said. 'You, and Mr Travers here, were pitch-forked into this inquiry, and you've carried it out thoroughly, and with tact – as far as it's gone. But I'd like to put a question or two that has occurred to us. What was for lunch here on Sunday?'

'Cutlets,' said Wharton. 'That showed nothing was to be left over, and that Miss Legreye didn't intend to be here for supper.'

'And did she ever make tea herself?'

'Frequently,' Wharton said. 'And she would do the trivial washing-up if Bunce and Ward were out. She rarely ate anything for tea. A piece of cake, perhaps.'

'She was said to be staying on to read a script. How long would that take her?'

Wharton looked at Travers, who replied:

'It depends on the degree of care with which she read it. If she stopped and visualized each situation and calculated the effect of every climax or point or curtain, that would be a very different thing from an ordinary reading, which would take no more than half an hour.'

'I note the condition of the script she read, and how she may have hurried towards the end. But she could have been away and gone soon after tea?'

'Most certainly,' Travers assured him.

The Chief Constable broke in. 'The tear marks on her face.'

'Oh, yes,' Aston said. 'Are you positive she had been crying, Sir Barnabas?'

'I'm not positive at all,' he said. 'I'm reasonably certain that she gave her face a hurried wash, which is consistent with the fact that she had been crying and made a hurried attempt to disguise the fact or remove the traces.'

'Her face was betwixt and between, sir,' suggested Wharton.

'Exactly,' he said. 'She must have been undergoing considerable mental anguish or she would never have been content to leave her face like that – I mean, a woman of her daintiness and taste.'

'Well, that fills in most of the gaps,' the A.C. said, and smiled over at Wharton. 'I wonder if you'd like to tell us what conclusions you've arrived at up to the moment?'

Wharton adjusted his spectacles, but he did no peering. He spoke altogether for well over half an hour, and the summary which here follows is brief and takes no account of interruptions. It should also be said that he began on a note of what Travers was soon recognizing as false, if well-paraded, humility.

'As Colonel Aston was saying, we were pitchforked into this case. We were told an unusual story at Arneford and we arrived here to find a situation which seemed beyond the capacity of the local police to handle. If we were to handle it, then the sooner we took charge, the better. Had I been satisfied that both suicides were no more than that, I should never have gone as far as I did. But I was not satisfied. All the evidence I had in the first few hours failed in each instance to produce any real cause for suicide. I was not then aware of the pregnancy, for one thing. Also I was most suspicious of the glass at Ward's hand, and of the theatrical lay-out of the drawing-room, both of which have now been satisfactorily accounted for.'

He cleared his throat, glanced at his notes and was off again.

'As to what took place, I now believe it was this – taking Ward's as a subsidiary affair and concentrating on the death of Miss Legreye. Everything shows that she did not intend to remain here after tea on Sunday, and I believe her intention was to go to Arneford and spend some time there with the man with the bass voice – the man, if you like, who was responsible for her condition. She took a case containing night-clothes, you will recall. She may, on the other hand, have intended to spend only Monday with him, because any longer stay would have meant restoring the rooms to the condition they were in when she arrived, and living a life absolutely confined to the cottage. In short, I'm fairly sure that she intended to spend the day, or part of it, only, and then go on to friends or a hotel in the neighbourhood.

'Well, gentlemen, she certainly did not sleep here on Sunday night, because the evidence of the maid is positive about the bed. But I will say this. If we have evidence that Ward slept out of the house on Sunday, then Miss Legreye may have slept in, making herself a temporary bed on a settee. If she slept out, then it was either with friends or at a hotel, and the latter probably, since no one has come forward to say she was with them on Sunday night. If she stayed at a hotel it was probably under a false name, since no hotel has come forward to say that she registered there.

'On that Sunday night the nephew, Percy Gray, and Bunce, the maid-dresser, were at Arneford and on Wednesday it was discovered that the house had been entered by means of a broken window, and though nothing of value had been removed except two miniatures, there had been a search of drawers upstairs and down. My idea about that is this. The man – call him the lover, or simply X – was hunting for letters that might incriminate him, and he also left behind him a letter for her. It was what we might call a letter of farewell, and its contents threw her into such despair that she was distracted. Her one desire was to get away. She snatched up her case and bag, and the two miniatures – the only things of her own she had brought down to that furnished cottage – and next found herself here.

'The rest of that we know, how the scene from the play was probably on her mind and how she set the stage; you being of the opinion, gentlemen, that she could have moved the furniture herself, and that she did not move the one really heavy piece – the sideboard. But, bearing in mind the breaking-in at Arneford and the searching of drawers, I was of the opinion that X returned here or came here – thinking she was away – and found her lying dead, and himself placed her in the chair. If there was likely to be anything incriminating at Arneford, there was still more likelihood of there being something here.

'Now as to Ward, and there the difficulties begin. If he was so attached to her that overwhelming grief drove him to suicide when he came in and saw her on Tuesday night, then everything's more or less plain sailing. She may have left the two miniatures on the table, and he may have taken them. If Miss Legreye left a farewell message, then it was taken by X; but there was no farewell message left by Ward, and that, according to our experience, is unusual. Wolters, for instance, left one. Did Ward go to Arneford on Sunday night and take the miniatures, about which he had heard his mistress express the opinion that they were valuable? Admitted that the bookmaker was after him for money – but the sum was nothing serious, and there is also the fact that Ward had the run of this house and never seems to have done a dishonest thing.

'As for motive, I'm still unconvinced that there was a motive in his case for suicide. Why did a racing enthusiast like him not get full value for his money and hang on at Warwick till the last minute? He would have had ample time to do his packing in the morning. And why did he bring in his breakfast if suicide were anywhere near his mind? I admit he had not done well at Warwick, well enough, that is, to repay the bookie, but a man like Ward would never commit suicide for the want of a paltry six pounds.

'I pass over other unusual points, such as why the sideboard had been left unlocked by her when it was always kept locked, because that may be covered by the state of her mind. Also why Ward took the poison in whisky, and helped himself to it out of that sideboard, and then came downstairs to drink it.' And there Wharton treated himself to his first ironical peer over the tops of his spectacles. 'In short, gentlemen, while the supposed state of her mind can cover a whole lot of extraordinary happenings, I fail still to see why the term unsound mind can cover a similar series of extraordinary happenings in the case of Ward. He was not pregnant, gentlemen, and no disgrace was staring him in the face. He was not faced with the problem of explaining away the refusal to play Mary Tudor in New York.'

The Chief Constable, who had put in many a shrewd question, could not refrain from a last dry comment.

'Granted all that, but the fact remains that this inquiry is merely into the reasons why two people killed themselves.'

'Presumably killed themselves,' said Wharton doggedly.

There was some exchange of words, and then the A.C. broke in with the question as to what lines might be the best on which to continue.

'It's no concern of ours to find out who X was,' he said. 'We'd all like to hear him get a severe public castigation, but that's nothing to do with this inquiry. Still, even the most trivial of cases has to be rounded off.'

Wharton gave a quick resume of what he had done, and what he proposed doing. For one thing he was now disposed to take into account a certain cameo brooch which was definitely missing.

If it could be proved that Ward had taken it, thinking doubtless it was more valuable than it was, then the problem of the miniatures might be cleared up. He was also proposing to interview every member of the Stony Heart cast and each person with whom the dead actress had been at all friendly, and to repeat every press request for items of information.

Aston smiled dryly.

'But still nothing in your mind but suicides?'

'Maybe, sir,' Wharton said smoothly. 'I'm an inquisitive man, sir. Unanswered questions always get my goat.'

Ten minutes later the conference was over. The last car departed and Wharton came back from the gate.

'Well?' he said, with an arch look at Travers. 'Did I make a good fight?'

'You put up a splendid fight,' Travers said. 'Discipline is a lovely thing, George, and I hate questioning our superiors, but I still venture to think that if they had entered this house last Wednesday night instead of us, they'd have appreciated the force of atmosphere. I formed certain ideas then, and I still believe – even against the facts – that there're things behind this case which we haven't come near discovering. Which, perhaps, we'll never discover.'

'Well, you saw and heard,' said Wharton. 'We're not popular here. The sooner everything's rounded off, as they call it, the better they'll like it.'

Then the phone rang. It was the Yard man ringing from the post-office at Cheney Magna. Miss Legreye, he reported, had never been known to visit the village, and indeed there was nowhere she could visit, except the vicarage. There the vicar was an elderly widower who had never even heard her stage name.

'Try the villages immediately around,' Wharton told him, 'and don't trouble to report unless anything turns up.'

So one likely source of information seemed to have been dry from the start. Then that same early evening something did come in. The local station rang up to say a man had come in with the information that he had seen Ward on Sunday night. The man – a frequenter of the Three Bells – had been coming home with his wife from a visit to their son, and had taken the short cut past the recreation ground, when he met Ward at about ten o'clock just going into the drive of Arden. The conversation was:

'Been to the pictures, Fred?'

'That's right, Tom.'

Good nights followed and Tom and his wife continued on their way; indeed, they had never done more than slacken speed.

'That settles Ward,' Wharton told Travers triumphantly. 'Now we know she didn't sleep in the house.'

'But you don't know if he had really been to the pictures,' Travers said.

'I'm getting more sure than ever that he didn't go to Arneford,' Wharton said. 'All we've got to do now is hawk his photograph round the local picture houses. Two or three days more and this case will look a bit different, or my name's Higgins.'

12
WINDING UP

THE DAYS WENT by and though there was no mention by Wharton of executing a deed whereby his name was to be changed to Higgins, he knew in his bones that the case was on its last legs. But he was still putting up a fight; there was no doubt about that.

'If I could only prove there'd been any sort of hanky-panky, then I wouldn't mind,' he said to Travers. 'You and I know there's more in it than just two suicides. Too many things happened that needn't have happened. Ward needn't have clung on to that glass. Wolters needn't have been brought round here on Wednesday night. Mary Legreye ought to have come home with her hat and fur on.' He clicked his tongue. 'And where'd she get the poison from? If it'd been a man, it'd have been different.'

If silence were anything to judge by, then the case was indeed dead. Bunce had gone from Arden, the funerals were over, and inquiries in the press remained obstinately unanswered. No one had come into contact with Mary Legreye on the Sunday night, and no one had seen her on the Monday. The cameo inquiry did bring several answers, but none of the specimens shown resembled Bunce's description of the missing one. No one had handled the miniatures, and there was no information about the poison. Since external contact with it was harmless and it was sprayed by machinery during an early process of the raw rubber, it seemed obtainable enough by anyone, though as the process was an ultra-modern one, its lethal qualities were none too well known.

In fact, the one thing which Wharton did discover was that the copy of the newspaper which Mary Legreye had brought with her to Arneford was a West of England edition, and on sale at an early hour. But that merely clinched the certainty that she had gone to Arneford, and though Wharton instituted an inquiry at railway bookstalls and shops in the immediate district, he was perfectly resigned when there was no identification of Mary Legreye as a purchaser of the paper.

Then there were interviews with the rest of the Stony Heart cast and a score and more people with whom the dead actress had been even slightly acquainted. Wharton, in fact, spread that net to its utmost width, and was never a pennyworth wiser at the end. Then he went down to Arneford with Travers and spent a morning there, seeking new inspiration and finding none. The window had been mended but the now neglected garden was growing like a wilderness, with the last of the daffodils and the early tulips climbing frantically above the rank grass.

'Reminds me of this case,' Wharton said. 'The grass is growing all over it. If nothing happens soon, it'll be buried out of sight.'

Percy Gray was resting, as they have it, after that week's engagement at Portsmouth, and Wharton twice had him up for interviews. The whole realizable estate would amount to somewhere round about eight thousand pounds, which was a magnificent windfall for him, and already he was posing to Wharton as one whose wild oats had been long since sown.

Wharton went to the limit of his powers of examination, and tried the old game of playing him off against Bunce. But Percy denied indignantly ever having abused his gifts of mimicry, and Wharton was convinced that it was not he who had rung up Wolters that Saturday morning. For the former uncle indeed, he showed a perfectly vindictive hatred.

As for that visit on Sunday night to the Arneford cottage, Wharton brought him to admitting that he had had something like blackmail in his mind. It now appeared, too, that when he had peeped into the windows to see if by any chance his aunt was there – as Bunce had led him to believe might possibly be the case – he had stayed no more than a second or two at each, since the blinds were not even drawn. That was why he was positive that when he saw the window which had subsequently been broken, it had then been in a perfectly sound condition, otherwise he must have been aware of the hole.

Bunce, as far as he was concerned, was plainly to be no more than a regrettable episode. According to him, she had always been the egger-on. He admitted that he had given her money and said that the trip to Portsmouth was only an attempt to keep her mouth shut, since she was already hinting at repentance and having to own up to Miss Legreye, which was a subtle form of blackmail of her own devising.

But the chief admission was a vehement repetition of the old, that he had never really known a thing about any definite man with whom his aunt might be compromising herself.

'You've had a lucky escape,' Wharton told him severely. 'You may not be out of the woods yet, and my advice to you is that if you think of anything at all that seems to have the slightest bearing on your aunt's death, or Ward's, then you'd better ring me up as quick as you can slip the pennies into the slot.'

When Wharton casually told Bunce that now Percy had come into money he would probably be less friendly, she remarked with a vast assumption of indifference that as far as she was concerned there had never been any friendliness at all.

'What would you say if I showed you a statement made by him that you were the one who instigated that spying on his aunt, and accepted money for it?' Wharton asked.

'He dared say a thing like that!' she said. 'He's a dirty liar, and always was. You ought to have heard Miss Legreye go on about him. If ever I –'

Wharton cut short the heroics. 'That Sunday night when you remained in the car and he looked at the cottage. Can you tell me just what he did?'

'He looked in all the windows,' she said. 'He was gone about five minutes, and when he came back, he told me. I said to him I knew she wouldn't be there –'

'Just a minute,' Wharton said. 'Don't tie yourself in knots. You're not going to make me believe it was he who had the idea she was going down there.'

'Well, he kept pestering me,' she said lamely.

'That's better,' Wharton told her. 'Now you tell me in confidence why you thought she might be going down to Arneford, after she'd distinctly told you she'd be arriving at tea-time on Wednesday.'

She frowned. 'Well, he thought they'd have to meet somewhere; her and the man she was carrying on with, according to him. Then when I was laying out her things, I didn't think she was staying anywhere important because of what she took.'

'What she was taking herself, do you mean?'

'Yes, in her own bag. It didn't look as if she was going anywhere important.'

'You saw the bag?'

'Well, no,' she said. 'I know what she asked me to lay out, though.'

Wharton smiled pointedly. 'And since that discovery was on Saturday at the earliest, you must have got on to Reading, and rung your friend Percy.'

An indignant look, then her eyes fell. 'It was him who rang me up. He used to make out he was my brother, and how my sister-in-law was ill. Then something else slipped out. 'I wish now I'd kept his letters.'

Wharton smiled grimly. 'A good thing for you, young woman, that you didn't. Blackmail's not the trade it used to be.'

The funerals were over and forgotten, and the case still dragged on. Then came the conference at which Wharton admitted himself bested. At the beginning of May, the adjourned inquest was resumed. The evidence was fully given with the hope that publicity might still produce something new, and ultimately the usual verdicts were brought in. Thereafter the case was pigeon-holed, though not altogether abandoned, and Detective-Sergeant Lewis held for some weeks a kind of watching brief. It had never in any case, except for a day maybe, been front-page news, and with the glamour of the Coronation and its attendant events, it was speedily forgotten.

But before that forgetting, one morning during the first week of May, Travers had the case recalled to him by Palmer.

'I see that that Mr Martelle is getting married today, sir; the one who wrote that play, sir, that poor, unfortunate lady was in.'

Travers's two papers were of the staid variety, but Palmer took one of the daily illustrateds, and Travers borrowed it to see the Martelle pictures. The honeymoon was apparently to be spent on the *Megantic,* on which the couple were sailing that same night.

That evening the papers had more photographs, with a particularly fine one of a small group on the steps of the Registry Office. There was Coralie Wain, clinging happily to her husband's arm; and Martelle, smiling diffidently and looking as big a fool as most men do in the particular circumstances. There was Wilfred Quorne, looking grave to the point of aloofness, and there was Frodling, showing as fine a mouthful of teeth as a man of his age could wish his own.

Next morning Travers saw Wharton at the Yard, and there was the General looking at yet more pictures of the wedding. He was not a bit abashed when Travers pulled his leg.

'What do you think happened this morning?' he said. 'The postman brought a tiny package and when I opened it, what do you think it was? Wedding-cake! Wasn't that thoughtful of her?'

'Quorne was sailing on the same boat, so I see,' Travers said. 'And young Abney. Both going to play in the New York production of *Stony Heart.*'

'Hm!' went Wharton, and laid the picture paper aside. A nod or two and he was philosophizing. 'That play title makes me think. It sort of sums up Mary Legreye; don't you think so? That's the impression she gave, like Mary in the play. Making out she was prim and proper, and all the time just as full of what you'd call romance as anybody else. A pretty sordid romance, her own, though; and some hell of an ending it brought her to. So did Mary's in the play, if it comes to that.'

With that vague epitaph, the case, as far as Wharton was concerned, was ended. Summer began to slip by, and when at the end of July Travers ran across Lewis and happened to mention the Westmead suicides, Lewis was momentarily surprised, like a man who has forgotten.

'Dead as a door-nail, sir,' he said. 'Of course you never know when anything may happen to turn up, but I doubt it after all this time. Curious case though, while it lasted.'

With that final epitaph from Lewis, the case indeed seemed over, and if it came back to Travers's mind it was only in the brief moments after waking. Then at last that dream, in which he stepped into a room and saw again the dead actress throned in that central chair, came less frequently, and soon he could think of that room, and its chill and inarticulate horror, with no more than a grave recalling.

Early in August he left for an old haunt of his in the Pyrenees, and spent the best part of a month there. Palmer accompanied him, and it was the first week in September when they arrived back in England.

PART TWO

*

Solution

13

TRAVERS REMEMBERS

IT WAS ON a Tuesday when Travers arrived back, and Palmer's birthday was on Wednesday, which was 8 September. That birthday was always a notable event. Ever since Travers had discovered the date he had insisted on its celebration, and, to be perfectly frank, he probably derived more pleasure from the day than did Palmer himself – at least at its outset. For then Travers would do the congratulating and begin suggesting the day's programme, while Palmer would be mildly protesting at unnecessary trouble. But when the day was over, Palmer would always admit that he had enjoyed the best birthday of his life, with Travers always wondering how much of the thanks was due to tact and a convenient lapse of memory.

From ten in the morning Palmer was free, with the flat merely as his headquarters, for Travers would take his meals at a club, and give himself something of a holiday too. A fiver was handed over, out of which a present was to be bought, and Travers would always insist that above all his old friend and valued retainer should stand himself a first-class dinner and end the evening with a show.

That Wednesday night Travers got back to the flat shortly before ten o'clock, and when Palmer returned, called him in, and poured two night-caps to seal the day's celebrations.

'What show did you choose?' he said.

'A play called *Saloon Bar,* sir.'

Travers broke in laughingly. 'That sounds like an amazingly good choice. What made you choose it? The title?'

There was nothing unkind about the question. Palmer's tastes were simple ones, with the music-hall of the good old days as a something to be regretted.

'I saw the author was that Mr Martelle, and that interested me, sir.'

'Martelle?' said Travers, and stared. He remembered now that on the cover of the MS, Martelle had described the title as tentative, but why a play about Pepys should have the title *Saloon Bar* was altogether beyond him. Saloons in those days, it seemed to him, were not yet even *salons,* nor were bars even coffee bars. But maybe there was some paradox or concealed joke.

'A costume play, wasn't it?' he said.

'Costume, sir?' He looked puzzled.

'Yes, Charles the Second period and all about Pepys.'

'Peeps, sir?' He looked more puzzled still. 'There wasn't any peeping, sir.'

Travels proceeded solemnly to explain. Then Palmer remembered the name of the great diarist and there was a chuckle or two at the mistake.

'This play wasn't anything about that, sir,' Palmer said. 'Would you care to hear the plot, sir, if I can remember it?'

'I certainly would,' Travers said. 'Just the merest outline will do.'

'Well, it was about a young lady who'd committed a murder, sir, or thought she had, so she ran away to her old nurse who had married a publican in the suburbs somewhere, sir, and asked her to hide her, so to speak. Quite a lady she was, sir – the Honourable Gillian Blaine – and a real self-possessed young lady too, sir. Finally, sir, as the landlady – the nurse, that is, sir – had been disappointed of a barmaid, they managed it that Miss Gillian should have the place.'

'Wait a minute,' Travers said. 'I think I've got the idea. A new twist to the old high-life-below-stairs theme. But I'd rather not hear any more because I may probably go and see the play for myself. What'd you think of it?'

'Very good, sir, very good indeed,' Palmer said. 'I laughed quite heartily in places. Mark Storton, sir, who took the part of the handyman, was very funny, sir.'

'Yes, he's always very good,' Travers said. 'A full house was there?'

'Well, no, sir – not what you'd call full. The pit looked rather bare, sir, from where I was.'

Travers sat on for a time when Palmer had gone to bed. That tragedy of the preceding April had been brought suddenly back, and there were a whole series of peculiar things in connexion with Martelle's new play that set his brain working. Maybe he had known that the Pepys play was not up to the standard of *Stony Heart* and maybe he had said as much to Mary Legreye that Sunday when he brought the play round to her, and maybe that was why she had not hastened to read it.

But why a man who had had such a success with a historical play should abandon the *genre* for modern comedy, he could scarcely at the moment fathom. Maybe, he thought, playwrights were like authors, and modern comedy was their magnet or will-o'-the-wisp, just as most authors – as a certain publisher had once pathetically told him – always arrived in the office sooner or later with a manuscript which, with an air of delightful diffidence, they described as stories about children.

Then Travers consulted the advertisements in the evening papers.

ODILON. (Tern. 0101.)
Evgs. 8.15. Th., Sat., 2.30
SALOON BAR
A Light Comedy by PHILIP MARTELLE
'A really riotous affair' – *Evening Record.*
'Mark Storton literally brought down the house'
– *Daily Picture.*

Now to the uninitiated those two quotes might have seemed a good enough recommendation, but to Travers, bearing in mind Palmer's description of the sparseness of the house, they gave the distinct impression that the play was not enormously far from being a flop. Then another idea occurred to him. How long it took an experienced hand to write a play he had no notion, but Martelle could hardly have begun that comedy of his till he was first of all convinced that the Pepys play showed no possibilities, and therefore the probable lack of success of the comedy might be due as much to hasty writing as to anything else – including, of course, an insufficient period for the try-out.

But in any case Travers was sufficiently interested to see the play for himself the following afternoon, which was a matinee.

He tested Palmer's estimation of a sparse house by not booking a seat, and was able to buy a centre front circle ten minutes before the curtain rose. The pit was reasonably full, though it was hard to tell how much of it was paper.

Amelia Cordage was the Hon. Gillian Blaine. He liked Amelia in anything: always getting the most out of a part, and always looking the gamine with that tip-tilted nose of hers. Connie Mace, the publican's wife, was one of the old school, but a fine character actress who had never let a play down. Mark Storton, the pub's handyman, was nearly always a riot. His was the dismal-Jimmy type of humour, and his face was no inconsiderable part of his fortune. Quite a strong team, thought Travers, and settled back in his seat as the curtain rose.

The scene was the saloon bar of a suburban pub on a spring afternoon, and the landlady, Lizzie Drew, was smartening up the place with the aid of Bob, the handyman. Talk, in which reminiscences by Lizzie of life at the Manor, and mention of the Hon. Gillian. George Drew came through. No answer to that advertisement for a barmaid? Very well then. Bob would take the four-ale that night, Lizzie the main bar and himself the saloon. Out he went, saying he'd be back at five. Hilarious comment by Bob on life in a four-ale bar, and descriptions by Lizzie of some of the customers. Hearts of gold plainly beat beneath her ample bodice and his cockney waistcoat.

Maid popped in. 'Lady to see you, ma'am.' Obviously an applicant for the post of barmaid. Bob sent down to cellar to do cask-tapping, and lady shown in.

'Miss Gillian!'

There she was: erect, defiant, and somewhat frightened for all the brave show. The story proceeded on the lines Palmer had indicated. Panic by the two women, recovery, panic again. 'I could say you was my niece.' Discarded. George had seen the niece. 'If only you knew something about barmaids!'

The project seized upon, discarded as preposterous, then toyed with again. Gillian suddenly determined. 'Of course I can do it, Elizabeth!' More dissuasions, then the initiation into the mysteries. Pulling of handles, where this kept and that, how much for a tot. Sudden reappearance of Bob. 'Beg your pardon, I'm sure.' Introduction of Gillian as new barmaid. Name Flossie Harris. Bob sent off again. Consternation and, 'Well, that's gone and done it!'

Rehearsal continued. Floss must show herself off more. Have more pep – more It. 'It? Yes, you know. What they call sex-appeal.' Rehearsal of that, clever and quite amusing. So to speech. 'Refeened' or cockney? Better be whichever Miss Gillian could do best; anything B.B.C. frowned on by patrons. So to return of George. Hoarse whisper to Bob. 'Who's she? New barmaid?' Bob: 'Not 'arf she ain't!'

George centre stage, with Flossie. 'Afternoon, miss. You the new barmaid?' Saucy look from Flossie. 'Not 'arf I ain't!'

CURTAIN

Maybe that earlier description by Palmer had spoiled things, for Travers had been faintly interested, and no more. His was also a sceptical and curious mind, and he wondered just where the Hon. Gillian had acquired that knowledge of cockney which she was clearly about to use in the coming scenes. Clever and well worked up to as had been that echo of Bob's, 'Not 'arf she ain't!' he failed to visualize Gillian as a barmaid to the manner born.

It was a hot afternoon and the theatre was somewhat stuffy, and he made his way out to the lounge. Then as he sat there he had a sudden, startling idea. *Martelle had first got the idea of that comedy from his experiences on a certain April morning with a rather flamboyant wench whom he had taken across the Arne estuary, and who had thrust herself on him later at the Beachington pub.*

He leaned back in his chair and tried to recall Norris's meticulously detailed inquiry into Martelle's alibi. That was it! Martelle had become aware that the Pepys play was a wash-out, and had hunted for a new subject, and his mind had been attracted by the showy personality of that talkative wench. She had talked about It, and sex-appeal, and had said, 'Not 'arf I haven't!' or something like it.

Frodling was passing through the corridor and caught sight of him. One look was enough, and he opened the door and came forward, hand extended. He looked plumper than ever, Travers thought, and as full of optimism.

'Well, how are you, sir? I thought it was you.'

'Trying to keep cool at the moment,' Travers said. 'You're looking remarkably fit.'

'Not so fit as you,' Frodling said enviously. 'Been abroad?'

'Just a short trip,' Travers said.

'Then you missed the first night.' He took a seat on the adjacent settee and mopped his brow. 'Been seeing the show? What'd you think of it?'

'I've seen worse,' Travers said.

'But not much.'

'Well, since you say that, I'll say I'm glad my money isn't behind it. How long will it last?'

Frodling shook his head. 'Till the end of next week, if it's lucky. What'd you think was wrong with it?'

'It just didn't hold me,' Travers said. 'For instance, I know that Gillian Blaine is now a barmaid, but I don't give a hoot what sort of a barmaid she makes. I don't mind whether she scoops the till, marries the proprietor, or is hauled off to Holloway, if you know what I mean.'

'Yes,' said Frodling, and nodded again. 'You're dead right. There's a good idea missed. We cabled Martelle after the first night but he wouldn't have it doctored, so what are you going to do? Still, there you are. They all get these ideas. Start off with a lucky break and then think it's dead easy, especially comedy. Situation or two and sprinkle a few wisecracks – that recipe's worked clean out.'

'When did Martelle write it?'

'Well, he was telling me –'

'He's been back in England?'

'Over in August,' Frodling said. 'Only stayed ten days or so. Saw the last rehearsals and then had to get back to Hollywood. Kevstein's begun work there on *Stony Heart*.'

'You were telling me when he wrote this new play.'

'Oh, yes. He had a sudden idea on the boat over – you know, the honeymoon trip,' Frodling said.

Travers nodded to himself, pleased at having made a good guess.

'It's his own money he's losing,' Frodling was going on. 'He put it all up himself.'

'Wealthy man, was he? I mean, he didn't give one that impression.'

'He came into a bit when his father died some ten years back,' Frodling said. 'You may remember the name. Martelle of Martelle and Lacey, manufacturing chemists. I rather fancy he got through most of it, though. Never did any work except spend the old man's money. He was pretty near Queer Street when *Stony Heart* broke lucky. Bit of a flyer too. Suppose you never saw that little place of his down at Arnemouth?'

Travers shook his head.

'I was down once. Many a bird he's had in that little aviary. A dark horse, old Martelle, but you don't fool Steve.' He gave himself a quick smile at that. 'No, Mr Travers. The luckiest day he ever had was his wedding day, though I doubt whether she'll always think the same. Nice little lady, though. Know what she's making a year?'

'I've seen the published lists,' Travers said, 'if they're any reliable guide. Best part of fifty thousand, isn't that it?'

'All that,' Frodling said, and mopped his brow again. 'Enough to make you sweat at every pore.' Then he glanced up at the clock and became aware of the time. 'Well, I mustn't keep you from the second act. It's been on ten minutes, in case you don't know. Glad to see you any time you're this way.'

Travers debated for a moment whether or not to go back to the play. Then he decided on tea instead, and made his way out of the theatre.

There was no particular wonder that that night he should have had again his old dream of entering the room where Mary Legreye sat in that lonely chair. But the dream took a curious and frightening twist, for as he entered, her head slowly moved, and she spoke.

'Mr Travers, isn't it? And how did you like the play?'

She was all at once gone, and it was Frodling who was speaking, seated on a settee and mopping his brow. But Travers woke then and found himself wet with perspiration. It was the bedclothes, as he knew – too many of them and too drawn up – and yet the vividness of that latest dream kept him from sleep, and it was not till dawn that he dozed off again.

All morning long the case was on his mind, and after lunch he leaned back in his chair and began to think back. He had reviewed the papers in the case just before the final abandonment, and with that tenacious memory of his he found it easy to recall its details, from the moment when he and Wharton had overtaken Bunce at Arneford in the dusk that April evening. But nothing new emerged from that revision, except perhaps one question.

Stony Heart had had a long run. What then had Martelle been doing since he wrote that play? Had he spent the months in idleness, and had he panicked when the run was coming to an end, and then hastily written that first draft of the Pepysian play? Had he not worked because he had had no inspiration? If so, and the inspiration had come on that short honeymoon voyage, then inspiration had proved a deluding jade, for if ever a play lacked fire and inspiration it was *Saloon Bar*.

Then Travers remembered what Frodling had hinted about various pretty ladies down at the Arnemouth bungalow, and how Norris's inquiries had elicited some mention of the same thing. Nothing against it, of course, if Martelle and they were like-minded. And he was not definitely engaged to Coralie Wain till her return to England from America. But Martelle was certainly a dark horse, as Frodling had said. Rather funny, in a way, the air of alarm he had assumed when telling of how that flighty young woman from Bristol had attached herself to him.

Then Travers realized he had never seen Arnemouth for himself, and all at once he had a violent urge to go down there. Then the mood passed, and as restlessness persisted, he rang the Yard instead and asked for Wharton.

'He's away on his holiday, sir,' he was told. 'We expect him back in about a week.'

'And Chief-Inspector Norris?'

'Up North, at the moment, sir.'

After that Travers felt that he and the Westmead case were locked up together in an empty room. Something must be done, either to rid his mind of it, or to get to real grips again from some new angle. Then all at once his mind was made up, and he rang for Palmer.

'I think we'll go away for a day or two,' he said. 'Pack for yourself and me for two to three days. Just a lounging holiday in the car.'

They set off in the Rolls after an early tea. The trip figures were set at zero on the speedometer, and it was five o'clock when they passed through Westmead, which is seventeen miles from town.

14
TRAVERS SUSPECTS

TRAVERS HAD a mind to see Arneford in daylight again. It was not much after six when he arrived at the tiny village, and he drew the car up for a moment, then slowly moved on. The young green of the beeches now arched the road and hid the river from view, but about a quarter of a mile through the village he heard the puff-puffing of a motorboat, and through a gap in the thin line of woods, saw a small, flat boat making its way up stream. Another hundred yards and he saw a stile, with a path that led to the river bank, and he pulled up the car and walked the short distance through the trees. But only a short stretch of the river could now be seen, for a bend and the trees concealed even the village.

It was half-past six when he reached Arnemouth, and just short of that village he found himself at a fork with a choice of ways. There was ample time and he tried both. That to the right brought him out on what was apparently the Southampton Road, with the garage and then the village about two hundred yards on. Then he reversed at a convenient field-gate and came back to the fork again. There the left-hand lane brought him along the winding bank of the estuary past the bungalow which he knew was the one that had been owned by Martelle.

Norris had seen no reason in his report to give a detailed description of the bungalow, and Travers was surprised at its quality, its conveniences, and its seclusion. And as he drove slowly past he thought he saw signs of the new owners.

'That's where Mr Martelle used to live,' he said to Palmer. 'Looks as if people are living there.'

'There was a lady working in the garden,' Palmer said. 'She was stooping, sir; weeding the front path it looked like.'

Just short of the squat church, Travers drew the car up, and let his eyes range over the view out to sea. Then they came nearer home, to the small landing-stage on the bank, and, gay in the evening sun, the red roofs of Beachington across the little estuary.

'I think I'll slip across to Beachington – that village there,' he said on a sudden impulse. 'I don't expect to be gone more than half an hour.'

There were two or three men on the shore below the bank, and there was no difficulty in getting rowed across. The man was told to leave the boat moored and come in the inn for a drink. His name was Gosling, he said.

The inn door was open and Travers marched in. The landlord was leaning across the bar counter, in talk with a man in fisherman's garb, but the talk ceased abruptly as the stranger walked in.

'What'll you have, Gosling?' Travers said.

'A pint, sir.'

'A pint,' Travers told the landlord, 'and a small whisky for me. Pour yourself something, and this gentleman too.'

'Thank you, sir,' the landlord said, and an echo followed from the fisherman, and greetings from the boatman who had rowed Travers across.

'Been a nice day, sir?' the landlord said.

'A lovely day,' Travers said. 'Your season over yet?'

'Well, won't be long now. You staying here, sir?'

'Not exactly. What I may be doing later depends on the weather. By the way, Mr Martelle has left his bungalow, they tell me.'

'Mr Martelle? He's been gone some months now. When did he go, Henry?'

'April, some time,' Henry said, and added a quick 'Good health, sir!' to Travers.

'That's it, sir – April. In America now, so someone was saying. My missus I believe it was. Saw it in the paper.'

'Middle of April, it was,' Gosling said.

'You're pretty modern here,' Travers said, pointing to the beer handles which the landlord had manipulated. 'Most country pubs I've been in still draw from the cask.'

'The brewers had the machine put in last year,' the landlord said. 'This little pub do a good trade when the season's full on.'

'Some of us aren't any too moist when it ain't,' Henry said.

'That's right, Henry,' Gosling said. 'There ain't no season, not for beer.' He gave a nod. 'Now Mr Martelle, who this gentleman was speaking about, he was as good a hand at a pint as most.'

'That reminds me,' the landlord said. 'He was proper interested in this machine, Mr Martelle was. He came over one morning before I'd opened and got me to let him draw a glass or two.

'Going in for the hotel business, sir?" I say. "Just interested," he say, or something like that.'

'I reckon he wanted to know so's to put it in one o'them plays of his,' Henry said. 'You remember when he reckoned he was going to write a play about us down here, and how he went out with the boats a night or two. Asking all manner o'questions, he was.'

Travers was listening with a curious intentness.

'When was Mr Martelle so interested? When the engine was first installed?'

The landlord thought for a moment.

'Why, no, sir. Round about Christmas time.' He chuckled. 'I remember something now. When I sort of pulled his leg, he gave a laugh. "'Stead of giving a Christmas party like a lot of people do," he say, "I reckon I'll hire a pub somewhere for the night and do it that way."'

'And did he?' asked Henry, mouth agape.

The landlord smiled tolerantly. 'I reckon that weren't only his foolery. But blow me! if I didn't take him serious at the time. Rare particular, he was. Wanted to know where this was kept and that was kept, and how to serve everything. Made a rare good job of it, he did.' He sighed. 'Perhaps he did scheme to hire a pub. You never know what some damn brewers will do. Nor what he'd be likely to get up to neither.'

Travers set down the glass and smiled across at Gosling.

'Well, we must be going. See you tomorrow, perhaps, landlord.'

All the way down to the boat his fingers itched to get at his glasses and polish them. Then the boat got going and he polished them in earnest. So Martelle had told at least one lie over that new play of his. He had not begun it on the honeymoon voyage, and there had been no sudden idea, for he had had the play in mind before Christmas, even if he had actually written no word.

Then as Travers hooked the glasses on again, he knew the lie might after all have been a partial truth. Martelle might have drafted that play at Christmas, and then have let it lie fallow. The real inspiration – or what he considered such – did come on the voyage, when he remembered the scene in the inn and that Bristol wench talking about It, and drinks, and cheerily rapping out her slang. She had been the inspiration that made him rewrite or recast the play to include her as a principal.

He paid Gosling, and then as he came up the steps to the bank again, he had another idea. Why had Martelle been in such a hurry to dispose of his Arnemouth property? Or hadn't he?

Perhaps the auctioneers might be consulted to see how long before April the property had been in the market. But even so, why sell it at all? If Martelle was marrying into Coralie Wain's money – a blunt statement yet plain fact – then why part with what would have been a pleasurable holiday headquarters when in England? – and after all, England was his home and hers.

Now though there were arguments enough why Martelle might have decided to sell the bungalow – that it was not handsome enough for his married prospects, for instance – Travers felt there was something queer about the business, and he uttered his thoughts aloud as he stepped into the car.

'I wonder what auctioneers or house agents sold Mr Martelle's bungalow.'

'There's a bill on the wall there, sir,' Palmer said. 'I was reading it, sir, while you were away.'

Travers found there were two bills: one for the bungalow itself and one for the contents, including the small yacht and the motorboat. The auctioneer was a W. Bleeve, of Whinsea, Southampton.

As he came back to the car again, Gosling was passing, and he called to him.

'How many years did Mr Martelle live here?'

'Just over two, I think, sir. May have been three.'

Travers moved the car on. He had no intention of making himself too conspicuous in Arnemouth and starting the first movements of what might become a dangerous avalanche of gossip attached to Martelle's name. Indeed, if nothing eventuated within the next few hours, he was proposing to carry no further what had up to then been merely friendly inquiries. Meanwhile he would spend the night at Southampton and call on the auctioneer in the morning.

It was nine o'clock when he entered the auctioneer's office. 'You handled that bungalow at Arnemouth for Mr Martelle, didn't you?' he asked the clerk. 'Did you sell it?'

The clerk smiled. 'It was sold on the sale day, sir. Fetched a hundred pounds more than its reserve.' At the first mention of the bungalow he had begun looking through files, and now he produced two catalogues. 'If these would interest you, sir, you can have them.'

'Thank you,' said Travers, and took them. 'By the way, had Mr Martelle been thinking of selling for any considerable time before the actual sale?'

'I don't think he had,' the clerk said. 'I believe I'm right in saying we had instructions to sell at the beginning of April or thereabouts.' He thought for a moment. 'That would be it. Allowing for all preliminaries, such as advertising and publicity, that would bring the sale to the beginning of May. Any other properties of the same sort I may interest you in, sir?'

But Travers courteously refused to be interested, and returned to the car again. There he stood for an indecisive minute or two, wondering just what move should come next. It was an indecision he was always to remember. At one moment he thought of heading back to town and relinquishing that preposterous attempt to bring life to a dead case, and then he began idly flipping over the pages of that furniture catalogue, and his eye fell by chance on a certain word – *hassock!*

When he afterwards came to look back on that brief minute or two outside the office of the Whinsea auctioneer, he found it hard to recapture the thrill of that blinding flash of revelation that came at the mere sight of a word, but a revelation it was: sudden, dramatic, and even fantastic. Maybe something of the subconscious had all at once leapt to the surface, but as he stood there polishing his glasses and blinking away in the morning sun, a score of mysterious happenings seemed less mysterious, and the insignificant acquired an ominous significance. It was as if he had for months sat before a vast jig-saw puzzle, and had never known where to plant a piece for a true start. Now piece after piece fitted snugly into place. Many, it was true, still seemed wryly out of all keeping with the shape of the final picture, but even they with patience might, as he somehow knew, be ultimately made to fit.

'Just a minute,' he said to Palmer. 'I must have another word with that clerk.'

In *Kensington Gore* or *Murder for High-Brows*, Travers has a paragraph or two on one whimsical aspect of police inquiry, namely, the enormous pleasure that comes from being able to lie with a perfectly good conscience. That was why he was smiling, though the clerk took the smile for some diffidence over so trivial a matter as a hassock.

'Who bought it, sir?' He once more began looking through files. 'Here we are, sir. Lot twenty-three – hassock and pair of bellows. Bought by a Mrs Lovecorn of Arnemouth. Two shillings.'

'I always liked that hassock,' Travers said. 'Rather absurd of me, perhaps. But the little yacht and the motorboat. Could you tell me who bought those?'

There was no need to look up the files for those. They had been bought by a Beachington firm – Hamble Brothers – whose business was the letting out of boats to visitors.

'A nice little yacht, I believe it was,' Travers said.

'Well – yes,' the clerk said dubiously. 'A yacht was rather a fine name for it, sir. I wouldn't have called it much more than a nice little turtle-decked sailing boat with a centreboard and a cabin got up spick-and-span.' He ran a quick eye over Travers's lean length. 'I think you'd have found yourself too cramped in her, sir.'

'I expect I should,' Travers told him. 'Still, I'd like to have a look at her, if only for old times' sake.'

At half-past nine he was at Arnemouth again, and inquiring for the house of Mrs Lovecorn. She turned out to be an elderly widow who lived near the church.

'Oh, yes,' she said. 'I bought the hassock and bellows, but I won't sell the bellows. It was the bellows I wanted. I didn't want that old hassock.'

'Then may I buy the hassock from you?' smiled Travers, who had talked about knowing Martelle and had hinted vaguely at keepsakes. 'Shall we say half-a-crown?'

The hassock was placed in the back of the car. The whole affair had not taken more than five minutes, and he lingered no longer in the village but drove on past Martelle's old bungalow to the fork. There he had a few moments more of indecision.

'You're not getting tired of rushing about like this?' he said at last to Parker.

'A very nice holiday for me, sir, if you'll pardon me saying so.'

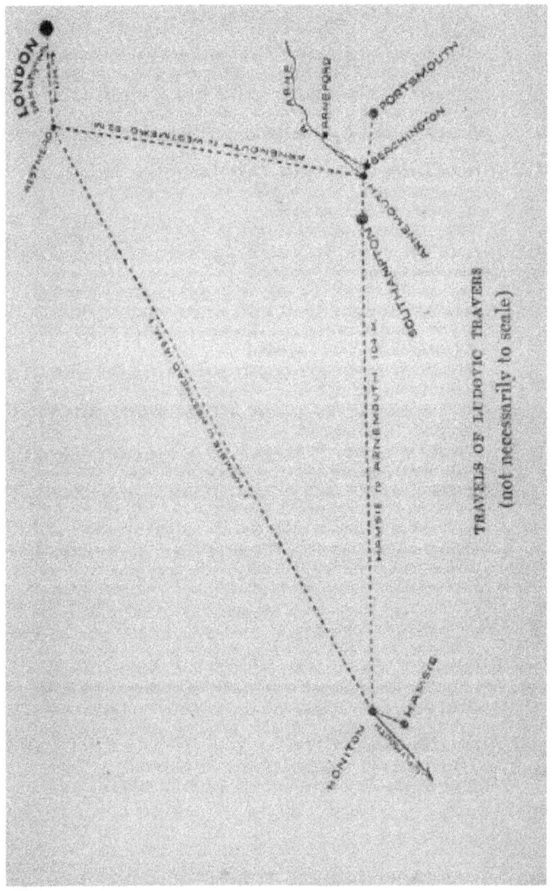

'Good,' said Travers. 'Then I think we'll do a whole lot more travelling.'

The trip figures were set at zero again and the Rolls headed for Southampton. There was no halt at Whinsea, or in the city itself. Mile after mile the car glided on through Dorset and Somerset, and then Honiton was reached, and a mile or two beyond it Travers at last pulled up and had a word with a road scout.

He remembered the spring floods well enough, and showed Travers the fork at which Martelle must have tried to avoid the mile stretch of one-way traffic.

'There was no real need for him to make a detour?' Travers asked. 'You people, for instance, didn't put up signs for the detour and advise it to be taken?'

'No need at all, sir,' the man said. 'As a matter of fact there wouldn't be all that traffic at night, so one-way traffic wouldn't make all that difference. I don't see why any driver of a private car need have paid any attention.'

Travers moved the Rolls on again, took the road that Martelle had taken, and, through the high-banked Devonshire lanes, came at last to Hamsie. The mileage indicator showed that from Arnemouth to Hamsie was 104 miles.

There was no need, as he saw it, for making inquiries at the garage where Martelle had come for petrol, though Travers had the tank of his own car filled there. He knew that Martelle had knocked up the proprietor at somewhere about dawn, but even that fact was irrelevant. After all, no one but Martelle knew how long Martelle himself had been driving about the lanes, or sitting in the car waiting for a lorry to give him a pint or two of petrol. All that Travers was anxious to do, in fact, was to return to Honiton for lunch, for it was long past the time and he was uncommonly hungry.

After the lunch he made a long-distance call to a certain firm of private inquiry agents in town, and it was an expensive call, for he was talking for at least a quarter of an hour to the senior partner in the firm. That done he took his ease for another hour, which included a short nap, and then he moved off again, and back to Southampton.

'If you'd rather stay here for the night,' he said to Palmer, 'please do so. As a matter of fact I'd rather you did. I shall be driving the car all night myself, and I can pick you up here somewhere between breakfast and lunch to-morrow morning.'

Palmer said with much deference and some obstinacy, that if it was all the same he would rather share the trip.

'Well, we'll have tea here at any rate,' Travers said. 'If you didn't bring any flasks, buy a couple and get them filled with coffee. And lay a stack of sandwiches aboard.'

The departure from Southampton was so timed that it was at precisely seven o'clock that Travers reached Arnemouth, and he turned left before the garage and avoided the village. Then he made for London by the Portsmouth road, pushing on the car at the highest speed compatible with safety. It was well on the way to dusk when he reached Westmead, and there he turned left and made due west.

The trip mileage was again set at zero and the car slipped along steadily through the dark. Palmer took a turn at the wheel while Travers ate sandwiches, and when Salisbury was reached Travers insisted that Palmer should take a nap in the rear seat. The car still glided on, pushed still to its best speed; Shaftesbury, Yeovil, and Chard were passed, and then Honiton, and once more the little lanes were taken and the Rolls came to a halt at Hamsie village.

It was still not one in the morning. The trip had been a hundred and forty-five miles, at an average speed of over forty an hour. And that speed, as Travers assured himself, had been steady and safe, for if he had been pushed for time he could have made an easy average of at least five more miles an hour. It was a fine, starry night, with a nip in the air, but he and Palmer took their time over the hot coffee and the rest of the sandwiches, and then began making quite a slow way back by the Dorset route. The almost sauntering journey ended at Southampton, where they had bath and breakfast. At nine o'clock they were making yet again for Arnemouth.

Now Travers was deciding to come out into the comparative open, and while using all tact, make every inquiry which the circumstances seemed to warrant. So his first halt was at the garage to replenish his petrol and oil. The garage man regarded him with no special interest, and it was reasonably clear that so far there had been no village talk about himself, and the car, and questions about Martelle.

'What happened to that car of my friend Martelle's?' he asked. 'Did he sell it when he went away?'

'The Dawburn?' he said, and shook his head. 'I haven't heard whether or not he sold it. He took it away with him when he left.'

'I was surprised he kept on driving it,' Travers said. 'After that narrow squeak he had, I mean. By the way, he never told me quite what happened.'

'It wasn't the car,' the man said. 'It was that big speedboat he used to have. He was doing about – well, what I'd call on land about fifty an hour and coming round Bishop's Bend, where all them trees are. Shot round the bend, he did, and slap into a couple of craft. Had about twenty yards to manoeuvre in and slipped between 'em. Told me he grazed the side of one and hit the other's propeller and slewed himself right round.'

'That was pretty terrifying,' Travers said. 'What did the other fellows say about it?'

The man smiled. 'I never heard what happened to them. Reckon he paid up and kept things quiet. All I know is he was shaking like a leaf for days after. Reckoned he was going to sell the Dawburn, only I talked him out of it.'

'Anything in the papers, was there?'

'Not him. He never let it get in the papers. He took the speedboat away and sold her, though.'

'And when was all this exactly?'

'When, sir? Let me see now. It was when we were having that fine spell – about the only one we did have this spring. Be about the end of February or the beginning of March.'

'You sure?' Travers said. 'I had an idea it was much longer ago than that.'

The man was sure. Travers paid his bill, then decided to leave the car there. Before he could mention the fact he had another idea, and reversed the car instead and turned back towards Southampton.

'I want you to go back to Southampton,' he told Palmer, 'and call up at the offices of the bus firm at the address we just got.

I'll write down the questions I want answered, and if the man concerned isn't available, you're to get hold of him at his house, or on whatever journey he is. Then bring the car back and draw up near the church where we stopped yesterday morning.'

When the Rolls had gone, Travers returned to the village on foot and was lucky enough to find Gosling mending nets on the narrow foreshore.

'I'd like you to row me over,' Travers told him, 'but I don't want you to wait. I've never seen Beachington, so I might as well have a good look round.'

The headquarters of Hamble Brothers lay towards the centre of the straggly village of Beachington, and there still seemed quite a number of visitors about the cramped streets and on the narrow beach. The Hambles evidently regarded the season as still on, for their boats were moored in the little cove and the sun made the scene gay as July.

'Yes, sir,' Herbert Hamble said, 'we've still got both craft. Which one do you want to hire, sir?'

'Neither,' Travers said, and decided the time had come for out-and-out lying. 'I wouldn't mind buying either if the price were right.'

'Buy?' he said. 'I don't know about that, sir. They're both worth more than what I gave for them.'

'In that case,' Travers told him diplomatically, 'we mayn't do any business. But may I see them?'

The yacht merited the deprecation bestowed on it by the auctioneer's clerk. The bunk could never have coped with Travers's length, and he had to crouch like a troglodyte in the small interior. As for the motorboat, it was equal to about a comfortable fifteen knots, so Hamble said, but it was a tiny affair that would hardly have held both him and Travers.

'She's an economical little boat,' Hamble said. 'Not one of those roaring great things that go cutting about up and down the estuary. That's why my customers like her. Just goes chug-chugging along and if you want to go reasonably fast, then she'll do it. Uncommon quiet, she is.'

But Travers apologized for taking up Hamble's time and said he would buy neither yacht nor boat.

'What petrol did the motorboat use?' he asked.

'She'd run on anything,' Hamble said. 'I've never tried her on ginger-beer but I don't know that she wouldn't run on that. Mr Martelle always used that Contrex. Fourpence a gallon less than anything else.'

He was pointing to a dozen cans that stood by the boathouse.

'Fourpence cheaper than the ordinary,' Travers said. 'That's a consideration. I wonder if I might try a can?'

Hamble also said he could have Travers rowed back to Arnemouth, and the can – on which a deposit of three shillings had to be paid, in addition to the price of the petrol – was left till he came back, which would be, he said, in about an hour's time.

15
INQUIRIES CONCLUDED

TRAAVERS WALKED ON through the village. It was so long that it seemed it never should have ended, and when it did, the end had a startling abruptness, for all at once there was nothing but a few inches of shore below the bank, and trees that came down to the water's edge. Every now and again there were paths that ran down to the sea or followed the winding bank.

A bus coming from Portsmouth way then caught Travers's eye, and he took it to save the longish walk back to Beachington Grapes. There he arrived just at opening time. He was the only customer and the landlord greeted him like an old friend.

'Going to stay here after all, sir?'

'I don't think so,' Travers said. 'Give me a half-tankard, by the way, and whatever you'd like for yourself.'

'The fact of the matter is,' he went on, 'this place seems different to me now Mr Martelle's not here. If he were still here, I wouldn't have minded a week in that bungalow of his.' He raised his tankard with a: 'Here's how.'

'Good health, sir.'

Travers thought hard as he took his own gulp. Since he would soon be out of the district he might as well go the whole hog in the matter of prevarication.

'As a matter of fact,' he said to the landlord, face sober as became the coming disclosure, 'I'm down here on a peculiar business. I happen to be connected with the biggest firm of inquiry in the country, and I'm really making inquiries into a certain young woman. Her name was Dolly, and she came into this public-house one day last April when Mr Martelle was here.'

The landlord's eyes were bulging. 'I remember, sir. A smart little bit of goods.' He frowned in thought. 'My missus knows more about her than I do, because she went with her to wash her hands, and them two got talking, same as women do. Nothing wrong with the young lady, I hope, sir?'

'Only that she's disappeared.'

'Disappeared! Well, I never!' Then his face lighted up. 'Portsmouth's where you ought to inquire, sir. That's where she was going.'

Two customers came in then. Travers whispered hastily.

'Is it possible for me to have a few words with your wife?'

'Of course you can, sir,' he said. 'Soon as I've attended to these two gentlemen, I'll take you through.'

A quarter of an hour later Travers had finished his talk with the landlord's wife and was being shown out at the private side door. Then he made his way to Hamble's yard again and was taken back to Arnemouth in less than no time in a motor-boat. He carried his can of petrol to the rendezvous by the church and there waited for Palmer, but it was not till one o'clock that the Rolls came round the corner.

'I'm sorry I'm so late, sir,' Palmer said, 'but the particular man who was wanted, sir, was on another route, as they call it, and I had to wait till he came in. The letter, sir.'

Travers hastily opened the envelope, and there were his two answers.

a. On the morning in question the conductor had taken over at the depot a package for Arnemouth, but he was unable to remember the addressee. The Company had no records but information might be obtained at Hillsons, the Arnemouth grocers, and local agents of the Company.

b. The conductor remembered that that particular morning a young lady boarded the bus about half a mile from the depot on the Whinsea Road stop, and went in the bus to Arnemouth. She was a pleasant young lady and was the only passenger who went to the end of the route. He could recall nothing of her clothes except that she wore a pink jumper and carried a pink handbag.

Travers pocketed the letter with a nod of satisfaction.

'One last call,' he said to Palmer, 'and then home. If you're as sick of this car as I am, you'll be glad to get there.'

The call was at the grocers', to ask if they remembered a biggish package being delivered by the Southampton bus on the morning of a certain day. There was further recalling, and at last the box was remembered.

'It was for Mr Martelle,' one of the men said. 'To be called for, and he did call for it that morning. I remember he had that little yacht of his outside at the jetty, so he said, and he carried it down himself. It wasn't heavy, though it was biggish.'

Travers headed for home, then pulled up again – at the garage.

'I thought I'd tell you I might buy that old Dawburn of Mr Martelle's if I knew where it was. I always liked it as a runabout, but there's just one thing against it. What does it do to the gallon?'

'Not less than fifteen,' the man said.

Travers made a wry face. 'There was some story or other I heard about his going to Plymouth and then getting stuck because he ran out of petrol. What did the tank hold?'

'That's nothing to do with it,' the man said. 'He was in a bit of a hurry when he left here that day. Only had about seven or eight gallons. What he intended to do was to fill up somewhere on the road, and then he forgot. You know how it is, sir. You keep saying you'll stop at the next one on the near side, and then there isn't another one, and there you are.'

Travers looked pleased. 'Well, that sounds better. Any idea of the number, by the way, in case I want to trace the car?'

The man went in to examine his books, and duly came back with the registration number.

'You don't want to give a lot for it, you know, sir,' he said. 'I wouldn't give a penny more than eighty pounds.'

Travers thanked him, gave a respectable tip, and once more headed for home.

It was his usual custom to spend his weekends at his sister's place in Sussex, but it was not till late that Saturday night that he was able to leave town again. For no sooner did he get back that afternoon to St Martin's Chambers than he was ringing up that firm of private inquiry agents.

Nothing had as yet been discovered, he was told, but he would be rung up at the earliest possible moment. So then he got into touch with his motoring association and gave the number of Martelle's car and asked if its whereabouts could be traced, if there had been any sale. Then there was his sister to be rung up, and the situation to be explained – or explained away – and after that nothing to do but wait.

But there was some sort of a reward at about seven o'clock. Frodling was speaking from the Odilon.

'Tried to get you yesterday, sir,' he said, 'but there wasn't any answer. Thought you'd like to know about the show. We cabled Martelle and told him the worst. He's sailing from New York in the *Empire* on Monday.'

'You mean, he's coming over especially to try to save the show?'

There was a grunt from Frodling. 'I leave that to you, sir. If he's not here on Saturday, he'll have a shock.'

'Why on earth didn't he cut his losses after your report?' Travers asked.

'Human nature, sir; human nature,' said Frodling wearily. 'It hurts their vanity to admit they're beat. Funny thing, the theatre business, sir.'

'I guess it is,' Travers said. 'Is his wife coming with him, by the way?'

'Not she, sir. She's up to her eyes in some new picture.'

Travers thought hard for a good few minutes after that brief talk with Frodling. Then all at once the phone bell rang again. The inquiry agents had news at last.

'Give me the gist now,' Travers said, 'and send the full report at your leisure.'

The information was as follows. The possible routes from Arnemouth to Westmead were so numerous that more men had had to be put on the job, hence the delay. True the post-offices were shut on the night in question, but each large town had various hotels from which a phone call could have been made. The wanted call had been traced only half an hour before, and the facts about it were these. That April night a man had taken a drink at the bar of the Coach and Horses, Bagshot, and had asked to use the phone. The charge had been the usual shilling for a distance call made at that hour of night, and the description of the man tallied in most respects with that given, though he had been wearing glasses and had a faint moustache.

After that there was no need for longer waiting, and Travers left for his weekend. As a special favour to himself it was extended till the Tuesday, on the afternoon of which day he came back to town. There he found the full report of the Bagshot call, and the information that Martelle's car had been sold to a firm of second-hand car dealers in Long Acre, and passed on by them only a few days ago to a firm in North London, who were using it as a traveller's car.

Then Travers rang the Yard and asked about Wharton. He would probably be in the next day, he was told. Thereupon Travers rang Wharton's private address, but the line was dead.

Before the likely closing time he paid a visit to the Regent Street showrooms of the London distributors of Dawburn cars, and there made some inquiries.

'Doesn't the petrol consumption go up enormously with age?' he said.

'Not at all, sir,' he was told. 'I very much doubt if it ever gets below fifteen to the gallon; that is if the car's had reasonable handling. How old was the particular car you knew, sir?'

'About three to four years, I imagine,' Travers said; 'and in quite good order, I should say.'

'Then on a journey of any length she should have done at least sixteen,' they told him.

'But you can't have speed and low fuel consumption,' Travers insisted. 'Thirty horses, mind you, and capable of doing an easy eighty.'

'That doesn't matter,' they said. 'Now if it was an English car with a heavy body, then it might be different. Everything's a question of engine design, and there's no hard and fast rule.'

Next came a visit to the hotel where Martelle had arrived with Coralie Wain from Plymouth on a certain Wednesday morning of April. There he made one inquiry only, and inside five minutes was away again.

There he left things till the following morning, but it was as early as seven o'clock when he rang George Wharton at his private number.

'We only got back late last night,' Wharton said. 'Had a pretty good time. And how are you?'

'Faint but pursuing,' Travers told him. 'But could you start off to the hurly-burly a bit earlier this morning and call in and see me on your way? Or better still, what about my being at your place at half-past eight and running you in ?'

'That sounds all right,' Wharton said, and then suspiciously: 'But what's the special idea?'

But Travers had rung off. Never a trace of shame was on his face when he greeted Wharton in an hour and a half's time. There was some pulling of Wharton's leg and congratulations on his holiday complexion, and then at last Wharton got the question in.

'You haven't come all the way here to tell me that. What's in the wind?'

'I'd like you to go with me to see a car,' Travers said soberly.

'What d'you mean? You're buying a new car?'

'It isn't a new car, it's an oldish one,' Travers said. 'I'd just like you to run an eye over it with me. It won't be more than twenty minutes out of your way. I rang up the people last night and asked them to have it there for us to see. I mentioned your name – in confidence.'

Wharton glared. 'Here, what's the idea? I'm not buying a car.'

'You never know,' Travers told him oracularly. 'You're like me, George. You'd buy almost anything if it was a good enough bargain.'

So Wharton consented grumblingly enough to get in the Rolls and be driven to Holloway. The firm who had bought Martelle's car were in the wholesale woollen trade, and it was their loading yard into which Travers steered.

'I want you to let me do all the talking,' he told Wharton. 'You follow the cues and don't shudder at the lies.'

But as soon as Travers announced his name he found he had stirred up quite a lot of trouble. A member of the firm was there, and the transport manager. Travers introduced Wharton and then at once assuaged the anxieties.

'Nothing wrong whatever, we assure you. Everything was open and above-board about the sale, and we know the car's history. The fact is that this car resembles one in which the Yard is particularly interested. It's the same age and colour, and Superintendent Wharton and myself would be most grateful if we could note down any other resemblances we happen to notice.'

That cleared the air and everything was smiles and affability. No sooner were they alone than Travers turned to Wharton.

'Well, what do you think of her?'

'Damn great elephant of a thing,' Wharton said. 'I wouldn't have her as a gift.'

'But very useful for carrying a traveller's samples,' Travers said. 'Look at all the room inside. And there's more luggage space in the boot. But run your eye right over her, George. Memorize her, if you can.'

Wharton gave one of his special glares. 'Don't you think the time's come to do some explaining?'

Travers's face sobered, and his fingers were fumbling at his glasses.

'You're right, George. Well, this is a car that used to be owned by Martelle.'

Wharton's eyes started. 'You've got hold of something to do with those suicide cases?'

'You're right,' Travers said. 'I've bust Martelle's alibi. That's why I want you to have a good look at the car in which he established it.'

'You've bust his alibi?' Wharton was still staring.

'Beyond all doubt, George.'

Then all at once he seemed to spring to life, and he was whipping open one of the back doors.

'I don't suppose there's a chance in a thousand but we might as well look.'

He was searching inside the empty car, then in a minute or two he was dolefully shaking his head.

'I knew it was hopeless.' He stared. 'But wait a minute. Here's something else.'

Then again his head was inside the car and he was stooping. Worn carpet covered the floor, held in its place by the usual press-studs. He tugged at the carpet and it came away, and beneath it was the undisturbed dust of months, a match-stalk or two and small unidentifiable objects. He stirred them about with his finger, and then all at once his heart gave a frightening leap.

'Come here, George,' he said quietly. 'Look through the other door and see what's here on the floor.'

Wharton's head came through and lowered till his eyes were almost on Travers's pointing finger. Then he looked up.

'A chip of paint. Green paint!'

'That's right,' said Travers. 'The dead spit of those we found in a certain house.'

There was the one chipping only, and Wharton slipped it into an envelope.

'There was jiggery-pokery then?' he said to Travers.

'More than that,' Travers told him. 'That chip of paint ought to hang Martelle. We could have made out a case without it, but...'

He broke off, shaking his head. Wharton's voice came in urgently.

'What've you got hold of? Come on, sir; out with it!'

'Not here, George,' Travers said gravely. 'Let's get along to my flat and look at a few more exhibits.'

16
MARY TUDOR

TRAVERS WAS singularly quiet on that short journey back, and even when they reached the flat. It was still early enough for more coffee, and while they waited for Palmer to bring it in, he assembled his ideas. Wharton made no attempt to hurry him, and when the notes were jotted down, asked the one question only.

'You can definitely prove there was jiggery-pokery?'

'More than that,' Travers told him. 'I can prove beyond any doubt whatever that Mary Legreye was murdered.' He smiled up as Palmer brought the coffee in. 'It's Palmer whom we have to thank for things. If he hadn't happened to have a birthday, and if he had chosen some other play that particular night, then the Westmead suicides would have stayed suicides.'

For Wharton's benefit he ran briefly over the visit of Palmer, and himself, to Saloon Bar. Then there were apologies before he settled down to his story.

'It's a pity that holiday of yours was abroad,' he said. 'I tried to get you, and I'd rather you'd been handling this than I. Sheer luck, it was really, as you'll see when I come to tell you.'

Wharton, notebook ready, did his best to chuckle.

'You get on with the story and I'll tell you if you were lucky or not.'

'Here goes then,' Travers said. 'It may be a muddled story in spite of these notes of mine, but there's one thing you'll be glad to hear. Unless I explicitly state to the contrary, everything I tell you can be vouched for by reliable witnesses. There's chapter and verse for everything, especially the improbabilities.'

'Good,' said Wharton, pencil poised over the notebook.

'Here we go then,' Travers said. 'If you'll bear with me I'd like to present the facts or lead up to them in my own way. I think it's essential, for instance, to have a preliminary look at Mary Legreye. She was at a dangerous age, as you pointed out. She was something of a prude, and very much of a shrew, and the theatre was her life. She wasn't a beauty but she had a certain amount of personality, could be very attractive when she wished, good company, and extremely likeable. The worst day in her life was when she fell in love with Martelle, and – still more unluckily for her – at a very awkward time. With that decree absolute a thing of the future, and a vindictive husband most likely on the watch, and then later a little cad of a nephew, she had to be more than circumspect.

'But I do think it will be essential to your case to insist that such circumstances were far from unattractive. Love, so I believe, is supposed to thrive on secrecy. Think how thrilling it was, for instance, to have Martelle call her up, using that deliciously preposterous bass voice! How exciting to buy with his help that Arneford cottage! To meet him on the river bank in the loneliness of the trees, where he could come in that shallow-draught, quiet little motorboat! To make out she was at a hotel or with friends or spending a day at Southampton, and really to be with him in his Arnemouth bungalow! A secluded bungalow with a boat-house from which one could enter the house quite unseen. A tiny yacht with a cabin in which she could hide while he was sailing in full view.

'Now Martelle, and a few facts of which you may not be aware. He was the spendthrift and the handsome philanderer. He had merely added Mary Legreye to his collection, but secrecy suited him even more than it suited her, for the simple reason that he was never serious. If there were ever jealousies and quarrels, then he must have come up against the shrewish side of her, but unfortunately for him, before he could break loose, the pregnancy intervened.

'That put him in the very devil of a hole. He had very little money and she had none – real, big money, that is, money in bulk such as was being made by Coralie Wain. It was to Coralie that he was laying siege, which was why secrecy suited him. She had been his goal all along; the other was merely another affair.

To be tied for life to Mary Legreye would be hell; and one imagines that the nearer he came to marrying Coralie Wain, the more desperately in love was he with the prospect.

'Now I conjecture that when he first heard of the pregnancy he tried to induce her to submit to an operation. Such things are only too common, and may be done with discretion. But if we have accurately assessed her, we know that she must have indignantly refused. After all, in a short time the decree would be made absolute, and then they could marry at once and regularize the position. Then, I imagine, he retorted, "But what about your career?" That would make her think. Once drop out of things and it's far from easy to get back. Mary Tudor had given her a solid position, and it was madness not to consolidate that position in the next play.'

'But she didn't have an operation,' Wharton cut in.

'I know,' Travers told him. 'I shall be referring to that later. Meanwhile let's move on till about six weeks after the pregnancy was known to be a certainty, or to be more correct, a fortnight before the murder, and assume that she had not made up her mind. He, of course, had been in the hell of a fix ever since she had told him. He couldn't bolt, for that would damn him for life. If there was scandal, he would almost certainly lose Coralie. In fact, he had soon seen there was only one way out, and as soon as he had begun to think of ways and means, he had found things far easier than he had first imagined. The great thing was that since their secret had been so thoroughly guarded, he would be a most unlikely suspect. Here I might say that I'm sure she never said a word to him about Percy. I'm positive that if he had suspected Percy of any real knowledge, there would have been three murders instead of two.'

'Ward was murdered?' Wharton could not help ejaculating that.

'He had to be,' Travers said. 'He was the pivot around which the murder revolved. He was an accomplice of the murderer, though he didn't know it. You might even say that but for Ward, she might never have been murdered.'

Wharton stared. 'How do you make that out?'

'I'm now about to tell you,' Travers said. 'But about Martelle first, and the planning he did during his ample leisure in the Arnemouth bungalow. He was a playwright, and what he was now confronted with was writing another play – a murder play in real life. What we must remember too is that Mary Legreye trusted him and put herself entirely in his hands. In her particular circumstances she couldn't conceivably do anything else.

'So to the actual murder scheme that he evolved. It was planned on the broad principle that the wood can't be seen for the trees. Or, put it another way, it was one of those puzzle pictures where, for instance, you see a horizontal line crossed by several almost vertical lines in such a way that the eye is deceived and you would swear that the horizontal line is really a curve. Complexity was to be the keynote, with one or two easily visible threads. The ultimate discovery of her pregnancy would be a fine thing, since it would account for the distraction and give the great motive for suicide. But there was to be nothing so simple as dumping her body in the estuary. If it ever broke loose, its very position might draw attention to himself. No. He planned for death to take place miles from where he could prove himself to be. In other words, if he should by any chance become a suspect, then he would be in a position to quell every suspicion by presenting the most perfect of alibis.

'I don't think, mind you, that he intended originally to be as complex as he ultimately had to be. He found as the scheme progressed that this and that had to be arranged for. He had to stage a burglary at the Arneford cottage, for instance, to see if there were any letters there or written references to himself. Also she might have left a will, in spite of the fact that he got her to destroy the one she made leaving everything to him. Still, you'll see those things for yourself as we go along. Now for the actual murder.

'What gave him the chosen idea was a play. He had been interested last Christmas in certain improvements at the Beachington Grapes, his favourite pub, and he had decided then to write a comedy about a pub and a barmaid in distress – the play, in fact, in broad outlines, that Palmer and I saw at the Odilon, and which you will undoubtedly have to see for yourself. But he didn't think too much of it, so he laid it aside and began toying with ideas about a play dealing with Pepys. But when he had finally hit on a scheme to kill Mary Legreye, that scheme involved a rewriting of the barmaid play, and, under a pledge of strict secrecy, he let her read it. The most hellish thing of all is that she was very much taken by it.

'Now do you see what happened? He said what a pity it was that the part was wholly unsuited to her. She denied indignantly. Versatility is the salt of theatrical life, and to keep to English queens and martyred historical heroines would be getting into a dangerous rut; besides she had served a long apprenticeship in the hardest and most versatile of all schools – repertory. Then he pointed out that her condition would make it impossible for her to take the part of the heroine, since the play would be coming on in early autumn. Perhaps then she consented to undergo an operation after all, because, if you remember, she was still expecting to be going on tour with Stony Heart. She couldn't have done that unless she had undergone an operation, and therefore I submit she had it in mind.

'But if she consented to an operation, the consenting came too late. All it did was to help to kill her, because what he would say to her was that after all there was no real point in discussing things from that particular angle since the part of the barmaid was utterly beyond her powers. Can't you hear the arguments and her passionate insistence? She, whose very breath of life had always been the theatre? And so to his master-stroke. "Very well then, Mary. There's one perfectly simple way of showing whether you can play the part or not. You prove to me that you can play it, and in actual life, and in the original scene where I set it, and I'll agree." She would confidently agree and then all that remained was for him and her to arrange that public – and dress – rehearsal.

'Now I think everything becomes plain. Each detail of their planning was complete by that Sunday afternoon, and deliciously thrilling and secret planning it must have been. Bunce had left, and Martelle was to see Ward off the premises so that she could slip out of the house herself. Either before she left Arden or else on the train, she underwent the transformation to Dolly, or she might have proceeded by easy stages on the other hand, not becoming the fully-fledged Dolly, the Bristol factory girl, till she left the small Southampton hotel where she spent Sunday night. But Mary Legreye's personal things were made up into a package and sent to the bus depot for delivery to Martelle at Arnemouth, and then, on Monday morning, with her face perfectly made up, and her pink jumper and almost gaudy garments in perfect keeping – down to her very underwear – she waited at a certain stop for the Arnemouth bus.'

Travers paused for a moment and shook his head.

'Doesn't it make you want to crook your fingers round Martelle's throat when you look back at it? Think of how she felt that Monday morning. What a lovely adventure! Everything going perfectly and just as arranged. The thrill of hailing him in his boat, of crossing with him to Beachington, of playing a parallel part in real life in the pub, and actually being able to use some of her heroine's very words in the script! Then at last leaving the village for the Portsmouth Road and coming to the lonely spot under the bank and waiting till his boat drew in shore for her. Then to hide down below while he came alongside at Arnemouth, went ashore and collected the package containing her bag and things, and so to the boathouse and the bungalow.'

Travers broke off there for a moment. Wharton, scribbling hard, merely nodded for him to go on.

'Yes,' Travers said. 'To the bungalow, where there would be great hilarity. Applause and congratulations for the perfectly wonderful show she had put up; and wonderful it certainly was – for him. All part of his alibi, for who could ever suspect that Dolly, the smart little bit of goods from Bristol, was Mary Legreye? Congratulations then, as I said. A cocktail to celebrate the glorious adventure and the triumphant success. The cocktail was her own special brand, but three minutes after drinking it, she was dead.

'What happened then behind the locked doors and drawn curtains? A new transformation, and a horrible one. Her face was cleaned of that garish make-up, but he did the job as a man would, and made none too good a hand of it, till perhaps he saw that it gave the impression that she had been crying, and so he left it as it was. She had dressed with infinite care for the part, and when he had put her into her own clothes, he destroyed Dolly's clothes, including the cheap silk stockings, but he didn't know enough about things to suspect that the smart cami-knickers were showy too, and not in keeping with Mary Legreye.' He broke off again, fingers at his glasses. 'There we'll leave her, George, if you don't mind, and go back to Arden, and the Sunday afternoon.

'It had been arranged, you may remember, that he should offer to take Ward and the luggage to the station, which was a guarantee that she would know where Ward was, and so have leisure perhaps to dress in comfort and slip out of the house. But Martelle wanted Ward to himself for a very good reason. I imagine the talk ran something like this.

'"Can you keep a secret? Like to be on a tenner, or more perhaps if everything comes off? Well, this is the secret. Some of us have planned a big surprise for Miss Legreye. A very big man, Kevstein by name, is over here from America and he wants her to do something from Stony Heart where he can see her, the idea being that he'd like her to play the part in New York, and maybe go on to Hollywood and do it there for the films. A fine trip for you, Fred? Well, this is the secret, as I said. She isn't to know a thing about it but you're to do this.

'"On Tuesday, when you get back from the races, sneak unobserved into the house. Don't let any lights be seen, but do everything in dead secret. First of all clear away some of the drawing-room furniture to the sides so as to make a kind of stage, because he'll want to have a scene or two acted just as it was at the theatre. That's why some of the others are coming along. Then you'll have every light out in the house and be on the look-out for me and have the gates open ready so that I can drive straight in. I shall have a trunk of costumes and props and things, and I shall want you to give me a hand with it upstairs. I should get here at about nine, but Kevstein and the others can't be here before ten. All the better. That'll give you and me the chance to see to things, and to have a word with Miss Legreye when she turns up here at half-past nine, wondering why she's been urgently sent for.

"'A real surprise it'll be for her, don't you think so, Fred? And that's the whole point of everything. A tremendous surprise, that's what we've all planned. A tenner for you, and more if everything turns out right and Kevstein buys the play. But not a word to a soul! If I have the least suspicion that you've dropped even a hint to anybody in the world – do you hear, Fred? – even a hint – then everything's off. Now let's go over again what you have to do."

'I think that was the substance of the talk. It explains why Ward tore that paragraph about Kevstein out of the paper on Monday, and it gives a meaning to that entry he made in his book when he had got back from the pictures that Sunday night –Job for Mr M. It clears up why he was so anxious to get back to Arden in good time on Tuesday, and why he was scornful about paying the bookie's trumpery six pounds on Wednesday morning. It also explains why Martelle was so uneasy when you showed him the entry in the book, and it proves that Martelle himself took the book in order to see what else Ward had written and to prepare answers which should explain anything that might incriminate himself. And now, back to Arnemouth.'

Travers unhooked his glasses and slowly polished them. Wharton watched with narrowing eyes.

'May I briefly review the position, George?' Travers said, hooking on the glasses again. 'We're coming to the really terrible part of the murder and it's essential to have the facts clear. Martelle had proposed from the beginning to bring Mary Legreye's body back to Westmead in a trunk he had, and I would say it was a smallish, narrow one. When he reached there he would need help upstairs with it, for it was vital that she should seem to have committed suicide in her own room. Ward would in any case be at Arden, and if Martelle had tried luring him away, then the fact might have emerged from any subsequent questioning of Ward. What I'm getting at is that Ward had originally seemed a danger to the scheme but nevertheless he was made to fit perfectly into that scheme.

'I also claim that this – and this only – was in Martelle's mind. He had to fake the Kevstein business to Ward but once Ward was dead he was proposing to put the furniture back again. He would have ample time, as you'll see later. Then, you may ask, why didn't he? I'll tell you. The answer is in the room in Martelle's bungalow where we left him with the body of Mary Legreye.

'He brought in the trunk, George, and began putting the body in it. Then, to his horror, he knew he had miscalculated. Though it was a long, narrowish trunk, the only way he could shut down the top was by drawing the knees up slightly. That made him think furiously, till out of his playwright's mind came an idea – perhaps when his eyes fell on a certain hassock. The very one that stands by your chair, George. Mary Legreye had one like it, he knew. And he knew all about rigor mortis, so it struck him that if he put her body into a chair and let it stiffen with the legs drawn up on the hassock, then all he would have to do when he got to Arden would be to put the body in a chair of similar width and height, with her hassock under the feet. Now why he chose to place her with her arms along the arms of the Arnemouth chair, I don't know, unless he thought that the pose was the very one which Sir Barnabas described as final relaxation. He couldn't have let the body stiffen naturally on the floor because then he might not have been able to fit it into the trunk at all. But place her with her arms like that he must have done, and later he found that the stiffened body would easily go into the trunk, which was just what he had finally calculated. It would have to be a handy trunk as to size, I should have said, so as to fit in the back of the car between front and back seats. Luckily she was a tiny, dainty soul. But all that you can work out for yourself. Let's stay at Arnemouth for a minute or two, and see how Martelle stood in his mind, once he had hit on the idea of the drawn-up legs. Was he satisfied so far, or not?

'I think he had every reason to be satisfied. He wasn't out of the wood but once he could make it appear that Mary Legreye had died in Westmead, he could prove that he was never more than a mile or so away from Arnemouth during the whole of Monday. Then he set about making himself visible to plenty of witnesses right up to the time on Tuesday when he was due to take the body away. His last job was to fit the body in the trunk, and fill the trunk with any light and valueless oddments. There were also two bags to pack with his personal things, and they went in the boot. But what he most certainly had to put in the car was four two-gallon tins of petrol. He had gradually acquired those tins for use in his motor boat. They were painted green, and this one here is one I bought from the same garage place.'

He showed how the tin might flake or chip, so that a flaking or two had adhered to the carpet of the car and so to the bottom of the trunk.

'The car was ready with its load,' he went on. 'He had told the man at the garage that afternoon that he was in too much of a hurry to fill the tank and he would fill up somewhere on the road to Plymouth, and he had made certain that the garage proprietor knew the tank then held only about seven and a half gallons.

'At dark he set off, avoiding the village. He had told everyone some time before about a narrow squeak he was supposed to have had, and all Arnemouth knew his nerves had so badly gone that he had become a laughing-stock for the mere crawl at which he had grown accustomed to drive his powerful car. But there was no crawl that Tuesday night. He drove fast to Bagshot and there paid to the owner of a hotel the usual shilling for a distance call made at that time of night. The call was to the Arnemouth garage, asking about an indicator which – I submit – he knew would not be in. But the garage man assumed the call was from the bungalow and would therefore be prepared to swear that Martelle had not left for Plymouth till after the time of that call.

'Meanwhile, somewhere secluded and handy, he had filled his tank from the four tins and disposed of them. By nine o'clock he was at Arden. Ward had the gates open and he drove right in, having extinguished his lights at the end of the road. The gates were shut behind him. Everything had to be secrecy and speed. You can imagine the low-voiced talk. By the way, I mention the obvious fact that till Ward was dead, he wore his ordinary gloves. Then perhaps he put on rubber gloves.

'"Here you are then, Fred. Lend a hand with this trunk. It's heavier than I thought. Full of costumes and props and things... Straight upstairs, I think. Switch off that light in case Miss Legreye should happen to turn up too early. Up she goes! Didn't think it was as heavy as this. Just inside the door will do... That's right. Good job you've made of the room. I didn't think you'd have moved so much. Still, it's a fine job... My God! I'm hot. Haven't done so much rushing about for years. Got a spot of anything to eat in the kitchen? Only cake? That'll do fine. Let's go and find it, and thank God I've got a flask."

'Out of that flask came a good tot for Fred, and that was the end of him. Then every light was put out downstairs and up Martelle went to the drawing-room. Out came the body and he began looking round for a chair that would fit the dead, stiff arms. There was one that Fred had left out – the chair that had been used in Stony Heart! So he placed the body carefully in it, and then all at once became aware of the full implications as they would strike those who found her body. She had had the play on her mind as she killed herself. That was it – that big scene with the ambassador! A wonderful idea, and it would save moving back all that furniture that Ward had been so damn silly as to clear aside.

'Soon everything was set – table, glass brought from Arnemouth, with her prints on it, the poison, whisky bottle with Ward's prints (which meant a quick trip down to the kitchen) and her prints on the cocktail bottle. He used her keys to open the sideboard but, you remember, forgot to lock it again. The attaché case was put beneath her bed and the handbag at her side. Last of all he had to turn out the lights so as to make it appear that she had died there at about midday on the Monday. At the door he turned them off, then had to move across the room in the dark to draw back the blinds and curtains. It was then that he trod on the top of the fountain pen which he had previously dropped. He was unaware of that, as he was unaware of the fact that a flaking of paint had adhered to the drawing-room carpet from the bottom of the trunk.

'Then he wondered if he dared leave the trunk in the spare room. I think it must have been her trunk, taken to Arnemouth for some reason or other before Bunce's time. Another chipping of paint adhered to the carpet outside the door, but when he looked inside he saw the dust was too thick to risk any disturbance. Then at the very last moment he saw to his horror that he had left a footprint just inside the door, and that had to be wiped away. Then at last he decided all was in order upstairs, and down he went with the trunk to the hall.

'Then came a last look at Ward. Two things should be pointed out there. As soon as he saw Ward that night he would make sure that no hint had been dropped to a living soul. If he was not certain about that, he could still have modified his plans by poisoning Ward and taking away the body after putting the drawing-room back to its original state. Then there were the miniatures. Sorry, but we've now got to go back to Arnemouth on the Monday night.

'That Monday night Martelle had to go to the Arneford cottage to make sure nothing was there that might incriminate him, and he had expected to find the key among her belongings. But apparently Bunce and Ward had the two keys, since they would be there before herself. So he had to break in, and on that Monday night he took with him her hat, fur, and gloves, and the paper with her prints. The back garden of the cottage runs down to the river bank and so there was no real danger, but I think he deliberately exaggerated the disturbance inside the house, and he took the miniatures. When on Tuesday night he stood looking down at the body of Ward, he had the sudden idea of connecting Ward with the cottage burglary, and so he put the miniatures in his pocket. He also had the idea it might look more natural if the poison glass were laid by Ward's out-stretched hand.

'Everything he did at Arden we shall never know but he must have been there a very long while, taking every precaution and staging everything with a desperate precision. One thing he did was to place in her bureau a special draft he had made of the

Pepys play, which would cover any slip she might have made in referring to a new play of his. But at last the time came to leave. He looked down the road and he listened, then out went the car, leaving a spot of oil behind it. Then he shut the gates and set off for Plymouth.

'Considering that the car could do eighty, he had ample time. Somewhere on the road he cut that trunk to pieces and disposed of it and its filling of oddments. I may tell you that when he reached the London hotel on Wednesday morning with Coralie Wain, he had only the two bags. When he got through Honiton all he had to do was to stage that running out of petrol, and no one would ever be able to prove the precise time he had – or had not – waited for a chance lorry before going on foot to find a village and a garage.

'You do see the ingenuity of that alibi, don't you? The man at the Arnemouth garage was prepared to swear two things: that Martelle didn't leave for Plymouth till about nine o'clock and that he had only seven and a half gallons in the tank. Martelle was also a very slow driver – as everyone knew – and as I just said, he could swear he had waited near Hamsie for just so long as suited him. I'd say he had explored every inch of that country beforehand. And, of course, the police would know he had not filled his tank. His was an easily recognizable car, and there would never have been found any garage at which he stopped for a fill – for the simple reason that he never did stop for a fill but used the four spare tins.'

Wharton scribbled on for a minute, then looked up, detecting perhaps the note of finality with which Travers had ended Martelle's night journey.

'That the lot?'

'I think so.' He leaned forward in the chair, beginning yet another instinctive polishing of his glasses. 'Heaps of minor things, of course. Why he got rid of his bungalow in such a hurry, and the two boats...'

'One minute!' said Wharton. 'What about the poison?'

'That will be for you people to work out,' Travers told him. 'Frodling may help you there. He seems to know all about Martelle's people and past. His father was connected with a firm of manufacturing chemists, for instance. That may fit in somewhere.'

'And one other thing – that play, Saloon Bar. If that was such damning evidence – at least, you found it so – why was he such a fool as not to chuck it on the fire?'

Travers smiled gently. 'Frodling will help you there as well. He knows more about theatre mentality than I do. But you and I know enough about human nature, George, to be able to answer your question. Martelle had to have a play ready. He had to keep in the limelight. He had to make a show to Coralie Wain. I'd say he tried hard to lick something into that Pepys play but couldn't. Very well, then, he risked the barmaid play. I should say it had no title when she read it, so he didn't have that risk to run.'

Wharton grunted, and made an entry in his book.

'And one other thing. Where does that poor devil Wolters come in? Why was he brought round there that Wednesday night?'

'Well,' said Travers, 'I submit that Martelle rang Wolters up on Saturday, using that easily mimickable voice of Ward's. I think he wanted the bodies discovered so as to avoid long suspense. But he intended to follow up with something else – to ring up the Westmead police at about ten to nine on Wednesday night and say he had seen something fishy going on at Arden. A man or two would have been hurried round and Wolters would have been seen. That would have made more complications; more upright lines to make us think the horizontal a curve. But Martelle didn't ring the Westmead police. Maybe he failed to find an opportunity, or lost his nerve, or thought after all the anonymous call might be somehow traced.'

Wharton thrust the notebook into his pocket and fairly leapt to his feet. Off came the spectacles and he was making for the door. Travers followed anxiously.

'Aren't you waiting to see if I can remember anything else? And what about the corroborations?'

'Your word's good,' Wharton told him from the corridor. 'I'm making for the A.C. at the double, and I reckon you'll be wanted. That's a kind of official warning.'

He went past the lift and Travers still followed protestingly.

'But, George, you're not putting me into the witness-box? Surely you can take over things yourself?'

But Wharton was waving a farewell hand. Travers saw the last of his bowler, then let out a sigh. A couple of minutes later he was filling his pipe with a methodical slowness, and his head was still shaking dolefully. No end of things he must have left out, and the A.C. would want them all. Now what were they? Oh, yes, the cameo brooch for one thing. Dolly had worn it at the neck of that pink jumper, and the landlord's wife had admired it and fingered it. Perhaps the bus conductor had noticed it too, and that might be a useful inquiry for the Yard to make.

He sank into his chair, legs stretched out and fingertips together, and all at once he was thinking again of that night at Arden: the chill of the stairs, the sudden glare when Wharton switched on the light, and then the dreadful silence of that room and the frightening repose of that regal figure, throned in its austere death. Mary Tudor – the climax of a career; a climax ironical and ghastly, for it had been followed by no gradual decline of powers but had held within itself the very means and end to furtive death.

Then suddenly Travers knew something for the first time. Those words she had let fall in an unguarded or sentimental moment, when Bunce had thrown out hints of a marriage; how, if such a marriage ever eventuated, it would be like the play. That was it; Philip Martelle and Mary Legreye – a new Philip and a new Mary! The vital clue that had been missed; too simple and too obvious to see, just as trees obscure a whole wood.

His head was shaking again at that, and his teeth were closing on a cold pipe. Mary Tudor, he thought, as in the play. Mary was deserted by Philip, and Philip, not Calais, was cut deep in a heart which the world knew was no thing of flesh but merely stone. And yet that latest Mary seemed to him more pitiful in her tragedy than the Tudor Queen. There had been all the gay bravery of her that Monday morning, the very waves rippling to her laughter in the dancing boat, and then the triumphant flaunting of her art in the Beachington pub; smiles and laughter over all, and a smile on her face even in that last dreadful moment as the cocktail was drained, and a something clutched at her throat, and her eyes stared for the horror of another something that she all at once knew.

Then Travers's teeth closed in a fierce grip on the stem of that cold pipe. A day or two and Martelle would be landing at Southampton. Wharton would be there and, by God! he would be there too. To hell with publicity and the witness-box and headlines in the press. Come what might –

The phone rang. Palmer glided in and was lifting the receiver before he could turn. A word or two and Palmer was reporting:

'Superintendent Wharton, sir. He says, can you come at once, sir. They'd like you there now.'

'At once,' said Travers, 'and quicker than that.'

He was smiling as he spoke, and it was with almost a defiant jauntiness that he was rising from his chair.

THE END